I0775474

THE COVEN ON 25 MILE ROAD

Amanda S. Holiday

Copyright © 2023 by Amanda S. Holiday

ISBN: 979-8-88615-148-0 (Paperback)

979-8-88615-149-7 (E-book)

All rights reserved. No part of this publication may be reproduced, distributed, or transmitted in any form or by any means, including photocopying, recording, or other electronic or mechanical methods, without the prior written permission of the publisher, except in the case brief quotations embodied in critical reviews and other noncommercial uses permitted by copyright law.

The views expressed in this book are solely those of the author and do not necessarily reflect the views of the publisher, and the publisher hereby disclaims any responsibility for them.

Inks and Bindings
888-290-5218
www.inksandbindings.com
orders@inksandbindings.com

Contents

Thank You

To all who have encouraged me, offered criticism and/or suggestions. Because I'd surely forget someone if I tried to list all, I won't list any. If you're one of those disappointed because you're not listed by name, then consider how much worse you'd feel if I listed everyone except you. Seems fair to me. Also, I don't want to bore others with names they don't know.

The Boiler Plate (Disclaimer)

This is just a fictional story. I've been assured that Magick won't change a person's sex but that's not the same as gender, and ignores shape shifting entirely. That was the consensus of a few witches with whom I have discussed the idea on line. Don't get your knickers in a twist if I take the liberty to make it possible in this book. Others have used the idea in books, movies, and even an episode or two of television programs, so I'm not alone. It's been either the realization of deeply held desires or fears, or random chance. I'm sure many of you have wondered at least once what you'd do if it happened to you. I know I have.

I've tried to avoid using any one personality to give my characters depth, but there are general traits universal enough that they must be used. If you think you see yourself or any other person in a character, it is strictly an accident. Same with ideas. I've tried to credit the originator of an idea if known, or at least give credit to the person others have credited as originator, or the group which followed it. Do the best you can to let me tell my story without nitpicking.

Foreword

Remember, this is fiction, so suspend disbelief. Allow yourself to ask "What if...?" Disbelief is the fault of modern science anyway. It limits where our imagination is allowed to travel. It denies anything not measurable and ignores the advice Hamlet gave, "There are things in heaven and on earth, Horatio, not dreamt of in your philosophy." (I work from memory, so forgive any error in that quote.)

Consider also, it is impossible to prove something doesn't exist, but only one verifiable observation to prove it does. Nonetheless, perhaps it is an extremely rare event that occurs once or twice a millennium. Or perhaps there are no survivors to tell the story. For that reason, I, for one, am on the fence for some ideas not yet verified. I neither believe nor dismiss the possibility.

Allow yourself to go back in time to when people didn't have more than a few, if any, books. Radio, television, computers, or cell phones weren't even possible because electricity only came in the form of lightning, and that was dangerous. Think about how you would explain phenomena without science to box you in. Or stay in the present but add events unexplained with current science. Or travel to the future with so much unknown.

To me, it makes more sense to stay open minded than trust to lucky chance that humans exist, as some "orthodox scientists" insist. Isn't it more logical to believe in a creator who put matter into the void in the first place and had the outline of an intelligent design that guides development?

But, most of all, try to enjoy the story as just a "ripping good yarn."

Surprise, Surprise

I woke, or should that be came to? You call it. My head hurts too much to be of any help with that. All I know for sure is that it went from color to black during a robbers against citizens gunfight and back to color when I opened my eyes. Took a couple of blinks to focus, but that happens almost every day when I first wake. Like screwing a loose light bulb into its lamp to make contact.

Found a large bump just above my right ear. I'm open to reasoned alternatives, but for now, that will take the blame for this pain. More like the worst hangover ever times two, maybe twenty.

Did I fall after drinking too much too quickly? I hadn't spent much time practicing to walk in four-inch heels. Unsteady on them sober, that was a real possibility when alcohol is added.

One other thing I knew. I don't want to find out I'm taking pain killers. If I was, when they wore off, this pain would kill me, at least make me wish I was dead. If more than a couple of aspirin, that opened the risk of getting hooked on prescription opioid painkillers. That would be a bitch from all I've read on the matter. If I'm not already dead, an overdose would probably finish me.

All those thoughts instantly faded into the background when nature called. Time to visit the bathroom. I got out of bed and noticed a few things, like this wasn't home, but no time to think about that until after I stood over the toilet and emptied my bladder.

Revise that. I sat on the throne to empty my bladder. No, I wasn't too dizzy to stand, though you'll argue that or call me crazy when you listen to the reason. When I lifted the hospital gown to urinate, it came as a reflex. I no longer had a male's outside plumbing to which I was accustomed. That was enough of a shock to cause me to sit down by itself.

I sat long enough to notice that I had pretty feet with bright red polish on my toe nails. It was the same color as I wore on my finger nails. My hands weren't bad either. The bowel movement that started when my bladder emptied gave me time to wonder how I looked. This wouldn't be too bad if I was attractive, like that barmaid I pulled out of the line of fire when those guys shot up the bar last night and some patrons shot back.

That was the last thing I remembered before I woke up here in the hospital. Yes, that's where I am. Just recognized it. As a subcontractor, my company did finish carpentry when this wing was built ten years ago. Just a little bragging here. We finished before the date specified by the contract and under budget.

I looked around and found the sink with a mirror above it. Would this please me or cause me to vomit? Did I want to look or not? Curiosity won the argument. I looked into the mirror.

Hmmm. Not bad at all. Allowing for some bad bed head, a pretty girl, the dream of most guys as the one who lives next door, looked back at me. Might even make the lead in a low budget movie. Skin was smooth, no wrinkles. The bumps on my chest seemed to be well proportioned to my size.

Size? I backed against the tiled wall, marked the top of my head with a finger, counted tiles to the floor. Sixteen and a half four-inch tiles plus a four-inch molding around the base. Give or take an inch or two, I was five foot ten. From what I've read, it would be hard to find a male lead tall enough for the movies unless I walked in a trench or he stood on a box. Not many of those since the old six foot or more tall stars retired or died.

I giggled at a thought. Instead of breaking through the opposing offensive line to stop the running back or sack the quarterback for a loss, I'd be on the sidelines in a short skirt and tight sweater to cheer for the players to do so. I busted some moves the cheerleaders on TV used.

Dang, but I looked good doing that in a hospital gown. Be even better in the cheerleader outfit. I would obviously be part of the foundation for the pyramid instead of the featured one at the top because of my size, but that was ok with me. I was still a team player, as I'd been all my life before this change.

I flushed away evidence of my visit and was back in bed before the nurse checked the room. We exchanged waves and greetings. After she left, a bright being with wings visited.

"Hey, girl. I've been assigned to be your guardian and advisor. The Boss wants you to succeed, and I've got experience in that line of work." It said.

I challenged, "Who and what are you? Why should I trust you?"

"Sorry. Thought you knew I was coming. Let me dim down a bit. " He dimmed to the familiar image of my grandfather in his mid-fifties. *"I'm your grandpa Pete. I'm your special need guardian angel. I got the job because I was with the State's Attorney's office until I retired. My unit specialized in busting up gangs of drug dealers."*

"OK. I'll take that for a test drive. Not ready to buy it just yet, but it warrants listening." I replied. "Keep talking."

"By now, you've noticed a change in your physical shape. In your spirit, you're still Victor 'Bear' Warsawski, warrior who fought a war already, but you're wearing my grand daughter's body. She won't need the memories

about how to maintain the body, so you've got those but you'll have to read her diaries to find what she felt, and what went into her growing up. You still have all your own memories and some of hers if you calm down and think a bit." he explained.

"Why?" I challenged.

"Because you know how to fight a war. You just needed the right combination of genes on your X chromosomes to gain some powers that will help you win the new one coming. Listen to Barbara Yeager for how to use those powers. " he stated.

"You mean the old widow out at Witch Woods?" I asked.

"None other. I'll let her know you're coming. She'll send somebody to help you in some pretty serious situations. Don't go naked into the world. Be prepared to defend yourself. Your enemies are of your time and place, so use weapons of your time and place to defeat them until you are trained in your new powers." he replied. He exclaimed, *"Got to go for now. Nurse is coming back. By the way, get to know the Vaquero."*

In a silent flash of light, he was gone. I was left to my own talents and abilities in a body I haven't tested yet to find its limits to get through this with help from unknown friends. I had a moment to consider that information and the observations I had of this new body. I needed a couple days.

Still, it seemed to me, I got this body to do some good with it from what I was told. Nobody hires a warrior without a war to fight. It was what I had. I'd use it and live with it as I had with the body I wore as Bear, all state tackle my senior year.

Besides, it was an answer to my secret dream to be a heroine since youth, or to be a hero more openly admitted. Been that way since first grade and the other guys laughed when I slipped and said heroine. I had only earned the National

Defense medal and a good conduct ribbon while in service, which left me short of that goal. I'd get another chance to be hero or, with this body, heroine. (Back when I grew up, use of words with masculine or feminine gender was still proper English, not this unisex politically correct foolishness.)

This would be as good as being a hero. Maybe even fun once I got used to it. One sure improvement, I'd get to wear some pretty clothes. Too, I seemed to be sound of wind and limb, and reasonably well coordinated. There was only one thing I could say. "Send me in, coach."

The nurse came in then. She saw I was still awake. "Good morning. Just checking on you. That was a nasty bump you took. We thought we lost you when you flat lined for a few seconds during the ride here." She checked the chart hanging on the foot of the bed. "Ursula Chadwick, what do you want for breakfast?"

That's my new name? Not bad for a hand me down. I gave my order, "My usual will do. Plain shredded wheat, not the frosted kind, with 2% milk, buttered toast, and coffee. Oh, and some jam or preserves for the toast."

"OK. Be back in about a half hour with your breakfast, if I can. Kitchen is busy today. Lots of kids with belly aches. Too much Halloween Candy. Happens every year." she grinned. She checked her watch. "Kitchen may have started lunch already. I'll see what they have." she said as she left with that purposeful, ground covering stride that is common for people at work before the new wears off. The good ones never feel that it's old hat. I had a good one.

A half hour, plenty of time to tell my story now. That will give me an anchor to my thoughts, and give me something to do while my breakfast is readied. Let me go back to the start. That should help us make more sense of this.

Yesterday was just another Friday at the end of October.

At least I thought it was. August 'Gus' Will called mid-morning and invited me to lunch. Gus was president of Will Lumber Company. As owner, he had to wear many hats. Today, he wore the one for paymaster. He found it boring and he claimed a visit by a friend helped him keep his sanity.

But don't think he was one of those pompous jerks who like to show they're boss by wearing expensive suits, demanding 'ambiance' in his dining room, eating gourmet meals that leave you hungry, or talking around a question without giving an answer. He was a straight shooter that usually took lunch in his office wearing work clothes. His lumber mill was neither suit & tie nor haute cuisine territory.

His eldest son would take over when he retired, as Gus had from his dad. Barring accident, that would be a few years down the road. Heck, like me, he was only in his early sixties.

Only reason I already retired was I had taken a fall at work bad enough the EMTs took me to the hospital. After those X-rays, I needed time to think and to heal from the limp. That was almost reason enough to sell my company. The doctor found no bones were broken, but reported a little extra something that made it a necessary move. She consulted with other doctors. They concluded the shadowy thing on the X-ray of my hip and pelvis was really a vagina. It was likely sewn shut when I was born.

There was no proven explanation, but many theories why that could be fact. One came closest to what I could accept. He lost me with medical terminology, but it had something to do with hormone levels at particular times in the womb. Not enough of one or too much of the other allowed both sets of organs to develop. She joked we could get rich publishing in the medical journal. I declined the honor of being a scientific curiosity. I did let her publish a story about "patient W", though.

I had enough to do to decide the question of my future -

where to from here? One question of this importance at a time was enough for me. Work would distract me from answering that question. That, I figured, was enough reason for me to decide to sell the firm. There was also the two months I was healing.

One of my older guys accepted the price and terms reached after negotiations, and bought me out. I left the company in good hands with a clear conscience that I sold a going concern and what I felt was fair compensation for twenty years as owner building a business worth buying.

During the two months since the sale, I visited a psychiatrist. Yes, the thoughts and dreams I had since childhood bothered me. I accepted them earlier as my cross to bear in life. After the diagnosis, I worried I was going nuts, or had been nuts all along.

After a test to find what my preferences were, when we found my brain was half male and half female, the shrink advised me to check out Two Spirit. I did. At first, I decided to play the game of life with the body I already had in the role it gave me. If anybody had a better idea, I was still open to change. Which road I followed was in God's hands. Still, it would be fun to dress on Halloween as the possible other me if I went with old, and now the current dreams.

But enough of me, back to the story.

I have done business with Will Lumber for close to twenty years, fifteen of those since Gus took over from his dad. This Friday lunch was almost a tradition, and I knew his order.

I stopped at the Spotted Horse Saloon on the way. On Fridays, they offered a deep-fried quarter pound fish fillet with lettuce, tomato, onion, and tartar sauce on a crisp hard roll with a huge order of fries and a small paper cup of coleslaw for a reasonable price. Add a pint of good beer, the total for a take-out order was only five bucks each. Bought two orders.

As I paid, the cashier reminded, "Don't forget the costume

contest tonight. It's Halloween."

Told her, "Send the cops if I'm not here and registered. Been planning my outfit for tonight since September. Be a head turner, I'll bet." Then I winked, grabbed both bags, and got to the mill shortly after.

Gus greeted me most atypically. Most times, it was a friendly, "How ya been? Pull up a chair and let's eat. I'm hungry." Today, he spat out, "Just heard something that has me riled. I need to get it off my mind before it eats me up and spoils lunch."

I answered, "Well, do it fast, before the food gets cold and the beer gets warm." But he had me thinking that I brought the wrong menu. If we have to solve that problem before we eat, there was a good chance I should have brought cold cheese sandwiches. They're still tasty at room temperature.

Gus continued, "You know James Forrest Junior took over when his dad retired? He came up with as bad an idea as I've ever heard, just behind Custer's decision to split his forces and ride into the Little Bighorn valley. Called me to ask what kind of price he could get on clear cutting all the wood lots from 24 Mile Road to 27 Mile Road, from route 17 to the boundary of Witch Woods."

"Why the hell would he do that? Is he nuts or something?" Those questions exploded from deep in me.

Gus said, "Nah. He's just greedy, like all the other land grabbers. Follows the business school dictum, 'take the money now, to hell with the future, you'll have moved on before the damage is bad enough to destroy the business.' All they care about is the bottom line this year."

Gus continued when I was silent, "He wants to buy all the farms out that way, turn them into a pair of golf courses at a high-priced country club with small tracts of high-priced homes on what's left over." he paused to take a breath.

"Sounds like I should have brought a fifth of something

stronger than beer if we're going to solve that problem during lunch."

Gus smiled. He knew my way of coping with problems was to make light of them. Turn them from invincible monsters into an ordinary problem that could be solved, given time. "No way to solve this over lunch. Let's eat. I think my stomach is ready for that now."

I handed him his bag and opened mine. "Good call. Food's still warm. Beer's still cool. We can talk a little about it. Get some ideas how to stop this scheme. Then think on it some more."

After some talk about the planned development, questions about his family, answers about my injury and latest news from the doctor, some teasing about being a man/woman of leisure while he was still a slave to his work, I remembered a possible ally for the fight coming up.

"Think I'll visit Barbara Yeager after lunch. She's named after the first defender of the Woods. Maybe she's got some ideas." I said.

Gus agreed. "You do that while I write and sign these pay checks. Got one question though. Why do you get the fun jobs while I get stuck with business?"

"Just lucky, I guess." Couldn't help myself. I grinned when I turned his dig back on him. I ate the last of my sandwich and fries, and drank my beer. "But this has its own dangers. If she's a witch, like some people think, no telling what will happen to me. Takes more than Dutch courage to follow my path willingly." I grinned. "And I haven't had enough beer yet to have even that kind of courage."

Gus almost choked on the fries in his mouth. "Yeah, but you were the best point man in the battalion. Seemed to know where the trails were booby trapped and where they were clear when we were in Indian country. If anybody can make it out of there in one piece, it's you."

"I'll be careful. Don't doubt that for a minute." I grinned again. "Actually, she's always been friendly since I built her cabin near the woods. I'll be all right."

"Well, time for me to get back to work. Best of luck on your mission, Bear." Gus ended our visit in his typical way - short and to the point.

"See you in church and next Friday, Gus, Lord willing and the creek don't rise."

"More to the point, don't let a witch cast a spell on you." He laughed loudly as I threw away the wrappers of lunch. I'll admit, I considered aiming them at Gus but controlled the impulse. Instead, I sunk the ball of crumpled lunch wrappings into the basket from outside the three-point line and grinned.

I shrugged and waved as I went to my truck. Started it and headed back to route 17 and north to 25 Mile Road.

It sounds like a long trip, but not really. The county named the east west roads by the miles from the south county line sometime around 1910. The Will Lumber yard was a half mile west of route 17 on 14 Mile Road. From the intersection of route 17 and 25 Mile Road, it was only a few more miles to the Yeager's homestead. Only about 20 miles total, I figured it.

With light traffic during the lunch hour, I didn't have to concentrate on driving. This is a good time to tell you how Witch, some call it Witch's, Woods got its name.

Back in the late 1700s, Austria, Germany, and Russia invaded Poland, took over the country and divided the land between them. Poland became parts of their claimed territory. The Poles never really accepted that but could do little about it except emigrate to the United States after it broke off from England. That lasted for 123 years until it became a recognized sovereign country again after WW1.

Some came early, like cavalryman Casimir Pulaski and the military engineer Thaddeus Kosciusko, designer of the fortifications at West Point. Both served in the American army during the Revolutionary War against England. Others waited longer, to the late 1800s. That gave them time to add legends from those other countries to the folklore which they brought with them when they immigrated. One such was the story of a witch from the Russians, Baba Yaga.

Some, the shopkeepers and laborers mostly, settled in Chicago, Detroit, and Milwaukee areas. The farmers came this far west to take advantage of the rich soils and the Homestead Act. They brought some stories about Baba Yaga with them.

Among them was a gal named Barbara Yeager. Because of her accent, people heard her say her name was Baba Yaga when she introduced herself to her new neighbors. Not long afterward, the town was filled with reports that normally sober people saw a witch flying on full moon nights.

Today, people would ask what the reporters were smoking, drinking, or taking. Back then, they'd ask "How sure are you that's what you saw?" because magic and magical beings, while rare, were still accepted as a possibility. I figured that's why seances and fortune tellers stayed in business during the early twentieth century.

One last tidbit since I'm almost there. During a serious dry spell in the 1910s, lightning started a fire that threatened the woods. Many heard Barbara Yeager / Baba Yaga vow to protect her woods and the critters that live in it. A rain started that day and lasted a week. Saved the forest which still stands as a result. Never any question to the locals then that it really was the Witch Woods.

Even though the state acquired the woods during the Dust Bowl years, and named it Casimir Pulaski State Forest, it was Witch Woods to the locals since the late 1800s, early 1900s. It still carries that local name frequently enough that the state put up a display in the visitors' center at forest headquarters that tells this story. I know, because I read it there.

Ah. Here's the drive. When the current Barbara Yeager and her husband moved here about twenty years ago, I built this house for them. Through the years, my company built the barn and granary. Since he died, I stopped by in the Spring and Fall just to let her know she wasn't left alone or forgotten. Today, I'd also ask if she had any ideas about how to foil the planned land grab Gus told me about.

First to greet me was Sasha, Barbara's dog. She was followed by the litter from last Spring. The pups were weaned now and nearly full size for an Akita X Labrador X Canis lupus (wolf) crossbred. (Read really big but gentle if not provoked. -grin). Sasha was starting to show gray around her muzzle. I gave them all a little friendly petting before I knocked on the back door.

Barbara yelled through the door, "Come in, Bear. Just mixing up something I think you'll need before the night's over."

"What is it?" I asked.

She answered through an impish grin, "Just a little something that'll make the change easier for you. I understand you're going to the costume contest tonight. You may not win, but this will help you compete with a smile. Hold your breath and drink it all at once."

I took the offered tumbler and noticed it was almost luminous green. That might be only because it caught the light coming through the window. I followed instructions and chugged it. It didn't burn my throat or turn my stomach but it tasted awful. "Dang it, woman. That's bad tasting stuff. You forgot to tell me to hold my nose."

"This should help you forget that taste." she said and offered a good bourbon and water to cut the aftertaste.

"This is much better. Got a serious question. Maybe you can help me with it."

"You mean about the land grab plotted by the Forrests, right?"

"How did you hear about that? I just heard about it at lunch and drove straight here." I responded.

The impish grin returned to her lips as she answered, "A little bird told me about it." Her grin faded as she warned, "Be careful when you take them on. There is someone else besides the Forrests, someone very dangerous, behind it all."

"Have any ideas? I think you're a descendant of Baba Yaga. At least that's what I've heard. She swore to protect these woods from any and all enemies." I stated.

"I just heard about it myself. Come back on Monday. That will give me time to think about it." She paused, then instructed, "Go home, get dressed for the contest. Have fun tonight. This fight is going to be hard and long, and you won't have much fun until it's over unless you get very lucky."

"OK. I'll be back Monday, Lord willing and the Cree don't rise. Uh, I meant creek."

"Don't worry about it. You just used the original version. That's just the 1800s version of 'See you later.' Back when it was commonly used for the first dozen or so years, the white settlers were concerned about the Cree Indians rising up to take back lands the settlers farmed. It's the potion working is all.

"If you say so. See you Monday if I can make it. Take care, Baba."

"You'll be here. I have a feeling you will want to talk about more than just a plan to prevent the land deal." she stated.

I went back to my truck and drove home. Felt strange sensations coming from my crotch followed by a tingle in my pectorals. I was ready to blame the drink for those sensations. I got home in one piece, showered, washed my hair, shaved close, and toweled off. I donned what I'd wear for the Spotted Horse Saloon costume contest, and added the final touches.

There was enough time to eat a PB&J on toast washed down with a glass of milk. I didn't drink on an empty stomach since that one time I did. I had time to wash the dishes and utensils, move my wallet and ID into the purse I'd carry tonight, and check myself in the mirror. I fixed my lipstick, and got in character.

"Hurry up, Sue. Get me there before I chicken out." I sent the message through the universe. I didn't need to fret. The doorbell rang and I let Sue in. It was seven PM, right on schedule. I should mention the reason for what I wore. My shrink thought I should try dressing before I decided on the course I'd follow. A good friend seconded the motion, so I was out voted, 2 to 1.

"Sue Driscoll, you look like a young politician on her way to the governorship." I greeted the one woman, beside the doctor who found my problem, I trusted with my secret dilemma. It was a trust earned since I went to her dad's architecture firm for a custom build for a large family.

She was a senior in high school when we chatted during my wait to talk to her dad that first visit. Now, eight years later, she confided in me about her life, and I reciprocated. Even told her about my condition.

I complied when she asked, "Walk for me." I walked away, then back. I gave my impression of a movie street walker looking for a John. You can learn some neat stuff from movies and TV.

She squealed in delight. "Ohmigod, girl. You sure you weren't a hooker in a past life? You sure have the walk mastered."

"Courtesan, if you need label me. Please. At my prices, at least a high-priced call girl." I said in a soft, sensuous falsetto, then giggled hard enough my breast forms bounced in my bra. "Let's get registered before I chicken out. I'm shaking more than I did during my first fire fight in 'Nam."

Sue issued her orders, "OK. But once you get in the car, I'm not letting you off the hook. Just breathe and go with the flow."

I pulled on a light jacket against the night's chill and bravely went where I had never gone before, at least not dressed this way. The night was clear, the nearly full moon bright, and I felt magic in the air. While still unknown to me, I was headed toward my destiny.

Maybe it was just wishful fantasy. Now that I was out in public, being dressed was kind of fun. Be more fun if I had a woman's body, though. I still looked like a linebacker in a dress.

The trip over was more or less uneventful. One slightly scary moment when the ape in the car ahead suddenly slowed to a crawl in front of us. Before you judge me as insensitive, or bigoted, I wasn't judging him or calling him any names. That was his costume.

Sue reacted and we quickly slowed too. We got close enough to see him straighten his mask so he could see again. She commented, "I hope he's going to a different party. I don't feel like playing Fay Wray to his King Kong all night."

"Don't fret about that. He probably has his sights set on the coed who sits in front of him at that class on classic horror films. I saw it advertised in the local paper. That was back before CGI and it was done one frame at a time so they could move the model of the ape." I offered.

"I hope you're right." was her response.

At The Spotted Horse

In a few minutes, we were at the Spotted Horse Saloon and parked in a back corner of the paved lot. It was an easy though, in heels, a long walk on the concrete. The distance to the door gave me time to concentrate on making an entrance rather than just walking in. When we went in, I was in character.

The line to register for the contest wasn't long. A mobster and his moll just finished. Next were Doc Holliday and Big Nose Kate. I recognized them as Fred and Wilma Stone. They ran the veterinary practice where I took my dog, when I had one.

I'd always admired their honesty and plain speaking. From some reading, those were the same major character traits the real Doc and Kate shared. That was a good costume choice for them. After all, they spoke honestly when faced with the task of telling me my dog was vomiting because the cancer was blocking his esophagus. They didn't sugar coat it. They gave two options. Not easy to tell a dog owner that it was a choice between major surgery with no guarantee it would cure the problem or put his dog to sleep.

It wasn't an easy decision for me. One fact decided it for me. He was too good a dog for the nine years he was my buddy to let him suffer longer. When he drank water, he couldn't hold it. That was a long slow death in pain. I had them send him to the rainbow bridge to frolic without pain. I planned to meet him there when I used up my time and joined him. I still get misty eyed when I thought of him. At least I got to say goodbye.

Then it was our turn. Sue introduced herself as Summer Holiday, Governor of the Great State of Confusion, and introduced me as Mona Hari, grandniece of Mata Hari, also a practitioner of the world's oldest profession, semi-retired. Then she laid it on thick. "When the town marshal tried to run her out of town, her customers rode HIM out of town on a rail. At least they didn't tar and feather him for that."

All in earshot grinned at that. A few of them were old enough to remember the last time anyone was ridden out of this town on a rail. That was only sixty years ago. A few nearby patrons who knew the story of Mata Hari chuckled in the background. The barmaid, Ursula, running the registration table smiled and wrote furiously to get it all down on paper. She seemed to get the joke, but maintained her air of disinterest as fitting for an official of the contest.

Ursula was quite pretty. While not likely to be a pageant winner, she was a shoo-in for Miss Congeniality. I judged that on conversations I had with her as a customer when she waited on my table on other nights. I sent out an old request. "Lord by any name You prefer, it would be a small task for You, like flipping the indicator for sex in that computer chat room I play in. It would be really great for me if You saw it as a good idea to let me try life as pretty as her before I decide whether or not I'll have the surgery."

Sue and I finished registering and swayed our way back to a table. She whispered, "You've got heads turning, Mona sweetie."

I answered in the falsetto I used back at the house with a wide grin on my lips, "You think I wouldn't after fifty years in the trade?" That's when I noticed the falsetto wasn't forced but really the new sound of my voice. I wrote it off. Must be that potion Barb gave during the visit.

Another barmaid, Francine, asked for our orders. Sue admitted she was designated driver tonight, so ordered an orange juice. Francine wrote VS. I asked what that meant. She replied, "Oh, that's my code for a virgin Screwdriver. Faster to write VS than orange juice."

She asked my order with a suggestion mixed with her question, "And what are you drinking, ma'am - a Tequila Sunrise?"

Her eyebrows rose when I replied, "No thank you, dear. I'll have a Manhattan, please." I noticed the look she gave so I used an old joke to make her feel at ease. "An old pro at the hen house where I worked in N' Orlins (New Orleans in the dialect of that town. At least it was for the cabbie I rode with for Mardi Gras once in my youth.) advised drinking those. That way, if and when asked, I could answer 'Yes, I still have my cherry.' without lying."

Francine blinked first, then laughed. "I'll have to remember that one. Maybe switch to Manhattans myself." She bent closer and whispered, "Nice costume, Mona. Seems to fit you for some reason. And that was a great joke."

I got her with the follow up, "What joke? That's what I was told once upon a time." I thought she would laugh herself to death. I guess I told her with a serious tone and face to make it that funny.

She was still chuckling when she brought our drinks. I paid and tipped a buck each. She bent low and whispered, "Working girls like us don't tip, but I'll take it as a donation to the fund."

I chatted with Sue and a couple of guys who sat at the next table while I sipped my drink. The older of the two asked me to dance after the music started. Gosh, he was good at buckle polishing. I felt the strangest sensation between my legs, like there was a hole there waiting for him to fill it with that bump I felt behind his jeans zipper. (Have you figured out what I meant by buckle polishing yet? -grin-)

The dance over, I walked back to the table. Ursula had finished at the registration table and took over serving this area of the tables. She brought me another drink with a very slight nod at the fellow I just danced with. "He bought this for you." she explained.

Sue danced more often than I did, but that was all right by me. She was younger and far more attractive than I was. I had my share of slow dances and even tried a few Texas Two Step numbers. Then things went dark.

Not literally, but the mood shifted from festive to threatening as two guys burst through the door waving what looked like AK47s. I'd seen a number of those in combat. They shot into the ceiling a few times and ordered us to sit still, don't move. Some of the patrons, licensed to carry concealed weapons, just didn't like that, at ALL!

Sue already hid behind the table I dumped over, but Ursula had that 'deer in the headlights' look as she froze in place. While others tipped over tables and took up firing stances from behind the barricades, I rose and grabbed her arm to drag her down out of the line of fire. That's when it all went black.

In the Hospital

I've already told you what happened after I became conscious again. Now, I just rested while I waited for the nurse to return with breakfast. I tried to remember what happened. I didn't remember anything after I pulled Ursula to the floor. I could remember up until I felt that punch in the back, then nothing.

The amount of lead flying by in both directions left me one logical conclusion. The number of casualties included at least one dead or nearly so in a deep coma, me. Or at least my old body was, since I inhabited this new body. I needed to accept that, for now anyway.

There's an old saying I needed to follow right now. "Don't look a gift horse in the mouth." This chance to try life as a young woman answered prayers I made on an irregular basis for my whole life. I needed it for whatever would come for some reason. Seemed somebody listened this time, so I went with it.

The nurse arrived with a hamburger and fries, a small paper cup of coleslaw, some green gelatin, and a small pot of hot coffee. I looked at the tray, then at her.

"Sorry. The kitchen had already started on lunch. They made this for you special because you're probably really hungry. You've been here for half a day already, and were at work for at least six hours before that." she explained.

"I'll take it." I answered. "Not your fault, so don't worry about it." I giggled a little, "But, leftover pizza with a warm beer would have been more appropriate after the night I had."

She chuckled, then said, "A detective will be here soon. Wants to ask you some questions about that. I told him to let you eat in peace, but he only offered a half hour. Eat fast." nurse Faith, from her name tag, advised with a grin. She started out.

"Before you leave, and I make a pig of myself, what's on the schedule for this afternoon?" I queried.

"You seem to be alert and thinking clearly, but doctors will check again. Standard procedure for a patient with a possible concussion. I'll see you to take the tray before that." Faith replied.

"Thank you. See you then." I turned to my meal and almost drooled at the thought of solid food and green gelatin. It would have embarrassed me if I had an audience and wasn't hungry. Twenty-two minutes later, I had nothing but an empty plate, bowl, and glass on the tray. Part of the coleslaw went onto the hamburger, and that disappeared quickly. When only the green gelatin was left, I ate that. A tasty mix of lemon and lime made a good dessert, though a piece of apple pie would've been better. Six minutes more to use the bathroom again and return to sit on the bed. I felt better and the grumbling from my stomach ended as it digested the meal.

That's when the tall, well built, good looking young man entered the room. If he's the expected detective, I wouldn't mind this interview at all. -grin- Then I saw the ring. Off limits. I vowed I'd never knowingly intrude on another woman's territory. I was surprised by that thought. Must be Ursula's.

He checked the patient chart, then his notes to check me off his list. He spoke, "Good afternoon, Miz Chadwick. I'm Detective Sean O'Doyle." He showed his badge and ID card. "If you don't mind, I'd like to hear your story about last night at the Spotted Horse."

"Please, call me Ursula. Miss Chadwick is for old spinsters." Instantly, I wished I had a do over. To me, it sounded like I was flirting. Maybe I was. I didn't know for certain. I hoped he took it as just friendly.

"OK, Ursula. That's the first time anyone has tried to set me at ease while I was questioning them." He paused and continued, "Can you tell what happened last night?"

I answered from my observations as I remembered them. "I started the evening running the registration for the costume contest. When time came to end that, I went back to working the section of the tables assigned to me. Just before midnight, two guys came in carrying what looked like rifle shaped squirt guns. When they shot into the ceiling, that shocked me. They shouted to stop moving. I did just that. A lot of the customers didn't, turned tables over and started shooting back. Bear, Victor Warsawski, grabbed my arm and pulled me down. He might have saved my life doing that." He asked, "What happened after that?"

"I don't know. I must've hit my head on the way down." I showed the bump above my ear. "I wasn't conscious of anything after that until I woke up here." I said. "The nurse told me I was out for half a day."

"OK. I can understand that. What do you know about Bear Warsawski?" he inquired.

"I know he was a regular for as long as I've worked there, about three years now. He stopped in for a beer or two after work Fridays with some guys that called him boss. He'd also stop by with guys from the VFW and American Legion posts in town after their meetings, so I guess he served. A few months ago, he fell at work and came in limping for about a month. That's about the time he had a minor celebration when he sold his company. I remember him saying he didn't bounce good enough anymore. It was time to let younger guys take over." I replied.

"Did he have any enemies that you know of?" he questioned.

"Not to my knowledge. He was a good tipper and friendly with the staff and customers there, so no problems that I know of. Whether he had any enemies at home or work, I can't answer that part, Detective."

"OK, then. Here's my card. Call me at the station if you think of anything else." He handed me a business card.

"I'll do that, Detective."

He turned to leave the room. I thought "Nice ass." Must have been the girl part of my brain working again. As he reached the door, I asked "How is Bear doing?"

He didn't answer, just kept walking. To me, that was confirmation of my conclusion. I left that body to reside in this one until the job, whatever that is, was done.

Pete materialized again. He spoke, ***"You seem to be a natural at this girl thing. How do you like it so far?"***

I answered, "So far, it's good. I just thought of a possible drawback, though. Will I keep what I learned in my previous life? I'd hate to pay the tuition again. Some of those lessons were expensive."

"I think you will. I was told you're going to keep your memories. That would include those expensive to learn life lessons." he responded.

A question came to me. "But how, why was I given this body?"

"Well, it's partly that free will thing you have as a human. The Reaper came for Ursula, but you got in the way when you left cover to pull her down. You took the bullet meant for her. After an emergency meeting, the Boss decided to switch your souls. Don't worry about her. She's got a nice house in the suburbs now. As for you, you now combine a good-looking woman, the combat skills of a

war veteran, the will to win as part of a team, all needed to save the forest, and a brain able to handle the situation." he replied. A faint smile on his lips, he added, ***"The deciding factor was your thought, 'Send me in, coach.' That got you a chance to show your stuff."***

I answered with a grin, "Dang. I'm in the game as a walk on." I didn't know angels laughed, but he chuckled anyway. Another thought came to me, "I've got some tests coming up. If I pass, the doctors will let me go home. I'll be suited up for the challenge after that."

"With your attitude, you'll pass with flying colors. Got to go now. The nurse is coming to take you to the first one." he said as he faded out.

A candy striper bounced through the door with the exuberance of youth, pushing a wheel chair. "Hi. I'm Dot. I've been told to take you to your appointment with the doctors. Hop on." She wheeled the chair next to the bed.

As I left the bed to sit in the chair, I asked, "Why is this chair necessary? Where's Faith?"

Dot answered, "You came in unconscious. You ride until cleared to walk on your own. Faith is covering two wards. I'm helping while the other nurse, Prue, is in the ER. Van full of fans on the way to the game had a wreck. Mostly minor injuries, but they needed an extra nurse in ER to triage them, and put bandages on their cuts and scrapes."

I noticed she took my chart for the exam. "OK. Let's go and get me cleared."

We rode the elevator down to the first floor and radiology. First thing was a new X-ray of my head. That done, we went down the hall and Dot left me in an examination room. A few minutes later, Doctor F. Williams came in. I presume he wore the correct name tag. He checked the X-ray of my head. He smiled as he examined it and commented that it looked normal. He was pleasant as he asked questions that needed thinking to answer.

One example, I had to think when he asked me to spell my name backward. Well, don't laugh. How many of you have ever spelled your name backward before, to a doctor that can let you leave or keep you in the hospital depending how you answered? Specially when it's a brand-new name?

After that, I did lots of silly little things to test my balance and coordination. After I hopped up and down on one foot at a time for a while, I got the hoped for news. He said I would be able to go home tomorrow. I'd spend the night just to make sure there weren't any problems that took time to develop.

I asked a question still unanswered when the exam ended. "So, is it ok if I walk back to my room instead of riding around in a wheelchair?"

Doc laughed and wrote a note that said I was cleared to walk on my own. "Keep that with you until you have checked out. The hospital requires that you get cleared to walk if you came in unconscious. I've put that note on your patient chart too, but not everyone reads the charts."

He handed me the clipboard with my chart on it. "Take that with you and hang it on the foot of your bed.

"Thanks, doctor." We shook hands. "Can I have a piece of tape or a safety pin? If I'm walking back to my room, I've got a necessary modification for this issue gown. Need to keep it closed so my cheeks don't show when they shouldn't."

He dug a safety pin out of the bowl of paper clips on the desk and handed it to me with a laugh. Then he said, "Make yourself decent. Then get back to your room." He left the room.

I pinned the back together, grabbed my chart and the note, and was in my assigned room before Faith came by to check my preference for supper. I took the spaghetti with meatballs and garlic bread. She noticed I had walked back and checked my chart, then congratulated me on the progress.

Now that I was free of subconscious worry that I had some serious lingering injury, I really enjoyed supper. After I finished it, I took time to think. I'd save consideration about the Halloween change, and whether it was a trick or a treat, for last. First was when I realized how good it felt to be alive and healthy. Then the tasty supper, compared to low expectations for hospital food, was another small blessing. Next was how I'd get some clothes to wear on the way home and how to get there. There were some low priority things I might think about before sleep, like how I was going to meet a Vaquero. Mexican cowboys weren't common around here, and most of those I knew about were married. It seemed like a good start.

When Faith came back to take the tray of empty dishes away, I asked about my clothes and purse. She giggled, "We hide that stuff until you're cleared to leave. Don't want you sneaking out."

She unlocked and opened the closet. I recognized my clothes on the hanger. Then she put my purse in the drawer of the night stand. "There you are. You're set to go now."

"Thank you, Faith. Can I dial out on the phone or is that for hospital use only? I need to ask a friend for a ride home tomorrow."

She said, "Dial 9, then the number. Local calls only, though. There's a pay phone near the admissions desk for long distance calls."

"No problem. She lives in town, Thanks again. I thought it was something like that, but haven't called from a hospital before."

"In that case, here's a tip. Eat early, check out early. If you're the first or second one in line, you should be ready to go by ten AM. Check out desk is part of the admissions desk. Ask for Louisa, She'll get you out faster than Millie." Faith advised.

"Once again, thanks. That helps narrow the time frame

when I ask that friend to help." I said with a smile. After she left, I called Sue.

"Hello?" Sue was well enough to answer on only the second ring. That was a relief. I had worried that she was in the hospital too.

"Hi, Sue. My name is Ursula Chadwick. I'm the barmaid Bear, Victor Warsawski, pulled out of the line of fire at the Spotted Horse. Really would like to talk with you."

A short pause, then Sue spoke, "I'd like to speak with you, too. How are you?"

"Doing well enough after last night, but I need to ask a favor. You and Bear came to the costume contest together, so I guess you were friends. He was a pretty good-looking retired courtesan, wasn't she?" I left enough unanswered question to trigger Sue's curiosity.

Yippee. She took the bait and answered. "Yes, you could say that. What do you need?"

'"The doctor said I could check out tomorrow unless something happens overnight. I need a ride to pick up my car. That will give us a chance to meet. I'd like to talk about Bear. Find out a little more about the Two Spirit woman that saved my life."

I was done for if she didn't catch that hint. She did. Her voice became noticeably warmer. It had been cool, business like, until then. Now, it was a friendly cool but warming. I had tomorrow morning to make her a close friend again.

"When will you be checked out? I'm glad to help a friend of Bear's when they need it." Then she added, "Even poke my nose into their business if needed." she chuckled.

"Oh, I'm asking for that. Look me up and trace my life if you want. I don't think I've anything to hide. Of course, after the bump on the head that put me in the hospital, I might not remember it." I giggled when I said that.

She caught the joke and giggled as she answered. "You read my mind. I'll do that tonight. Internet never closes just because it's the weekend."

"The nurse, Faith, advised me to check out early. I'll try to be waiting for you by ten AM. If I can, I'll be in the lobby waiting or at the admissions desk checking out."

"See you then. Sleep well. Good night." she offered.

"Good night to you, too." I wished her.

We hung up and I started to back plan. To be checked out by ten AM, I needed to be at the admissions desk by nine when they opened. To do that, I needed to finish eating breakfast by eight forty-five. Allowing forty-five minutes to eat, it needed to be served by eight. That meant I'd have to order it tonight to beat the morning rush and make sure it got here by then.

Other things needed to be planned also. I needed to be showered and dry before I put on my clothes. Then I needed to dress and put on makeup. Allowing forty-five minutes each, which built some slack into the schedule, it was going to be an early morning.

I walked out to the nurse's station, and talked to the duty nurse about breakfast. She knew that to stay on the schedule I outlined to her, my best bet would be cereal, toast, and coffee. The forecast indicated hot oatmeal would be a good choice. I ordered that for next morning. I also borrowed an alarm clock so I didn't oversleep.

Back in the room, I set the clock to ring at six-fifteen AM. I moved my clothes from the closet to the hook on the inside of the bathroom door. I checked my purse and found just enough makeup and a hair brush to get by for the morning. I settled into bed and relaxed.

'Whew! That was a burst of activity.' was my first thought. Following that, I realized I hadn't needed a painkiller since lunch. While one would have helped, I was good to go without one. Just needed to keep to my schedule in the morning.

I let my mind wander. I had mentioned the Two Spirit concept in the conversation with Sue, so that came to mind first. In case you don't know what I'm talking about, it was a concept accepted by many, but not all, Native American tribes until the European missionaries taught the male OR female binary model.

After I read a few articles on the computer, I accepted the Two Spirit model as more correct than the binary. As many subtle differences as I observed during my life, I felt the bookshelf that held the books of our individual lives was infinite. It had to be to hold the stories for six billion people, give or take a few millions, alive right now and all those who came before back to the first humans and all the variations that contained. That's allowed by the Two Spirit model. In contrast, the European binary used the bookends as the ideal, and only option.

It just made sense to me. With as many gene pairs go into determining eye color, all the different properties of hair, height, weight, muscle, bone, fat, and intelligence, why not accept, or at least consider, that some genes influence preferences in life too. We don't all look alike, do we? Except identical twins, not even siblings can claim that, and even then, some differences let mothers identify which of the twins is guilty of raiding the cookie jar.

That led me to the idea that sex is different than gender. Sex is physical and obvious from the different organs. Gender is psychological and has no clear boundaries. Don't many women like to fish and hunt, usually considered masculine pursuits? Many men like to cook or bake, usually considered feminine traits. Few if any ever do more than notice that as unusual.

The Apache even taught their children to learn both roles from necessity. Small tribes, like the scattered Apache bands, faced annihilation during wars unless the men knew how to sew, cook, and care for children, and women knew how to hunt and fight.

The Native Americans who accepted the Two Spirit considered it a blessing. Some tribes considered it a gift because it conferred the ability to see both sides of life. Just be what you are is the lesson I took from that study.

But that's enough of that. I was happy to have the chance to experience both. I thanked the Maker for the chance, then settled into a restful sleep.

The New Me

I woke at six, anxious to try out the new me. I had a few minutes before I had to start my plan. I started thinking, trying to remember things from Ursula's past. One thing I remembered clearly. Didn't count as the old Ursula, but it did count as my first dream as her.

Of special note, I don't usually remember my dreams, but one last night stuck with me. I wore armor, like St. Joan of Arc. Mounted on a sorrel charger, I led a mixed unit of cavalry, archers, and foot soldiers of an army. Three other units were on my right flank. The knight to my far right led another cavalry unit. He had obviously seen recent combat. His armor was dented, muddy, and bloody.

The other two had bright and shiny armor that appeared to be recently purchased. They led the charge, but were quickly routed because their troops were tired from the run before they reached the enemy. Those knights were the first to break and run for safety.

As the infantry from the first wave neared the top of the hill we held, I rode over and rallied some of them and moved slowly over the hill to the reverse slope. The proven knight on my flank did likewise. We stopped and waited while the infantry got its breath back as I assigned some of the junior leaders to instill some semblance of fight into those who stayed for the battle.

The enemy misread the situation and chased what they

thought was a fleeing foe. They were tired and disorganized when they neared the top of the hill. We marched over the crest into them and rolled over them. Their knights and foot soldiers either surrendered or died on the field. Their king was surrounded by the dark knight's and my cavalry, captured, and finally surrendered.

The shiny knights rejoined us when the battle was over. They tried to take credit for the victory, but our king laughed them out of the tent. He honored the proven knight with a title and a large estate, me with a title and a nice though smallish estate near the proven knight. I wondered if he had plans for us.

Only thing I could make of it was that I needed to be wary of the untested. Untested for what was open to further discovery. But it had awakened me before the alarm sounded. That was good. Better an early start than rush to catch up. I turned off the alarm five minutes before it rang.

I showered and shampooed, dried my hair, brushed my teeth, and applied a light coat of war paint. (They do call it the battle of the sexes, after all.) I wore mascara, eyeliner, eye shadow, a light hint of blush and some lip liner and lipstick. I dug out the brush and did my hair in a pony tail after I removed the tangles. I found an emergency change of bra and thong panties in the purse's zippered pocket. I donned the blouse and skirt, and checked the image in the mirror. The flannel lined jacket would wait until closer to time to go outside. These heels were comfortable and sexy. That was a new experience I savored.

Back in the room proper, I sat in a chair at the small table and considered my next move, or moves. That's when Pete arrived with a soft glow compared to the blinding light of his first visit. "Hi, Pete."

"Good morning. I see you're ready to go. Do you like the new body?" he asked.

"Very much, so far. When I get fully used to it, I may change my mind, but, for now, it's great". I replied.

"Good. You're making points. Keep this up and you won't be breaking too many rocks in purgatory when it's your time. When Sue picks you up, clear out your old studio apartment and spend some time tonight seeing where the former Ursula came from. " he counseled.

"How am I going to do that?"

"Her diaries would be a good start. She kept good records. Also check the file box in the dresser. " he suggested.

"Thanks. I forgot you mentioned that before. Thanks for the reminders. I likely wouldn't have thought to check those." I responded.

"See you later. Your breakfast is almost here." He left as the door opened.

The nurse knocked and came in. "Good. You're up. You should be first in line at checkout."

I started giggling. She looked at me quizzically. I explained, "I just had an image of a grocery store checkout lane. Just seemed funny. 'And what did you buy?' 'Nothing much, just a tonsillectomy and two quarts of ice cream. Put it on my insurance card." She chuckled with me.

Then she apologized, "The oatmeal is a little off. Breaking in a new cook in the kitchen."

I checked the clock when I finished eating. Eight twenty AM. Still on schedule. Actually twenty- five minutes ahead, but the wallpaper paste they passed off as oat-meal would stick around for a while judged by how long it took me to choke down a bowl even with the milk they provided. Thankfully, they sent two of those individual containers of strawberry preserves for the toast. The coffee wasn't bad either.

I used the spare time before going to checkout to make a

final sweep of the room. Nothing I had was worth that much until you added the memories. That's not to mention the aggravation of replacing a favorite item lost at an inopportune time.

I remembered the note that gave me permission to walk out rather than ride a wheelchair. Came in handy just a little after I vacated the room with my belongings.

As I walked to the elevator, a handsome dude wearing scrubs came up ahead of me. I tried to go around him, but he told me, "Sit down. You're not cleared to walk yet."

I faced him. First impression pegged him as a guard or tackle, but, from his pale skin, one that spends too much time in the gym rather than outside. He should be more tanned by the end of summer.

"Hate to spoil your fun, but I've got this." I showed him the note. "Same note as on my chart. Doctor told me not everybody reads the chart, so I carry this with me."

He muttered, "Dang it. I finally had a chance to wheel a looker, and now all I can look forward to all day are those overweight prune faces from the geriatric ward."

I laughed. He laughed. "Maybe I can save your day. If it means that much to you." I sat in the chair and instructed, "All right, Jeeves, to check out. Chop chop. Quickly, quickly."

He looked shell shocked, but was quick enough to ad lib his line in the script. "Of course, Madam. Fasten your seat belt."

I mimed fastening a seat belt in the exaggerated pretense of the stage to ensure the back row saw the motions. "I'm ready, Jeeves. You may proceed."

We chatted on the elevator. I found he was a sophomore studying civil engineering and held the grade of sergeant in the local Army Reserve unit of Engineers. I congratulated him for picking a real job for his study and related my bad choice as an example of blowing it. I couldn't help noticing that he was quite pleasing to the eye. Tall, athletic, easily capable of any sport played in the vertical, or horizontal, plane. I really needed a queen bed, I decided. Not for him, but for a guy old enough to interest me.

"I'm Ursula Chadwick, barmaid at the Spotted Horse Saloon. Why don't you come by some time? I'll even tell the other barmaids you gave me the ride of my life." I winked. "That will break the ice even before you get there." Seemed almost a perfect match for Francine. Maybe I could help Cupid with this one.

He took it well. "Thank you, Miss Chadwick. I'll remember that. My name is Hugh Long. When is a good time for that visit?"

"Probably the night before your day off would be good. If you work this shift regularly, you don't want to come to work tired, drunk, or hung over." I replied. He nodded as he made a mental note.

The door opened and he wheeled me to the check-out section of the admissions desk. "You can stand up now." he said.

"Thank you for the ride. It was quite fun." I stood and shook his hand. He reciprocated. I felt tingles where I didn't know the human body tingled. I wondered if he was one of the knights in shining armor I dreamed about, or if he was the battle tested one. Or was he just the joker in the deck? Useless unless the game was Jokers Wild poker.

I took a place near the checkout window. Louisa, the administrative clerk Faith recommended, opened the window five minutes later. She asked my name. I gave it and mentioned that I was injured at work. She checked and found my file.

After going through the charges on the statement, Louisa drew my attention to a waiver of coverage for future charges for any conditions not in my medical records related to this incident. Any such future conditions would require a new claim. Since it sounded fair to me, I signed it as understanding what it said. Too, it was quicker than waiting for a lawyer to nitpick it. Plenty time to choose a lawyer if it went to court, but I didn't see that happening. Louisa explained it very well.

Then I signed the statement that I agreed to cover any charges refused by the insurance company. It was pretty clear to me that I only had a couple nights, meals and tests related to transport to and a stay in a hospital after an act of violence at work. I didn't expect any rejected charges since I stayed only at doctor's orders. Another time to trust to luck that I'd find a good lawyer if it went to litigation.

When we were finished, I looked at the clock. Only nine thirty AM. That was fast. If Sue came on time, I could relax for a while. I spotted a seat in the waiting room that would let me watch the entrance. I sat there and looked through the stack of months old magazines until I found one that might interest me. As I thumbed through the first magazine, it dawned on me I had no trouble walking in these three-inch heels. Must have worn them a lot.

Two articles later, one on fashions for Fall, the other on Fall makeup trends, for last year, the clock showed nine fifty- three. I returned the magazine to the stack and started to watch the door for Sue. My vigil was not in vain. She came through the door five minutes later. I walked over to her. "Hi, Sue."

She looked at me for a couple of seconds that felt like years to me. The glimmer of recognition flashed in her eyes. "Hi, Ursula. How are you? When they took you out to the ambulance, we were worried." She paused to bring the conversation to the present. "How's your checking out coming along?"

"I'm ready to go. Finished checking out a few minutes ago. Those jeans fit you well." I pulled on my jacket as we spoke.

"Thanks. I got some stretch leggings that look like jeans this time. A lot of people call them jeggings. Don't keep me from breathing, but really hug me nicely. You should try a pair." She preached to the choir, then said, "If you're ready, let's go.

Found a spot and parked nearby."

We left the hospital and its unpleasant aromas behind for the fresh air of November on the High Plains. Just a hint of a nip started me thinking about an insulating middle layer. Winter was still two months in the future, but the lining of this jacket wasn't up to the job alone, not with the thin blouse I wore for work at any rate.

I felt uncaged, loose and dangerous, as we walked out to the vehicle. I spotted the Hunter Green pickup. As Bear, I owned the only one in town because I ordered it instead of buying one of the metallic silvers, grays, blacks, or reds on the dealer's lot. Took a lot of haggling with the salesman to get the work truck. He kept trying to talk me into one of the pricey models with fancy names. "Brought my truck. Good move. If I weren't me, I wouldn't have recognized it. You were screening me without saying a word."

Sue's head snapped around to look at me. "What did Bear wear to the costume contest?" she questioned.

It didn't take long to describe the salt and pepper long straight wig, tight hot pink sweater with deep Vee neck worn over a bra with breast forms, the miniskirt of snake skin grain black pleather, and black patent leather four-inch heels. "I also enjoyed what you told the other Ursula when you registered us, madam governor."

"You really are Bear, then? How? Where? When? Why? her voice trailed off as she wrapped her mind around this minor miracle.

I answered, "How is likely a minor miracle I can't explain. The nurse said I flat lined for some seconds in the ambulance. That would be my guess about where and when. I had a dream about, or maybe an actual visit by a spirit that claimed to be my guardian angel. He said I was needed because I am a tested warrior, and, with this body, said I now have powers that I'll need in a battle coming up. Again, that's just my guess at why."

"What battle coming up?" Sue asked.

"Gus Will told me about a proposal from Junior Forrest." I repeated the story he told me, and continued, "That would destroy the boundary ecosystem between the crop land and the woods. Add that I've heard that some people who opposed the Forrests wound up dead. That's what will turn this into a battle not resolved in court or by protests on the streets."

"From what I know about you as Bear, I'm glad you were picked for the fight, though not anxious for it to come to that." Sue commented.

"Same here." I replied. "But nobody hires a soldier unless there's a war coming."

We reached the pickup. Sue opened the doors and started to go to the passenger side. I stopped her. "You better drive. Doctor told me to be careful for another day. Make sure I don't rattle a blood clot loose. If I did, I'd likely crash."

I got in the passenger side. That was a trick with the long step up and a short skirt. Good thing it didn't end with me on my ass in the parking lot or exposed to God and the world because the skirt rode up too high. I managed adequately.

She just jumped into the driver's side, but didn't start the engine right away. "This is as good a time as any to tell you what I found on the Internet sites. Can you handle it that Bear Warsawski was your grandfather?"

"What?" I felt a bit light headed at the news. "Either you got the wrong people or the web was wrong, as far as I know."

"No. I double checked it because I didn't believe it either." She pulled out a sheet of paper with the notes she took. "From the dates, I worked out that Victor proposed to Joyce but got called up and enlisted rather than be drafted. He shipped out to Viet Nam before the planned wedding. Joyce had a hard time being fiancée to somebody never home because of service.

From the dates, she broke it off with Bear before she knew she was pregnant with your mom."

Seemed pretty thin to me. I was skeptical until I remembered some things. Grandpa Pete rarely talked about family and never about his service with me, though a member of the VFW. It was possible grandpa Victor was the same close-mouthed type. Also had a memory from Victor's trove. I remember that last night when she gave the ring back. I thought it was temporary until I got back. It wasn't the best memory I had. Less enjoyable than some of the fire fights I had been in.

"OK. What next? Give me a heart attack while we're close to the hospital." I laughed.

Sue reported, "Joyce met Peter Kovac. He already finished his enlistment. Aided by two missed periods, he swept her off her feet and they married. She had Victor's daughter less than seven months after that. They claimed she was just premature rather than fathered before they met.

Holy Mackerel! So that's why she wrote that Dear John letter saying she met somebody new. "What else?"

"They named your mom Victoria in Bear's honor. Loved her like she was theirs, but without much discipline. She became a very wild child. When she grew up, she married Louis Chadwick. He lost control on some ice and crashed his car on the way to the hospital for the birth of their only child. That's you, Ursula."

"What happened after that?"

"He died at the scene, so Victoria moved back in with mom and dad. When she died from pneumonia, Peter and Joyce took you in, and became your legal guardians. You must have been about ten then. They did a better job raising you, based on the rank in class you managed." Sue related.

"How did I get here, to this spot in my life, a decade later?"

"Pretty straight forward, really. You finished grade school

and high school near the top of your class, then went to college. Your freshman year, Joyce died from cardiac arrest, a heart attack. Peter died your junior year." She finished her thought. "You've never been in trouble bad enough to be listed for an arrest."

I had a vague recollection of that. He was down in the dumps when I visited that Christmas. Two weeks before finals that spring semester, I buried him next to Joyce. The medical examiner's opinion was some long medical term. I called it a broken heart. Closer to the truth as a reason, he lost his will to live. That was a painful memory.

"I can finish the story from there. I graduated with a B.F.A. in theater. Spent a year looking for a role to break into the business, but got rejected at every audition. Went to work at the saloon because the tips were good and my godfather owns the place." I chuckled. "Speaking of the saloon, still time to make the Sunday brunch special. While there, I can let my boss know I'm all right. Maybe even find the car I own."

Sue turned the key, The engine started, and we were going to the saloon like a thirsty cow that smelled water and was headed that way at a fast walk. Nothing was going to stop us except old age... or an assassin. I was taken aback by that thought from nowhere, but hid it.

"I suggest we drive as quickly as possible and still get there safely. If we get there before noon, we can get the Sunday Brunch special.

"I know. I'm doing the limit." Sue answered. Then she laughed. "Didn't they give you any breakfast in the hospital?"

"The spaghetti and meat balls for supper last night was tasty, but the tile grout they passed off as oatmeal for breakfast today sucked." I snorted. "I want something that tastes good and digests easily." Both of us chuckled at that.

We got to the saloon shortly and found a spot near the

employee parking. I pointed out the pink ten-year-old compact four door alone in the back row. "Bet that's mine."

Sue studied the atrocious vehicle. "Get a camper top for the pickup instead. You could deliver your services that way, Mona. Or get a van and set it up as a mobile boudoir." Sue started laughing as she listed what she thought needed to go into such a contraption. She didn't finish until we were at the front door. We stopped again before we went in.

Part of the blame fell on me. I asked if she meant the old geezers at the Shady Rest. "I can see the line of walking frames and oxygen tanks lined up outside my pink van now."

She broke up again, that was a shorter fit than the first one, but still kept us at the front door instead of through it and ordering brunch.

I applied the brakes to this trend of conversation. "I've had an idea. I need to vacate my apartment and move into Bear's place. We can do that after we eat, though."

Sue stopped laughing. She agreed that was a good idea, but I might want some help. There might be some furniture to move. She had to check the records to find whether or not the original furniture had been put in storage and replaced with the tenant's own.

"I figure I might get some help from the crew of my old firm. They would work only a few jobs now. The construction season for framers is about over. Still want to get some belongings tonight. It was suggested by that angel I mentioned. I can get the big stuff after you check the records to find out what if any is mine." I offered a compromise proposal.

We went in, found a table, and ordered. Since the smoke alarm went off whenever I fried bacon at home, I rarely made it. I like it crispy, which means a hot enough fire to trigger the alarm located too close to the stove. But I did like some when I didn't have that distraction. This was a restaurant and I ordered bacon, eggs, and hash browns, with toast and coffee. Sue had almost the same except had sausage in place of the bacon.

When our food was served, we ate despite the interruptions of well-wishers. The longest such came from my godfather/ boss, Bob Josepski. He talked a lot, but did deliver some good news. He gave me time off until after the funeral for Victor. When I asked why, he said I'd find out sooner or later that Victor and I were related. He'd been with Victor when they met Pete and Joyce and Joyce bragged about how their baby Victoria was getting along in the terrible twos. Didn't take rocket science to figure out he was Victoria's father. Bob figured I'd want to be there now rather than kick myself for missing it later. I thanked him.

We finished our food, had a second cup of coffee while we planned the afternoon. After we finished our coffees, and paid the bill, we were on our way again. I drove the Pink Lady, Ursula's car, to Bear's house and put it in the garage. Sue followed and I joined her in the truck. This time to my apartment.

As we arrived, I commented, "This seems like I know it for some reason." Of course, I did. I lived here. Just played the amnesia card as a joke. I spoiled it with a chuckle after I said it.

Sue answered, "It should. Besides living here, you and your guys did all the carpentry when it was built. The studio and one-bedroom apartments are quite popular with young adults and with empty nesters."

"Yes, I remember now. Your dad designed it and just about every contractor and subcontractor in the county bid on the project. One of the few that were done two weeks before the contracted finish by date. Who owns it now?"

Sue grinned when she admitted, "I do. Dad built it on speculation, kept it for the income, and left it to me in his will."

"Looks in good shape. Glad to see you're not a slum lord." I managed the statement with a straight face. The follow up smile and giggle made my intent to tease obvious. We laughed. "Well, landlord, I've got bad news for you. I think I've inherited a house, so I'll move out."

Sue replied, "We'll check the apartment for damage first, but I think you'll get your damage deposit back." She thought a bit, then added, "In fact, this will be the inspection as well as moving a grumpy tenant out." She made it to sentence end before she started giggling. That started me laughing.

We parked out front and went in after I found the key. The apartment was on the second floor to the end of the hall on the right, I let us in. Smallish studio apartment, obviously home to a romantic young female, greeted us warmly, figuratively, almost with a hug. "No wonder I still have a ten-year-old car. Spent all my money on pictures, drapes, and furniture." I joked. "Or did you furnish all the apartments this well?" I asked Sue. She said she would check the records tomorrow and let me know. That brought another round of laughter.

I looked around. A four drawer 'campaign style' chest (the kind with brass corner bracing to stand a lot of moving) anchored one corner. A single bed disguised as a sofa during the day was located along the longer wall. A campaign style night stand held a converted to electric light oil lamp. Other bits and pieces took care of the living room. The kitchen held what in my youth were called apartment sized stove, sink, and refrigerator with cabinets in an ell shape arrangement around the inside wall. A small dining table with two chairs marked the dining area under the outside wall window.

Two doors led off the kitchen. The first door led to a three-quarter bath-sink in a cabinet, medicine cabinet behind the mirror, toilet, and a good size shower, with enough space to turn around or dress comfortably left over.

The second was entry to a walk-in closet. The clothes would provide me a starter wardrobe. A rain coat, a trench coat with zip in liner, and a winter coat almost hid the brilliant sapphire blue formal still in the dry cleaner's bag. Two suits, several skirts of varied length and fabric, some dressy pants, blouses and shirts, and several pairs of footwear were there also.

Took a couple of big leaf bags to make short term garment bags to move the clothes on their hangers. Two heavy duty tall kitchen bags held the footwear. Another to clear the shelf above the rod, and I was ready for a beer, if any was around the house.

The cupboard was sparsely loaded with some canned goods, bran flakes, and oatmeal. All fit easily in another tall kitchen bag but I used two because the cans threatened to fall through the bottom with the load. The refrigerator held milk, butter, eggs, and a six pack of beer. I had one and gave one to Sue. We agreed to take the rest with us to the house. After we drank our beers, we emptied the refrigerator and freezer into the kitchen trash can.

The dresser contained jeans, sweaters, sweat shirts, shorts, underwear, stockings, and socks. There was also one of those portable file boxes insulated to minimize fire damage. I looked inside and found documents of interest. Also found diaries from sixth grade to high school graduation, a second one from then to present. It looked like I had my evening's reading, and that recent diary was going to be first book read.

We carried the bags out to the truck and loaded the back seat with the clothes. The diaries and file box went into the front seat with me. The stuff that didn't fit in the back seat wound up in the pickup's box. At my house, we put the perishables into the freezer or the refrigerator first. Clothes on hangers were hung in a closet. Shoes and boots also went in on the floor.

We each had a beer as the sun neared its setting. I gave Sue a ride to her house before dusk became night. When I got back, I opened the file box and found enough evidence to support a claim that Victor was my real grandpa, but Peter was married to grandma when mom was born and was on the birth certificate as her dad. There was still a stigma attached to children before marriage then. Politely ignored inside families, but not everyone was family. The old timers handled it well.

Then I opened the current diary at two weeks ago and read up until last entry 30 October, Thursday. I took the liberty to finish entries for the weekend. It pleased me that the handwriting matched. It was going to be a strange change of topics, but no one would see it until I died. That wouldn't be for a few years yet, I hoped.

I read for a while longer. Started at the front and worked my way back. One, no three things, caught my attention. The first was the ability to do things not in the usual repertoire for normal humans which she discovered a long time ago. She tried not to use them at all unless to save a life.

The second was her long held desire to own an Appaloosa mare. She wanted one that would carry her to victory in barrel races, and have foals that would carry on that heritage. Until I remembered she was raised out here among horses and cattle, that struck me as a little strange for a young woman. Not so weird when even a lot of town folk had horses.

The last was a lament that she wasted four years to study acting when she could have studied to be a veterinarian, or at least an assistant in a vet's office. That came after the twelfth rejection by local amateur theater groups for productions since she graduated, and minor roles in movies filmed in the state. The one that broke her was rejection for a member of a crowd scene in a production filmed locally. She asked herself, "Why would I get rejected for a non-speaking role in an uncredited spot in a crowd?"

She concluded the reason for rejection was that she was too tall for the movies with male leads filled by guys shorter than she was. In heels, she towered above them. That or the fact she refused a producer's invitation to 'audition' on his casting couch put her on a black list. It moved me to sympathy for the girl who had been in this body just three nights ago.

I went to sleep a little misty eyed. That happens whenever dreams are dashed and trashed, whether mine or those of someone I liked.

Second Day

I woke to a chilly house. After the bathroom call, dug out a sweatshirt from the pile of clothing still to be put in the dresser. Decided I needed some fleece lined slippers if this was a normal thing. For now, I pulled on some socks, and checked the thermostat.

That was the problem. Ambient air temperature was 64°, noticeably cool without the blanket I slept under. The thermostat was set at 60°, I reset the dial to 68°. The furnace kicked on after a short delay. That should make it comfortable soon.

In the kitchen, I looked out the window. 'That dog doesn't belong here.' was my first thought after I noticed him. 'Not going out in just a pair of socks and a sweatshirt to shoo him home.' was the second. 'That can wait until after breakfast.' was the third.

That decision made, I started making breakfast. Nothing spectacular. Just a bowl of cereal, bran flakes if you need to know, with milk, some toast with butter, and coffee. I washed the dishes and let them air dry in the rack near the sink.

I looked out the window again and didn't see the dog. I thought his wanderlust led him away. It eased my mind to think he had a home to return to. It was coming on winter, and he needed a warm place to sleep with a family that loved him.

Time to get dressed. I found and donned a pretty pair of hot pink bikini panties and a pair of snug jeans. Next was to try shoes that fit over socks. The mid-heel loafers did as long as the socks weren't too thick. Their saddle tan color just went with the faded blue of the jeans. They might be my favorites for casual wear. I better start looking for replacements. Favorites have a tendency to wear out quickly.

Pete visited, again coming as a glow. "Hi, Pete. What's the skinny this morning?"

"Nothing much. I saw you check the documents. Don't forget you need to show those to police to prove you're a relation. Simplifies claiming the body for burial. " he answered.

"Forgot that. Victor deserves priority attention. I'll do that this morning, then go see the lawyer. I'm glad I, unnh, he signed that will last summer. I need this house to live in."

"Another thing you need to do is make friends with the guns he owned, specially the handguns. Now that you've started down this path, you're a target. Not sure just yet who will make that call, but somebody will. You can bet on it. Bye for now." he said as he faded out.

"Oh great, now I need to worry about killers after me." I thought. Then I remembered that revolver I saw in the night stand last night. It was a Colt Single Action Army, also known as the Peacemaker. That or a look alike. Wasn't in fashion now that everybody thinks they need a semi-auto, but it was the one Bear had depended on during times of danger. If good enough for him, it was good enough for me.

I changed from sweatshirt to a plaid flannel shirt, got the revolver from the night stand, unloaded it, and stuck it in my purse. It rested alongside the documents I needed to show my lineage included Victor. Grabbed a heavy cardigan sweater, and headed out the back door.

"Dang dog. You almost tripped me." I told the dog sleeping in the doorway. He looked at me with a sheepish grin on his face. I was done for once I looked him in the eyes. He didn't have a collar, so he was mine. Finder's keepers would be my defense if an ownership dispute ever made it to court.

"What do I call you? Rover? That would fit since that's how you got here." He yawned, I felt that was a no. A name popped into my head. "How about Shadow, Shad for short?" I swear, he smiled at me. "OK. That's your name, but remember, you picked it. Don't blame me if the other dogs make fun of you for that." I felt his confidence that wouldn't be a problem.

"OK, Shad, have a drink before we go. Just a little one, though. You'll spend a lot of time alone in the truck while I take care of some important business." He acted like he agreed.

In the kitchen, I dug out a steel mixing bowl and gave him about a pint of water. He lapped it up quickly. "OK, Shad. Time to roll. We're burning daylight, as John Wayne said in one of his movies."

First stop was the police station. I walked in and went to the desk. I inquired, "Is Detective O'Doyle in?"

"I think he is. Let me check for you. Your name please?" the desk sergeant replied.

"Ursula Chadwick. This is about the shoot-out at the saloon Friday night."

He dialed and spoke to whoever answered the call. "He'll be out shortly. Take a seat until he gets here if you'd like."

"Thanks." I said. I turned to my right and went to the bench. It had only one other person on it. She looked like a young runaway from the Hollywood rendition of a runaway's 'uniform', down to the holey panty hose below ragged jacket and skirt. That or she rebelled against her parents' affluence. No telling what she had done to wind up here. Might be anything from shop lifting to mass murder or a minor trying to buy booze. I stood at the opposite end of the bench to keep my distance. Better safe than sorry. After all, she was wearing handcuffs and leg shackles. Shackles meant she was more dangerous than average.

A few minutes later, Detective O'Doyle came out and invited me to follow him. Well, it was more like a command. He said, "Follow me, please." with a sharpness that brought visions of a drill field and he was in command. He turned to go back the way he came. I followed.

The detectives' squad room was at the end of a short hall. He indicated I sit in the visitor's chair and took his seat behind a rather cluttered desk. "How may I help you?" he asked.

"I think this is related to the case. I remembered grandma Joyce gave me some papers and said to check them if Victor died." I pulled the papers out of my purse. "It makes more sense if we start from oldest and work up to newest."

He looked interested. I started and fifteen minutes later, we both knew that Joyce had been in love with Victor. She just had to let him go to war the first time, and find somebody else when he volunteered for a second tour in Viet Nam. Joyce admitted that she just wasn't cut out to be a soldier's wife. It was in the Dear John letter she sent him. She married before their (Victor and Joyce) daughter was born. That was my mom. She married and had me. I was raised by Joyce and Peter after mom and dad died. Then grandma died in my second year at college, granddad my junior year. But it showed that I was blood kin to Victor Warsawski.

"I think I'm the next of kin. Want to get that on the record so when you folks are done with Victor, you let me know. As the only known surviving relative, I owe him a proper funeral at least." I explained.

He said, "Looks good to me, but, if you don't mind, I'd like to present this to the City Attorney. Making legal decisions of that kind is above my pay grade. May I take copies of those papers?"

"Sure. Just make sure I get all the originals back." I agreed conditionally. "How soon do you think you'll know?" I queried.

"Don't worry. As the lead detective on this case, I can put a hold on him until further notice for that decision. You'll have the answer before we release him and you can bury him." O'Doyle promised.

"Then make the copies. After I get the originals back, I'll be on my way. I've got some other errands to run before noon." I said.

"Sit. I'll be about five or ten minutes at the copy machine." He smiled and continued, "Unless the copier jams or something." We both chuckled because both of us had experienced that frustration.

He gathered the stack of papers and went to the copier. I looked around the room. Looked like one from those movies set in a busy big town with one difference. Instead of many rooms like this, our town had only this one.

A few minutes later, Detective O'Doyle returned with two stacks of papers. He handed one to me, put the other into a folder, and that into an inter-office mail envelope. He lined out his address and wrote 'City Attorney - Priority' in the next empty space.

"Since the official business is finished for now, have any suggestions where I can try out one of granddad Bear's guns? They need to give instruction to new shooters?" I asked.

"You thinking about buying a gun?" he asked.

I replied, "Not buying, just need to learn to shoot one correctly. I found one in the night stand, and thought I'd keep it as a memento of the man, my granddad, who saved my life. I believe in knowing how to operate any new tool."

He smiled, then said, "Try Northwest Sportsman, about a half mile west of town on 16 Mile Road. The old Gunny was a qualified instructor in the Corps. Semper Fi, Ms. Chadwick.'

"Thanks, and Semper Fi, Detective." Hmmm. That came

easily, like I had done that before, often, a long time ago.

I left and rescued Shad from boredom and loneliness. I know because he told me so. After some petting, I drove over to Victor's lawyer. Gene Washington had opened his practice last spring. Bear was one of his first customers. I walked in and laid out the same story with the same results except he didn't need to check with the city attorney. He agreed that I had a good case to prove I was kin. I asked him to recommend an administrator for the estate, since I was the only known heir. He said the county, under State law, had an elected Public Administrator to take care of cases like this. I said fine.

As he handled the paperwork, I noted he didn't wear a ring. That got my interest. I might just try to make him think of me as more than just a client. Small town lawyers don't make as much as the big city ones, but better than average, if judged by the cars they drove. Didn't want to be too pushy though.

I decided to ask his advice on the potential land grab. He said another client asked the same thing. With two of us asking, he'd make research about it a priority and get back to us. I thanked him and swung my hips a bit wider than usual on the way out. That was as much flirting as I was prepared to do on first meeting not in a bar.

From his reflection in the window, it was enough. He watched my departure at least until I could no longer see his image. I rated that as a good start.

"Only one, maybe two more stops, Shad. I'll try to keep them short." He mumbled his reluctant agreement. On the way to the gun shop, I spotted Farmers Supply. Their roadside sign offered dog food on sale. That was fine by me, considering the circumstances and immediate need.

I parked and went it. Oh, my. This was a lot of stuff. Might be a good place to look for everything I needed, starting from the ground up. I found a couple pairs of heavy wool socks that will be handy when winter comes. Also found some slipper socks and smiled. Wool tops meant warmth to me, and leather soles minimized slipping on shiny floors.

The frost on the lawn this morning would melt and leave wet grass behind. That meant rubber boots, and if snow or sleet, wool socks in them. I looked around and found some 'Made In the USA' chore boots. Equivalent look and construction to the 'Wellies' I'd seen in those British movies on PBS, but at a third of the cost for English made ones in the catalogs, the last time I looked.

Put on a pair of the heavy weight wool socks and found some boots just a bit snug but very comfortable. That should make them loose but comfortable worn with thin socks when it was just a warm rain. I went back to the entrance and got a shopping cart to make lugging my purchases around easier until I was ready to check out.

As I passed the racks of coats, the sign for chore coats caught my eye. 'I've got chore boots. I need a chore coat to go with them.' I thought. I think I smiled at my reason. It seemed my sense of style carried over to dog ownership. I tried one on over the heavy cardigan I wore, and it fit quite well. Unlike the fashion boutique versions, I was still able to move my arms freely. Yes, this was really a work coat, not a fashion clone fake that bound my arms. If you haven't guessed by now, it went in the cart with the boots and socks.

Next rack down, I found lightly insulated jackets. One of those in the chore coat would handle chilly weather not yet cold enough for a winter parka. Inside the chore coat, might even handle freezing temperatures well enough. With their nylon shell, one would be easier to put on than the sweater I wore. Another item in the cart.

In for a penny, in for a pound. The old saying came to mind as I looked at the wide brim hats for rainy weather. Yep. One of those went into the cart, and a USA made watch cap for colder but dry weather.

On the way to the companion animals' section of the store, I came across the rope and cable display for purchases by the foot, pre-measured hank, or spool. That brought memories of some leashes I'd made in the past. I found the pre-measured packages and chose 50 feet of half inch kern-mantle rope with an interesting braid pattern for the mantle layer. The half inch diameter would be more comfortable if Shad tried to pull away suddenly. The memory of the discomfort when another dog did that when I used clothes line for the leash when I had him, and he was much smaller than Shad, made that decision inevitable. Also bought some snap fasteners like those used to attach the lead line to horse halters. If they held a horse, they'd hold Shad. -grin-

Finally in the pet department, I found some stainless steel five-quart bowls. One each for feed and water joined the other stuff in the cart. Add a forty-pound bag of brand name dog food that guaranteed use of real grain for about ten dollars less than two twenty-pound bags of the same brand at the grocery.

Sure, there were cheaper brands available, but I was reluctant to buy those. Caution became necessary after a story broke about a Chinese dog food manufacturer. He wasn't smart and added melamine pellets to raise the protein level. Amine in the name indicated the presence of amino groups. The test for protein measures only the content of nitrogen in a sample regardless of source. Amino groups registered as protein even if from plastic. Not considered is whether or not digestible or safe for animals to eat.

In the ignorance that amino groups could kill dogs and cats, their product used ground melamine to cut costs. That one Chinese manufacturer sickened or killed many dogs and cats. The veterinarians noticed the deaths and tracked the source according to that article in the paper. There was a nervous atmosphere because that story also affected families that used melamine for dishes because they were darn near unbreakable. That ended when eating from those unbreakable plates became suspected dangers. It faded when grinding for pet food that made it dangerous. People went back to the melamine table ware. My dog was lucky that I stuck with the made in USA brands that guaranteed use of natural ingredients.

Flea and tick collars and a sturdy nylon web collar went into the cart also. Just guessing, I bought the biggest size collar they had on display. I got the ok to try the collar on the dog, since he was in the truck. It fit with a bit to spare, so I went in and paid. The receipt showed my total cost this purchase was about half what I would have spent at a department store or boutique and in a grocery or pet store, and would be more durable since made for work rather than the fickle fashion of the day. Who says that the old patterns are old fashioned, not worth the money? They are wrong as can be if durability is one of the criteria.

I loaded my plunder into the truck and continued to the sporting goods store. The parking lot had only one other truck in it, but the 'open' sign was lit. I went in. I didn't see anyone so called out, "Hello? Anybody here?"

A deep rumbling voice came from the man who appeared from behind a display of fishing lures. From the handful carried, he was buying or restocking the lures, "Hello yourself." There was a merry tone to that greeting despite the deep rumble of the voice. "How may I help you?"

"I inherited this gun from my grandfather, and admit I need to find out how to shoot it, Will you help me?"

"Got it with you? Show it to me at the counter." He came over and led me to the counter on which the cash register sat.

I opened my purse and brought out the Peacemaker with a

firm hold on the grip, fingers well away from the trigger. "This is the one." I laid it on the counter.

"Don't see many of these anymore." He checked whether it was loaded or empty before he cocked the hammer. "Hmmm. This is one of the Stainless Ruger Vaguero with transfer from hammer to firing pin. Handles and shoots about the same as the old Colts. Looks like the one I sold to Bear. Are you the granddaughter?

"Yes, though I just found out about the relationship after he died. He and Grandma broke up when he..."

He stopped me short. "Save your breath. I know the story. I was his fire team leader when he got the Dear John letter. Of course, I'll teach you what I can. He saved my bacon a few times. I owe him."

I learned the caliber was .45 Colt. It was a single action revolver. Loaded with care, it would shoot hot loads, but for general use, the old factory load was more than ample with much less recoil. After he showed me how to load it and unload it, he took me to the range. I opted for ear plugs instead of muffs, and a pair of clear shooting glasses for my first lesson.

I also learned again what was a good sight picture and a bad sight picture, and the practical difference between them. With a good sight picture, it's like shooting down a pipe, with a bad sight picture, it's like shooting down a funnel. Old memories rose from their storage area. I recalled the two-hand hold, strong hand to hold the grip properly and squeeze the trigger, weak hand to cock the hammer after firing, and steady the aim during a shot.

He started me at seven yards, more or less. I hit paper with the first shot. He had told me about calling my shot after I fired before checking the target. That was why I knew it would hit low and right but still on paper. After that, I paid attention to the sight picture superimposed on the target. I hit in the black regularly after that, and called my misses accurately. Only practice would improve my score. In actual use against someone who wanted to hurt me, the targets left a lot of chest showing around the edges. I had confidence that I'd hit him/her/it or even them.

He gave me a tip if I ever HAD to shoot an attacker. At short range, the single action revolver could hit near the point of aim by pointing at the target. The grip design was such that it fit a hand pointing at a distant point. "Handy in a gun fight." he chuckled.

He left me to my own devices to serve another customer. I shot the ammunition in the boxes. I could hit paper at fifty feet, in the scoring rings at thirty, and in the black at fifteen feet or closer, including when I tried the finger pointing method. I cleaned up the proximity of the shooting position I used and put the used targets in my purse to study later. Then went up front.

I hung back a little because Gunny, Gunnery Sergeant Leonard Sharp, Retired, conversed with a deputy sheriff. When done, he signaled me to come closer, and introduced his son, Stan. The son's handshake as we were introduced was firm but not bone crushing. Impressed by his looks also, I checked for a ring. He wore neither the physical gold band nor the pale skin of ever having worn one for any length of time.

If Gene doesn't respond in a reasonable time, I have an alternate target. That wasn't a formal thought. It was a strong feeling that would either fade with separation or lead to romance. Only time would tell.

Hmmm. Hugh, orderly at the hospital, Gene, lawyer, and Stan, deputy sheriff. That's three eligible guys, plus Sean, the married detective, like the knights in my dream. Wonder if there's a correlation? Only need to see which one has the battle tested armor to pick my favorite even if not correlated.

After my train of thought left that siding and returned to the main line, I bought another two boxes of .45 Colt cartridges with cast lead 255 grain flat point round bullets. This was about the same load that was first used in the original Peacemakers, or Single Action Army, revolvers, Model of 1873. At that time, it was the most powerful handgun in the US.

A side note. If you're among those who think I messed up, I didn't. The official name of the cartridge is the .45 Colt, not .45 Long Colt. When Smith and Wesson introduced their Schofield break top revolver, the engineering to avoid patent infringements, and the rivalry with Colt at the time made them use a shorter cartridge to fit the chamber. That ensured the cartridges ejected when the action opened and used lower pressures so the action didn't pop open during combat.

The .45 Colt was too long so they shortened it. The cavalrymen issued that revolver called that the ,45 Short Colt, and the longer one for the Colt Single Action Army was the .45 Long Colt to them.

Originally, the Army simplified the supply chain by just issuing the shorter cartridge because it fit either weapon's chamber. Currently, the short cartridge is called the .45 S&W Schofield. That allows use of the original name for the longer .45 Colt cartridge. That's what Gunny told me anyway.

I told Gunny I'd be back soon for lesson two. Might even ask for more lessons with other firearms. He laughed as he responded, "I don't doubt it. I knew your gramps. He had a thing about making a collection of all the firearms he and his family carried during service to this country. That was from 1880 to present. You'll need to look for them. When you're ready, I'll tell you what you need to know."

"I'll do that, Gunny. Semper Fi." I said as I left.

Again got in the truck, apologized to Shad about taking so long, He said he understood. We stopped at the house for lunch and to unload my plunder for the day so far. I checked my watch as Shad made his rounds of the yard. He left deposits at the four corners to mark this ground as ours. I figured it was animal for "Strangers enter at your own risk and stay only at our sufferance."

You never knew a little puddle carried so much information, did you?

I rinsed out the pans, dried the one to be used for his food, and served four cups of kibble based on an estimated 100 pounds of dog. Gave him water too. Made a sandwich for myself.

"Ok, Shad. Eat." He didn't need to say anything. His chomping was clear evidence that he was hungry. So hungry he finished before I had half finished my sandwich. I tore off a piece and gave it to him.

I tapped him on the nose because he tried to take part of my fingers with it. I tapped him on the nose and said, "No. Take it gently. I am sharing with you. Don't bite the hand that feeds you." He hung his head and apologized. "Just don't do that again. OK?" and I pet him gently. He grinned and said thanks.

At Barbara's

"Well, I've got something to report to Barbara when we visit this afternoon. Oh, shoot. Better hurry, It's already twelve-thirty." I thought. "Come on, Shad. Need to visit one more friend today. Barbara Yeager is expecting us."

He jumped up and waited at the door with tail wagging as I pulled on the chore boots and the coat. "Where we're going, might be muddy and has potholes on the best of days." I explained, "Better to prepare for the worst and be surprised when it's not as bad as expected." As afterthought, I loaded the revolver and put it in my purse. "Let's go."

Traffic was light, but the parking lots at any place that served food were full. When I cleared the last chain fast food server, the speed limit increased to sixty-five on route 17, and the road was empty of traffic. The road conditions on 25 Mile Road caused me to slow to about forty-five for the first four miles. Slowed to twenty-five after the pavement ended for the last four. "Made it by one." I told Shad.

Barbara met us on the back porch. "You've had a busy morning, Ursula. Have a seat. Hi, Shad. Glad you found her. Is she treating you well?" I heard him tell her I had. She commented, "Glad to hear that. You'll be with her for a long time even if nothing happens."

She turned to me. "Let me get you a drink first." She rose spryly, disappeared through the door, and returned in a flash. She handed me the drink, and said, "I heard you like Manhattans because, when asked, you don't have to lie that you still have your cherry." She grinned widely. Her face got serious. "Does anybody still care about that?"

"A few, but seems to me that most expect their dates to be experienced."

"That's too bad. Good thing no one expects we witches to be virgins, right?" she giggled like a school girl though she was at least three quarters of a century old, maybe older.

"We witches?" I quizzed.

"Oh dear. You haven't figured that out yet. Have you had any experiences with powers you didn't know you had?" she replied. As I shook my head, no, she said, "Looks like I've got some explaining and teaching to do first."

"Well, tell me what happened this morning. Maybe you missed some clue." Baba stated.

"When I woke, I saw Shad in the yard. I seemed able th hear him when he answered my questions. Later in the day, he seemed able to carry on a conversation." I related the rest of the morning's events and all seemed pretty normal to me.

"Speaking to and understanding what animals respond is the first power to wake. If you follow the usual learning curve, next two should be telekinesis and freezing any non-magical humans, inanimate things around you, and demons." she explained.

"Won't argue about that, but tell me how I got to be a witch."

"You still have questions. Let me put your mind to ease. Your family tree goes back to the original Barbara Yeager. She had three sons and three daughters. One of those daughters, Helen, married and had children. Another generation later, her daughter, Lucy, had a child she named Joyce. Victor was born to another daughter two generations removed from Barbara Yeager. They met in school, dated in high school, grew to love each other deeply, planned to marry, but never did because he went to war. Even though they never married, they had a child. Her name was Victoria. Victor is your blood granddad while Peter was your legal one because he married Joyce when she discovered she was pregnant."

She smiled, said, "You have powers because of genes linked to the X chromosomes. Has to be on two chromosomes, one X from your father and one X from your mother to be really strong. Victor Warsawski had one because his mother was a witch. Joyce was a witch in her own right so your mom was one but she never had the discipline to discover that before she died. The Chadwicks had about the same story. There was the very good chance that you have the genes. When you reported you could understand the animals, you proved you're a witch too. I thought you already knew when you called me Baba your last visit."

"I felt Victor and I were related, in spirit at least. By itself, that took some getting used to. Now, you tell me that I have genes that really give me magical powers." That revelation had my mind spinning. One thing when I thought it was a fun game. Entirely different when it was presented as fact. What she proposed was at the least daunting. I wanted time to consider it calmly before I answered either yea or nay. "I need time to think about that. May I call you later to talk after I digest this news? Will I be able to do any more than those three things you mentioned?" I queried.

"Yes, but first, you must decide to be a good witch or a bad one. I can only tell you, I've found being a good witch has a few benefits that evil witches can't get. Then you must study and practice." Baba answered.

"I can think of one or two right now, without thinking about it. I imagine there's no such thing as a clear conscience and a good night's sleep for evil witches, or talks with your guardian angel, either." I said.

"Must be your grandpas are putting in a good word for you. That or you've already decided without realizing it." Barb smiled.

"Would a decision to fight to save the nearby farms and woods to protect the ecosystem count as a decision to be a good witch?" I questioned.

"Oh, heavens, yes, child. That would." The youthfulness for one of great age returned to her face and her smile.

Another question popped into my head, silly but I wanted to know, so I asked it. "Will I have to wear all black outfits all the time now?"

"Heavens, no. That isn't a rule for witches except in the movies and most of those are bad witches Sometimes black is appropriate for the social occasion, but, generally, you can wear what you like. Maybe once upon a time it was a rule for all, but not since the Great Depression of the thirties has any good witch worried about it. The patterns on the cloth flour sacks and feed bags were bright for a depression, and many had to use that cloth for clothes." Barb answered with a chuckle in her voice Then she invited me to the next meeting of the coven.

I accepted, maybe "If I'm lucky, I might make it if the wake is over before Saturday." I realized what I said. How did I know that?

"Good. I'll let the others know the meeting will be on Monday. You should be free by then." Barbara said. "Be here by five in the afternoon for the meeting. Come earlier if you like. Bring Shadow. His momma worries about him." She smiled warmly.

"I think you'll fit into the coven quite nicely. You have the smarts, the attitude and the will for it."

"Don't know diddly squat about magic or witchcraft, though. You sure I'll be able to help?"

"Oh, my dear. You've forgotten that a gathering of witches

is only one meaning of coven, though the one most commonly used." she reminded. 'The dictionary shows that's a common mistake. Lazy writers are responsible for that. They stop at the easy definition if they open a dictionary at all. That makes people think it means only that as a result.

She sipped her drink and finished. "Actually, it means any gathering or meeting. The word comes from the old 'covin' which connotes a secret meeting is stated 'specially for witches.' The 'specially of witches is added in deference to the most common usage. In our case it's a secretive meeting because it needs to be if we will protect the forest from greedy, moneyed folks. We call ourselves 'The Coven' and my place happens to be 'on 25 Mile Road'. There's little witchcraft involved, unless you call lawsuits, or raising public awareness and sentiment witchcraft. Some of our members, as you do, have some powers not usual for humans, but the membership works with the laws on the books. Some of our foes over the years have used 'itches' because we annoy them. Others start it with a W or a B, depending on who says it."

That was worth a chuckle. When I stopped, I quipped, "Whew. That's a relief. I can understand keeping it on the down low if the Forrest family is involved. They don't have a high regard for nature at all. Just want to make more money even if their projects destroy an ecosystem. Too, I've heard rumors that they contract killers to remove serious opponents. They're short-sighted sons of bit - beaches."

"That's not far off the mark, Ursula. There should have been a fourth servant in that parable" Barbara commented. 'The one who drowned after straightening a river and planting right to its banks. The rains came and the river couldn't hold the flow so it flooded the valley. He drowned in the flood.

"The same problem we have now. Lots of folks ask 'can we', answer yes, then do it. Too few ask 'should we' and stop if the answer is no. A total lack of common sense." I added.

"See? You already think like a coven member. You'll fit right in." Barbara said with a grin. "Your last point just proves common sense isn't common anymore."

Subconsciously, I checked the lengthening shadows, then my watch. I finished my drink in one gulp and said, "Sorry to leave, but I'd like to get home before night fall. Can we continue the discussion next visit?"

"Certainly. You should be able to fit that in your schedule after Bear's funeral. Before you go, though, do you know what your name means?"

"Not really. Never thought about it much." I answered and stayed seated.

"Do you know how to find the North Star?" she asked.

"Yes. Find the Big Dipper and use the two stars at the bottom of the dipper cup to determine the line to the Little Dipper. The North Star is at the end of the Little Dipper's handle." I answered.

"Not bad, but the Dippers are only parts of constellations known as Ursa Major and Ursa Minor. The Greeks had some mythology to explain how they were formed, which gave them those names. The Romans changed the names, but the basic story is very similar."

She continued, "Callisto, which means beautiful, was one of the hunter maidens with allegiance to Artemis, goddess of the moon, wild animals and hunting. They swore to remain virgins for life. Problem was that Zeus noticed Callisto because of her beauty and lusted after her. He made many attempts to seduce her, finally succeeding. She got pregnant. Tried to hide it. She couldn't. Artemis, angered by the broken oath, turned Callisto into a bear to run wild in the forests until killed by hunters. Callisto gave birth to Zeus' son, Arcas, which means born of a bear. Raised by a lesser goddess, he never knew his mother's story. Out hunting, he spotted a huge bear and threw his javelin. Zeus intervened to prevent matricide, turned Arcas into a bear also, and threw them both into the sky to become the Ursa, or Bear, constellations. Next time you look at them, think of them as protectors of earth and mankind, and the North Star, Polaris, as a guiding beacon for travelers, and has been for a very long time."

"That's some story. But how does that tie into what my name means?"

"Ursula is a variation of Ursa, so you are 'little bear'. Chadwick means 'from the warrior's village'. Remember that you fight to protect the wild creatures."

Then Baba commented, "To me, a real life huntress is better than one just known for being known, like the Hollywood stars. She would be a much better protector of these woods than an empty skirt who talks more balderdash than should be allowed."

"I'll consider that, but I'll have to work out how it fits into what I know and believe. But thanks for the story. It was very entertaining." I said, and meant it. "Now I really have to go. Until the next time we meet, Lord bless and keep you."

"Have a safe trip, and sleep well, Little Bear." Barb offered.

I headed for the truck and called, "Shad, wherever you are, I'm leaving. Come on."

Shad came from the shadow of the truck. He asked if I understood now how he got his name. I answered with a chuckle. "Now I do, and I see you….you sneaky dog."

Barbara and I waved good-bye. Shad and I left while still light, though storm clouds gathered on the western horizon. That storm might miss us if it followed the southwesterly wind blowing at ground level No telling where it was headed if it followed the winds at higher altitudes.

In the first leg of the trip, we drove into the setting sun. I realized I disliked that cliche. When I was a kid, it signaled the end of the movie, period. Now, to me, it signals the ignored sadness of the girl is left standing alone while the hero leaves behind to seek his next adventure.

My adventure was just starting and too early in the story to know whether I'd be a heroine or bystander, in the front lines or left behind them. We got home before the storm hit and were warm and cozy for the evening.

Shad ate first. I gave him water and added some hamburger to the kibble in the other bowl. I wanted a hot meal but didn't feel like cooking. I checked the frozen dinners. The chicken fried beef patty struck me as what I wanted for supper. I put one in the oven. In the thirty-some minutes before I ate, I checked the answering machine for messages, there were two.

The first call was from O'Doyle. The M.E. (Medical Examiner) needed results for two more tests before he released the body. He expected the lab's report by Tuesday afternoon. If those came in, he'd release the body by Wednesday noon. He added that it looked definitely like a shooting. The test results would allow a conclusion whether an accidental death or an intentional shot fired to kill a specific person - a murder.

The second call was from Sue. The records showed I had asked them to store a queen bed and some other items, and use my own chest of drawers instead of the one they provided. She also asked me to call her tomorrow. She had an unexpected date tonight.

That left me time to consider the stories Baba told me. I allowed that man as a species was still working without real science, or a universal ability to write in years BC (or B.C.E if you prefer). That would mean they wanted explanations for things unexplainable with their contemporary knowledge. That was focused on survival at that time. A god or goddess with specific responsibilities and a chief riding herd on the bunch would make sense to them. It was the same form of 'government' as they used for their tribes.

They also made for good stories to explain what was without the science to explain how the thing came into existence. The traveling story tellers would get a meal and a relatively safe place to sleep in exchange for a rousing tale. A good story still sells. Ask the programmers for TV or the producers of movies how much they make. Same principal.

The tribal start man got from the first group of people that joined together for mutual assistance still evidenced itself. Politicians and church fathers are the current chiefs and fear consolidation. They still preach the differences between groups and religions rather than the commonalities. I decided I could accept the myths as explanations for things once upon a time, before books were commonly available outside the nobility and richest common folk.

For myself, I believe in One God Who wears many hats, just like any business man, but had differing personalities depending on which hat was worn. That squared with the Trinity concept, one God in Three Persons. Those taught otherwise might put emphasis on a few specific powers in one individual, or have different names for the Great Maker. Others went back to ancient polytheistic religions, some because they couldn't accept a single god with that much power, others because it was just the fashionable alternative. Others just rebelled against all common religions. They might have any number of gods, or no god at all. As long as I was free to believe and worship as I chose, I'd let them follow their conscience.

Says to do so in the first amendment. But that doesn't make me choose to be friends with them if I don't like them personally or have political differences, like the groups that want to tear down our laws and install theirs instead. For example, it was a long fight from the founding until 1920 and women finally got the right to vote in federal elections. For another the fight to be considered people with rights equal to those of men is still waged. I'm not fond of those who want to make me a piece of property again, or to think the same things they do without question with a death penalty if I don't.

Instead, I cherish the rights to associate freely with those of my choice and to voice my opinion if I think others are blowing smoke. I do a lot of that during election years. --grin-

That brought a new thought. Professional politicians strike me as snake oil salesmen when they shill "one world government" like a street vendor. It's worth extreme efforts to avoid knowing them personally. That's one of the reasons I have never gone to see a politician, though during election years, some of them have come to see me at work or while shopping.

No, not to see me personally, but as a member of the faceless monolithic group they call voters which they recently decided were also members of conflicting subgroups. Just because they think so doesn't make it correct, and I try to avoid the political BS.

Worst one I have ever met that way is the current governor. He blew into the store, shook hands, gave his name, office sought, and solicited votes from everyone. Then he blew out to torment the folks in the next store. As far as his terms in office, let me just say I'm proud I have never cast a ballot for him. I refuse to accept blame for his term. Maybe I'll add that I'm amazed he hasn't been jailed yet. I still await an explanation where the budget surplus went that the previous governor left him. But he was elected and I call him governor with a smile, albeit a thin and forced one.

That's not to bad mouth statesmen. The difference between statesman and politician is easily remembered by the thought, "A statesman does what is right while a politician does what's popular." Got that one from a PBS broadcast of a political science course I watched one rainy afternoon. That's also where I got the joke about the origin of the word politics. "In Greek, poly means many. The word ticks means blood sucking insects. Thus, when combined, politics means many blood sucking insects."

That train of thought almost caused me to have an overnight stay on a siding to the main track. I left it and checked my watch. Dinner would be ready soon. Just had to remove the film covering the tray and let the food cool enough that I didn't burn my mouth. I grabbed a pot holder and did the pre-meal ritual specified in the instructions from memory from many previous such meals.

After I ate, I allowed myself a sour mash and water and turned on the radio. The station played old time, 1950s and 60s, country songs. Good background music for making leashes for Shad and cleaning the revolver after a day at the range. The coffee table made a good workbench for the tasks at hand and I found the mat to protect it from scratches.

In about an hour, I tied a twenty-foot-long leash, and one of six feet. Add another half hour, and I had cleaned the revolver. I counted that a minor success. I put it back together with no spare parts, and it functioned as smoothly as it had before I took it apart.

I gave myself another whiskey to celebrate. When finished, I took Shad out for the last walk of the day. The storm was now a gentle, warm rain, but still wasn't comfortable if we got soaked. We made it a quick trip. He shook off before he came in. I hung the wet coat over the back of a kitchen chair to dry.

I found a pair of flannel pajamas and put them on. I turned off the lights in the other rooms.

I remembered the gun on the way to bed, grabbed it from the coffee table, loaded it, and put it on the night table next to the bed. I turned off the bedroom lights. I said my prayers and climbed into bed. Didn't take long before I went to sleep. Tomorrow would start early to do everything I wanted or had to do.

I woke to a cold nose, attached to a large dog, poking me in the neck repeatedly. "What is it Shad? Need to go out?"

"Shhhh Somebody is trying to get in the back door." Shad whispered. He also whispered advice, "If you're not sure about your magic yet, nothing in the rule book against using weapons of this time and place to defend yourself, and me. Bring your revolver."

In the silence after he finished, I heard something, or someone, trying to get in through the kitchen door. That doesn't sound good. I heard the squeak of the hinges as the door opened. As I grabbed the gun and cocked it, I willed the kitchen lights on. Holy smoke, they turned on.

I sneaked into the hall where I could observe the intruder. The language coming from the kitchen was a mixture of very angry drunk and surprise. I peeked into the kitchen. The man struggled to take off a pair of night vision goggles with his left hand as he filled the air with foul epithets. I've been told, when you wear night vision goggles and the lights come on, it causes temporary blindness like when you come in from a walk after a new snow on a sunny day or look at the flash when photographed. He was blinded until he got his vision back. But I saw the long knife in his right hand.

I ordered him to freeze as I lined up the sights on the third shirt button up from his belt buckle. I willed him to freeze. Neither had the desired effect. It only fueled his rage.

He came toward me. "Where's the old man that lives here? Tell me and you won't die too, bitch."

Something in his voice warned me that what he said wasn't true. Whether or not I answered, he intended my demise. "Doesn't live here anymore. Get out." I answered.

He took another step toward me. I fired. He lost to that big bullet as the hole in his chest spurted red. He staggered, surprise on his face, then fell face first with no effort to break his fall. I dialed the emergency number.

"9-1-1. What's your emergency?"

"A guy broke in, threatened me with a knife, wouldn't stop coming toward me. I shot. He's down in the kitchen."

"Without taking a risk, can you tell if he's alive?" 9-1-1 asked.

"I'm about ten feet from him and I don't think he is, but a slim chance he might be." I answered.

"I'll get a car and ambulance there as quick as I can. Stay on the line until they arrive." she instructed.

"I'd like to turn on the front porch light, let them know which house. Don't want them going to the wrong one and waking the neighbors by accident."

"Dang, girl. You're awfully calm after a gunfight." she remarked.

"I've always been calm in an emergency. It's after it's over when I get the shakes and my brain goes into neutral." I replied. Well, it was the truth as far as I knew. My knees were shaking now, not before.

"OK. Don't hang up, just put the phone down, turn the light on, and talk to me when you're back." she issued more instructions.

I followed her plan, turned on the porch light, came back, and said, "Hello. I'm back."

"Boy, you're at the edge of town there. While you were gone, I tracked where the call originated to give a good address to the patrols and ambulance." she chattered on to keep me calm. I guess she didn't want me to shoot the police when they got here. Or make sure the police didn't shoot me. That thought made me shudder a bit. I wasn't done doing whatever I was supposed to do yet.

"Do you see a police car out front?" she asked.

I turned to look out the front windows. A patrol car with flashing blue and red lights on the roof mount bar pulled up and parked. I reported that "I see one officer, can't see anybody else."

"Can you see his rank?" she asked.

"Three chevrons on his upper arm."

I could hear the triumph in her voice. "Damn. He was a mile farther away than the rookie. Guess he can still drive faster than that new kid." she chuckled. "Serves the kid right for betting he'd get there first."

"The other car just arrived. I'll be witness to that if they argue about it later. The wall clock in the kitchen shows zero three-ten." Hmmm. Where did I learn the twenty-four hour clock?

I let out my own damn. No wonder I was getting grumpy. I only had five hours sleep, forced to wake and kill the intruder. Enough to make anyone grumpy. One good thing, my knees quit their dance.

"They're coming up the stairs now. I'll answer the door. Want me to stay on the line?"

She said, "Just tell sarge he won fair and square. You can hang up now."

"I'll tell the sergeant. Thanks for listening." I signed off, hung up, and left the Vaquero on the coffee table. I opened the door for the officers. "Sarge, the dispatcher said to tell you that you won. Pay up, rookie." I giggled a little as the rookie's face soured into a pout.

He managed to be business like despite his lost bet. "Where is the man you called about, ma'am?"

I backed a little and pointed as I said, "Right there. Hasn't moved since he landed there."

"Cover me, Sam." Sarge instructed as he approached the body on the floor. He exclaimed, "Jesus Jenny. This is

Alfonso Diablo if I'm not mistaken. Just got another federal wanted notice for information or for his arrest the other day. Remember that one, Sam?"

Sam answered yes, then spoke to me, "The one for the ambush of two DEA agents. Ma'am, you deserve a medal for getting rid of that scumbag.

"No medal. Don't want one. I just saw a guy that threatened me with death, had a weapon big enough to make good that threat, and he moved toward me. I figure he did that because to him I was just a girl with a big gun, unlikely to shoot and hit him. He figured wrong. As my granddad told me, 'Walk your post from flank to flank. Take no shit from any rank.'"

Sam whistled softly, then said, "Remind me to never piss you off, OK?"

Sarge finished handcuffing Diablo and rolled him over. "This the knife?"

I moved a few steps closer, and replied, "Sure looks like it from here."

He whistled and said, "Put me down for that reminder with Sam. That would have scared me too."

Those exchanges were worth a laugh, but, while my tenseness diminished it to a lopsided grin, they succeeded to take the edge off the situation. "Do you mind if get a robe? It's getting a bit chilly."

"Go right ahead. You'll be a while yet. The detectives and CSU will be here shortly, so if you'd rather get dressed, you can do that instead." Sarge said.

"Thanks. Be just a couple of minutes." I went to my room and changed into nearly street clothes - sweat shirt, jeans, and slipper socks. That this might be the new normal for me was on my mind the whole time. I hoped the follow up wouldn't take long. I had a lot to do later and wanted to be presentable for two of the stops. I wasn't comfortable with taking a shower with all these strangers in the house.

I returned to the living room. Sarge and Sam looked tired. "You fellas want some coffee? I'll put on a pot if you do."

Sarge spoke up, "I'd appreciate a cup, thanks." Sam followed the senior and echoed him.

I tip toed around the blood Diablo left behind him to make a full pot of full caffeine coffee. I exercised the cook's privilege to take the first cup before I announced it was ready to the others. Sarge got the second cup. Sam got the third.

"The detectives are here." Sarge announced when his cup was about half done. "Thanks, Ma'am. That will be a big help getting through the rest of my shift." Sam just said, "Thanks." and swallowed the rest of his coffee. Sarge downed his in a few gulps. Their rinsed cups went in the sink before the detectives knocked on the door.

The detectives came in. "Just made some coffee, plenty of clean cups if you want some." I offered.

The gray haired one declined with the excuse, "I'd like some, but doctor said not to have any stimulants after midnight."

Detective O'Doyle, on the other hand, accepted the offer after chiding the gray hair. "Yeah, you get to sleep at end of shift while I'm still filling out the report. I'd like some, please."

I told him where the cups were, pointed to the pot still on the coffee maker's hot plate, with the invitation to "Help yourself." He released the uniforms to return to their normal patrols before he poured a cup for himself. I noticed he wasn't wearing that ring now, though the pale skin where it had been was evidence it had a long acquaintance with his finger.

As he did that, the Crime Scene Unit arrived and came in as the uniforms left. They examined the back door and 'dusted for prints', just like on TV. Then they measured the distance from the door to the night vision goggles, and from the goggles to the blood. One drew a sketch of the scene.

Another took photographs.

One asked, "What took him so long to get to the place you shot him?"

"Dog woke me while he was still fiddling with the lock. I grabbed the revolver and investigated. I turned on the kitchen lights. He wore those goggles. He started cursing. I think those are night vision because he was temporarily blinded when the lights came on. He finally pulled the goggles off and dropped them where they are. He asked for the old man or he'd kill me." I stopped to breathe, then continued. "I told him Bear, my grand dad, wasn't here and told him to get out. He started toward me with that knife in his hand. I shot him in self-defense."

The CSU tech picked up the knife, held it up to the bag he held, and got out a bigger evidence bag. "Yeah. I'd say that's big enough to take him as a serious threat to me. I'd have shot him, too." He turned to O'Doyle to show the weapon. "What do you think, detective?"

"I'd say it looks like self-defense, but I need to ask some more questions." He turned to look me in the eyes. "Is that the gun you were going to have to learn to shoot?"

"Yes, it is. I went to the range you suggested. Gunny Sharp walked me through it. He also gave me some instructions and taught me how to shoot if close and forced to shoot and really needed to hit the target. I shot two boxes of ammunition practicing yesterday morning. Got pretty good by the last half box I put into targets."

"Gunny Sharp taught you?"

"Yes, he did. I've shot handguns before, but not a single action revolver before the lesson."

"Do you remember aiming?"

"Yes, like Gunny Sharp taught me, at the third button up from his belt buckle. Why?

"Self-defense it was. Gunny is a damn good teacher. I've taken a few lessons from him myself." Sean admitted. "Not impossible after a hundred shots on target just the morning before to be able to hit a man size target at five paces. Not even for a shooter with an unfamiliar gun if they have the nerve to aim. She aimed."

The crime scene unit had its photos. When told it was all right, the EMTs carted poor old cold Diablo to the ambulance for his ride to the morgue. The CSU packed up and left. O'Doyle finished his coffee. Gray hair finished writing in his notebook, flipped it shut, and grinned at me. "You are one tough lady. Many women, and a lot of men, would be too scared to shoot, or followed the commandment 'Thou shalt not kill."

"Might have slowed me down too, except I read some place the church had checked the translation made in medieval times. They rewrote the translation using current, more complete knowledge of the original language when one of the scholars showed that kill was a secondary meaning of the word. Now, the commandment reads 'Do not murder.' At least there was an Imprimatur and Nihil Obstat on the version I checked, which was good enough for me. As I see it, it isn't murder when the other guy is armed and means you great harm or death. That's self-defense." I explained. "Besides, at least one granddad served during a war, and told me he wouldn't have come home if he had hesitated when the shooting started. That was the only thing Bear told me about his war."

"Thank you, Miss Chadwick. That's the fastest we've closed a case in a long time." O'Doyle stated. Gray hair nodded agreement. "Be safe. Hope we meet again under more pleasant circumstances." Sean and gray hair left after I wished them the same.

The eastern horizon showed hints of dawn's first light. I had time for another cup of coffee before it would be light enough to go out with Shad. Or I could start to clean up the blood. The latter had priority. "Dumb ass thug. Why did you pick my house to die in?" kept coming to mind as I worked. "At least you died far enough back in the kitchen you bled onto the linoleum, not on the carpet." came to mind as I picked up the first layer of paper towels. They went into a separate trash bag. I didn't want them in the house.

Bright enough now to take Shad out, and that was far more pleasant than cleaning up blood I had spilled. "Shad, come on, boy. Time to go out."

We were greeted by the squirrel living in the oak tree. It objected to the interruption of its hunt for acorns.

I listened to it as it scolded us and thought, 'My word, that's foul language even for a drunken sailor.' "Take it easy. We'll be back inside soon. We yield to your claim to the acorns. But get used to the intrusion. Dog needs to go out too, you know." The scolding stopped and the furry critter laid on one of the bigger branches where it could watch us. "See? I expect we'll be gone soon, Mr. Loudmouth."

The sunrise was exceptionally pretty this morning. I thanked the Creator for the opportunity to see it and that both Shad and I were in reasonably good health for our day. Shad finished his ritual visit to the yard's corners and came to me. We went in.

Back inside, Shad went around the blood spot as I went back to work removing the remaining blood. Then I made a strong bleach and detergent solution to mop up the last remnants of pink tinge, and to kill anything infectious left behind by Alfonso Diablo, permanently retired killer for hire. I grinned with satisfaction at that. Then I apologized to the Great Maker that I had taken a life, no matter how misspent it had been.

I fed Shad and gave him a hug for waking me in time. While not the most welcome chore, better that I was the clean-up crew rather than on a slab in the morgue. At least I thought so. I could wake from my nap. He would sleep forever, or until the Second Coming. But now that the adrenaline ebbed in my system with the completion of the task at hand, I was getting drowsy. I had some toast with butter and preserves, a cup of coffee, and flopped on the sofa for a nap.

Two hours later, I woke. Took off my 'emergency outfit' - the jeans and sweat shirt - donned my robe and took a longer than usual shower. Some would say that, subconsciously, I tried to wash the blood off my hands. I dried off, applied my make-up, and dressed for the day. Walked Shad again. Then started to check the yellow pages for a funeral home. Victor deserved a nice burial. I intended to do my best for him.

A note in the phone book, written in Victor's hand, had the names of local funeral homes. All but one were lined out. Well, that was easy. So was picking St. Michael's for the funeral Mass after I found the box of donation envelopes in the cupboard when I put away the coffee cups. I looked at the clock.

Still time to visit the Rossen establishment before lunch. I called the undertakers to let them know I was coming.

"Come on, Shad. We've got work to do." In a flash, he was at my side. He was well behaved, more than usual if that's possible, as if he sensed the missions we were on were quite serious. Both in the truck in our assigned seats, I drove to the Rossen Funeral Home.

"Sit. Stay. I'll be back as quickly as I can." Shad would lay down as soon as I was inside, but that would be OK with me. He pretended to mind very well. I wouldn't fuss over details today.

Inside, a tall, older gentleman approached. "Are you Miss Chadwick?"

"Yes, I am. You're who I'm supposed to meet?"

"I'm Albert Rossen. We spoke on the phone. I am the one that will discuss the arrangements for your grandfather's funeral."

"This came up suddenly, and I didn't know him well, so

what do I need to do now?"

"Please follow me to the office. We'll discuss it there and I'll show you the caskets we have in stock afterward. My son is there with some others in need right now and we try to offer privacy to our clients." he answered.

He led the way about a quarter step ahead. We reached a comfortably furnished room where he held the door. I sat in an armchair in front of the desk. While he went around behind the desk to sit in his executive's swivel chair, I noticed the pastel shades of the paint, carpet, and curtains. Even the chairs were in a bright, cheery pastel green, far from the somber colors in the office I visited for my adopted Grandpa's burial. I actually felt good rather than depressed as we discussed the situation and Bear Warsawski's burial. Those details settled, even the uncertainty what time the medical examiner would release Bear. Albert said he'd give the ME a call to let the morgue know they were the undertakers for the deceased and ask for a call when the body is released.

Finished with the preliminaries, we went to the showroom for the caskets. One caught my eye. Grandpa Bear was a carpenter, so I thought he'd like the idea of a plain wood box. That wouldn't meet local ordinances for caskets, but the one I fancied did. It was a plain metal box with a thin veneer of what looked like varnished oak, with antiqued bronze hardware. I asked, "How much?"

The answer was surprisingly low, though not the cheapest on display. Much cheaper than the ornate ones for sure. That would make Bear happy in the bargain. I heard him once declare about people who bought luxury models when they would be as well served by ordinary level trucks, "They have more money than sense." It wasn't about really expensive coffins, but was applicable here and now as with cars, or anything for that matter.

The negotiations continued back in the office. Bruce Rossen had finished with his clients and joined us. I noticed that he wasn't looking into my eyes, but rather than call him on it, I crossed my legs. That drew my skirt up just a little until I showed just a little bit of the lace tops of my thigh highs. His gaze shifted from my chest to my legs and back up to my face. He had taken the bait and realized he was caught, judged by the blush he now wore. I felt confident the deal we'd make would be the best possible, allowing them a reasonable profit but keep it in budget for me. We agreed on the details discussed. That left just one question more to consider. The question took me by surprise.

"How would you like him dressed?" the elder Rossen asked.

"Huh?" I answered. Not very eloquent, but I was surprised. Give a girl a break. OK?

Albert clarified, "I heard he was killed during the attempted robbery at the saloon. He was dressed as a woman for the costume contest. We had talked about his desires a few months ago. We can make him a very pretty woman. In the alternatives, he was a carpenter like the Lord, so we can dress him in work clothes. There's no shame in working for a living. Or we can put him in a suit as is usual practice."

I replied, "A business suit is out. That much is certain. I've learned enough about Bear to know he wasn't a suit person. Give me a little time to decide between the other two. He faces eternity, or at least until his body returns to dust, in how I dress him for the funeral. Maybe I can find something in his home to guide me to what he wanted."

"As long as we know before the body gets here, no problem either way. When you decide, bring a change of the clothes you want him to wear. That saves you buying the suit." Bruce said. Obviously, Bruce didn't follow the company line if judged by the quick but stern look I caught Albert give him from the corner of my eye.

"I'll try to let you know by tomorrow morning, and bring the clothes in shortly after." I replied.

Albert responded, "Fine. Either Bruce or I will be waiting for the delivery. Have as good an afternoon as you can, Miss Chadwick. I'll walk you out."

Bruce interrupted, "I can do that, dad. Organize the notes and I'll finish the contract when we find if we'll make the major changes or not."

He rose and held his hand out to me. I took it, stood, and started to follow him, but stopped and turned to Albert. "Thank you both so very much. You made this trying time for me a little less so." I hurried to catch up to Bruce.

Oh my. How my hips swayed. It wasn't intentional, at least I don't think it was. Still, Bruce gave me about a $200 savings by not requiring that I buy a suit from them, and was a fine-looking young man that seemed infatuated. Then again, might be the wiggle is just a normal consequence of high heels, a long stride to keep up, and a tight skirt. Plainly, from the gleam in his eyes at our parting, he had been pleased with the earlier display. I'd experiment with the walk later under controlled circumstances.

I felt compelled to keep it up on the walk to the truck because he watched from the door. I didn't want to disappoint the young man observing me. Neither did I want to dissuade him from the bargain we reached. A few hundred off was nothing to sneeze at. Feminazis be damned. I wasn't too proud to pay for the savings with a hooker's wiggle.

Next stop was St. Michael's because the collection envelopes led me here. A few minutes later, I parked near the rectory for the unscheduled meeting. The extreme hip sway disappeared as I got out of the truck. It wasn't appropriate when dealing with clergy. I filed that away for consideration later.

I rang the doorbell. The assistant pastor answered the door. I stated my purpose. "Hello, I need to speak with someone to arrange a funeral for Victor Warsawski."

He replied, "Father Leo isn't here. He was called out suddenly to administer last rights to an old friend. But I can help schedule a funeral if Father kept his calendar up to date. At the least, I can take notes and he can get back to you. By the way, I'm Father Joe."

"Pleased to meet you, Father Joe, for Joseph?" He nodded. "You may have heard about my grandfather's death. He was killed when the customers shot back at the robbers during the attempted theft at the Spotted Horse on Halloween. I need to arrange for a funeral Mass, but it's going to be tricky. Granddad's body is still at the morgue, and the coroner hasn't signed the release yet. The detective in charge said it would likely be released tomorrow, though."

That raised an eyebrow. We sat in his office and discussed the situation. We reached a compromise. I'd let them know as soon as I heard confirmation of the expected release. I was to call him when I knew. He allowed two days for the wake If I wanted the funeral Mass at nine in the morning on Saturday if no more than two were scheduled that day. and that it wasn't on a Sunday. If Father Leo had filled out his calendar completely for other commitments already made, he would say the Mass. If not, Father Joe would, since he had an open calendar for this Saturday.

I saw a chance to bring a little order to the chaos if they overbooked Father Leo and scheduled it with Father Joe. He agreed and penciled Bear's service on his calendar. Sounded good to me. I gave him Grandpa's name again. He said the name was familiar for some reason. Then his eyes lit up.

"Oh. Yes. Now I remember." He leaned back in his chair. "Bear visited to discuss a problem he had. If you've been to his house, you may have already found what I mean." He paused. "With his medical condition what it was, if he asked to be buried as a woman, it would be all right to honor that request."

That was a response I never expected, but was a relief for me. I answered his question. "Yes. I found a note to confirm or cancel the reassignment surgery on the calendar. Thank you for the help with my decision."

An answer had popped into my mind before I saw the evidence. What's going on?

The priest said, "You're welcome."

After we said good-bye, Shad and I headed home. When at home, I traded the stilettos for my moccasins. The heel didn't sink into the lawn like the stilettos. Then I walked Shad. Maybe that should read Shad walked me. He sure pulled me around. That continued indoors. After he took a long drink, we followed his nose. Well, in truth, he followed his nose. I followed him.

He parked his butt in front of a closet in the hall between bedrooms. A long garment bag hung from the closet rod. I lifted it from that location and laid it on the bed. Bear's stash of pretty dresses was revealed as I opened the bag.

One stood out. I smiled when I held the tight red charmeuse dress against my chest, and again when I tried it on. This was a dress he must have bought in hope to one day fit into it, or to use to prepare a pattern in his size. Whichever, it fit me quite well. I enjoyed the freedom of the hip to hem slit skirt and the plunging neck line high enough to be almost, but not quite, modest, but more so than some of the dresses on the red carpet at awards shows.

More than the handgun and to be discovered collection of other firearms, this would be my memento of Victor. While two or three pounds of machined steel was more likely to have greater utility if needed, the dress had much more meaning for me. I would wear this next Halloween to see who took notice. Or if my need changed, I'd wear it next Valentine's Day for the guy I was with.

Hanging next after the red dress, a skirt suit in dark and light brown tweed carried an interesting maker's tag - Mama Bear Warsawski's Fashions. That old dear sewed it herself. A tan button front blouse was on the next hanger. I just knew she'd be happy to wear this at her funeral, but would his/her friends?" I set the suit and shirt aside to give to the Rossens tomorrow morning for Victoria's last outfit. Laid out a set of work clothes for Victor, too. I'd think about it overnight which he or she would wear for this last time.

I also found his notes from discussions with the surgeon who was to be in charge of the sex reassignment surgery. I read about the conversation when he was told about his vagina discovered on the X-rays that could be opened. He hadn't decided whether or not to have that surgery. Too, it explained a lot of things no one had guessed during his life as he-Bear, all state two way tackle his senior year. He noted it might also explain the aunt with a linebacker's build.

I remembered those strange urges I felt when in Victor's body his last dance. Not so strange with this information. It explained why, when other guys wanted to have sex with the starlet in the female lead of the movie, he wanted to be the starlet having sex with the male lead. I now understood her desire to be Maureen O'Hara in any of her movies with John Wayne as her husband. I still measured the men in my life compared to the Duke.

The rest of the dresses were early purchases for the rest of his life had he lived after the fateful night. They were too large for the body I wore now even if altered, and would go with my blessings to the parish clothing bank. Also in that bag were a wig, some jewelry, and a pair of mid heel pumps in brown, which I put with the suit and blouse. The leftover jewelry, wigs, and a pair of good quality boots with soles and heels suited for walks on blacktop or lawns went with the other clothes for the clothing banks.

I wished the boots were keepers, but were way too big over nylons and even over a pair of mid weight socks for me. I copied the maker and style number to purchase a pair in my size for winter. I could look for some on the Internet later.

Not a magic trousseau, but it reflected her sexy grandma mind in his grandpa body. Beat the mini-skirt I sometimes wore for work at the saloon six ways to Sunday at any rate. The women who got one of these would be satisfied.

Thinking clothes raised a thought. I called the hospital and asked about the clothes Bear wore when admitted Saturday morning. The duty clerk on the desk at the time said the police or the coroner had them by standard procedure. She gave me the coroner's phone number. I thanked her, hung up, and called the city morgue.

A short conversation with the clerk that answered assured me the body would be released to the mortuary handling the funeral after the coroner signed the death certificate. That would be about mid-morning tomorrow in Bear's case. The clothes would go to the mortuary with the body. I thanked him and dialed the next number on my list.

"Hello. Rossen Funeral Home. This is Bruce Rossen. How may I help you?"

"Hello, Bruce. Ursula Chadwick. Just spoke with the Coroner's Office. Expect the call to notify you about release of Bear's body mid morning tomorrow, Wednesday. They also said they return the clothes worn at the time of death with the body. This may change your plans some. I found a note. He hadn't reached a decision about what he wanted to be or whether or not he'd have the surgery. I've decided to have you make him as he was before his death. I'll bring over his work clothes to wear. Also, I'll bring clothes, shoes, jewelry, and a wig to hide around his feet for the funeral. He sewed what he wanted to wear some day. Only right to let him/her choose later, after he is judged."

"You want him as a him, then?"

"Yes. The additional information I found since we talked last made up my mind." I said. I continued, "I would like Bear to have two days for the wake. Father Joe said he should be able to say a funeral Mass on Saturday if the wake starts Thursday. If it starts Friday, the burial will be next week, probably Monday, because they don't do funerals on Sundays. Can he be ready for the wake on Thursday if you have him later than noon Wednesday?"

"If you want him buried as a him, I can answer that question with a yes, probably. Depends if he was badly damaged by the bullet and whether it would be visible. Also, we'd be able to do the necessary work as long as we had all normal work hours on Thursday."

"I'll give you an estimate so you don't have a heart attack when we sign the contract tomorrow morning."

"Just a second. Need to check my price list." Muzak, a.k.a. elevator music, played. A couple minutes later, Bruce was back on the line. "Still there?" he asked.

"Yes."

"OK. Standard price for a rebuild of damaged limbs is $250 if not visible. That's pretty common with gunshot wounds. I don't think you'd want him buried in his birthday suit, so I'd guess about $500 total above the standard fees. Those are in the neighborhood of a couple thousand with embalming and other preparations for burial, the wake is held here in a visitation room, the obituary, a cemetery plot, the coffin you picked out, a standard vault, and grave digger fees. (The clicking of key strokes came through the phone) Be about seven thousand." he reported.

"Is that payable when I sign the contract, or after the insurance money comes in?" I inquired.

"After, but we give a five percent discount if paid within the week, if that's doable for you."

"I'll see what I can do about the payment." I responded. "What do you do with the clothes he wore when he died?"

"If not used to clothe the deceased, and if they have useful life left in them, we have them cleaned and donate them to one of the clothing banks around town." Bruce replied.

"OK. I'll bring the replacement clothes tomorrow morning before you'll need them. I'll be there by nine in the morning to sign the contract, Lord willing. See you then." I replied.

"Until morning then. Stay safe." Bruce answered.

As I hung up, I felt tired. Decided that was enough for today before supper. When I finished a walk with Shad and had supper, I pulled out the first volume of Ursula's diary. Another night's reading called for a whiskey. I made a double and settled in for the evening. Three hours later, I finished both the diary and the glass of whiskey.

Still only seven thirty pm, I made another stiff bourbon and water and dialed the phone. When she picked up, I spoke. "Sue, feel like having a drink? I've had a rough day and think it will be better shared rather than kept to myself."

"Be right over. Save some for me." I grinned and stifled a laugh. Sue almost yelled her answer loudly enough she didn't need the phone to be heard.

"Don't worry, just opened the bottle. But don't dawdle. Can't guarantee there will be much left if you waste time getting here." The click of the receiver at her end told me she took me literally. That comic relief for my day raised my spirits, just like the gag used in some old movies still does.

If you remember it, it's the one where two of the characters are on the phone. One says he or she needs help and wants the other to come right over. Before the phone is hung up, the other character says 'Hello' from feet in front of the caller. And this was before teleportation was used in Sci Fi movies.

Less than ten minutes later, Sue sat on the other end of the sofa. She held a drink in one hand and a cheese and cracker sandwich in the other. There was a small plate of more ingredients at the middle of the coffee table. She told me of her day. I told her of mine, finishing with "And Victor told the priest and funeral home director his story. I wonder if I was the only person who didn't know."

Her comment was, "Not really surprising. Not the kind of thing you tell folks, even family, at the first meeting. More likely to wait until you have a sense of how they'll react."

I replied, "We never had contact except as barmaid and customer, so that would leave me out of that loop. I guess it was meant for me to find out now, not sooner."

After some silent thought, we chatted for about an hour more. When she went home, I finished my drink, and rinsed the glasses and plates. Shad got another walk, last one for the night, and I washed up and got ready for bed. After this morning's unpleasant visit, I checked to make sure the revolver was in the night stand drawer, loaded. That accomplished, I said my prayers and went to sleep for the night.

Wake Minus One

"Wake up, Ursula. Got some talking to do before you start your day."** He only spoke loudly enough to wake me, PLENTY loud enough. -grin-

"Morning, Pete. What's so urgent?"

"You need to be ready today. Things won't go as smoothly as you hope they will. Just know that you have the strength of body, mind, and spirit to get through it. Actually, come to think of it, keep that thought for the rest of your life. You'll need it. " Pete commented.

"Going to be that bad?" I questioned.

"Not really, but it will feel like it at times. Don't let it get you down, or like that joke Latin saying that made the rounds a while back, 'Non tatum illegitimate carborundum', translated, it means 'Dont let the bastards wear you down. ', at least in the joke. Fight the urge to give up or take the easy road. Do it righteous and right every time." he preached.

I acknowledged his talk. "Best mini sermon I've ever heard. I'll try to remember the lesson come hell or high water." I sat up and asked, "Any specifics that you'd care to mention?"

"Oh. Can't do that unless it's vital to your mission. Just got another lecture about that from Michael AND Gabriel. It's that free will thing the Boss gave you folks. Not allowed to give you anything more than guidance.

Up to you, as individuals or groups, to make the choice." Pete explained. He continued, ***"That's why there are so many churches, like the one that worships the false god, money, and they do anything it takes to get more of it, even murder innocents."***

"What about the drive by shootings and the innocents killed by stray bullets during gang wars?" I asked.

Pete replied, ***"Those injured or dead because of drive by shootings really bother the Maker."***

"Then why doesn't He do something about them?" I demanded.

"He could but won't. He can't interfere every time or it wouldn't be free will, would it?" Pete answered.

That answer slapped me on the back of my head, like the ones that Gibbs gives Dinozzo on NCIS. "Put that way, it makes sense. Sorry I didn't think of that myself."

"Don't beat yourself up over that. Lots of folks older and supposedly wiser haven't figured that out yet either. That or they forget that and try to shift blame." Pete smiled as he answered. His head jerked alert. ***"Got to go. Got a call from one of my other charges that could be an emergency. See you next time."*** He faded out.

I thought, 'Heck of a way to wake up.' The clock showed four-thirty, still before day light by the stars instead of the sun in the sky. I had about three hours until day break. Lots of time but none to waste. After I took care of the usual bathroom tasks, I shampooed my hair, showered and toweled off my body, and blew dry my hair. 'First task for the day deserves an A+.' I giggled at the thought. Laughed at the next one. 'Let's see if I can keep on this roll for breakfast.' That was a pun to beat all others.

I put on my robe and slipper socks. I gave warning, "Kitchen, get ready." Then attacked the day. After all, I was 'burning daylight'. Sounded better when John Wayne said it. My tenor voice didn't do it justice. It needed to rumble, not sound like a squeak in comparison. Still, it was true. If I waited for day break, I lost three hours to no purpose since I was awake already.

Breakfast of sausage, eggs and toast with coffee was done, dishes left to soak in the sink. Time to dress for the dog's walk. When back from that, I changed into the skirt suit I wore yesterday, a multicolor hounds tooth check with long jacket and short skirt. I planned to save the black one for the funeral. I put on a light tan tank top under the jacket to look less like a street walker. Maybe some night I'd stand under a street lamp if things ever got that tight. For today, I needed to show a little decorum.

I checked myself in the mirror. After yesterday's meeting with Bruce, I clearly showed too much leg. Skirt went back on the hanger and onto the closet. I got out a pair of tan gabardine slacks. Much better image for a visit to a funeral home. The tan loafers got the call again, as did the tan purse. The light coat of makeup was well suited for a sunny morning's business.

"Let's go, Shad. We've got business to do." He was ready and at the back door before I finished calling him. At revolver on the mental checklist, I fetched it from the night stand. "Now I'm ready too." We went to the truck and got in. Something bothered Shad. He hadn't said a word since I put the revolver in my purse. "OK. Something bothers you. Tell me what it is."

Shad just looked at me like I had the brains of a brick. He also commented, "You're really ready this time? ...Get organized, girl. Yesterday's run in with that hired killer should have put taking the gun with you everywhere first on your checklist by now."

"It was just behind Driver's License and keys. I knew where the revolver was, but had to move the other things first before the gun was a factor." Without conversation, we listened to the radio on the way to Rossens. There was a breaking story instead of sports to end this hour of the show. A bomb or something had exploded in my old apartment building. My first thought was 'I hope no one was hurt.' Second thought was 'If that's true and not a leaky gas connection, I'm not paranoid. They really are after me.' Third thought bordered on the philosophical, 'Who in hell are 'they'?

Once at Rossens, I parked in a spot near the door since the parking lot was empty. My thoughts centered on how to pay the undertaker's fee to get the discount. I didn't have enough in my checking account to just write a check, and the credit card couldn't take the strain either. I'd have to move money from savings to my checking account. I'd promised myself a vacation this winter, at least a week where it was warm enough to thaw. That was out of the picture now with the battle coming up soon. I felt that more than had any proof of it.

Looking up at grass roots, even with the critters that crawled around between them, wasn't as attractive a view as looking down on a green lawn, or even one snow covered. That's where my body could be for a long vacation if I lost sight of my surroundings and any threats. And it's too hard to hide a Vaquero in a bikini, even the short barrel one I had now.

That question settled, I started to listen to the music seriously. Nothing like a sad song by Patsy Cline to realize I didn't have it that bad. I wasn't taking walks after midnight looking for a former lover, or going crazy with memories of lost love. At least not right now. There were some memories left behind a few lost loves in my history when I lived those songs of sorrow.

The memory that went with the story of one cigarette left in the ash tray still hurt. It had changed my life and signaled the time I first paid dues to the Sisterhood of Soiled Doves as self-prescribed therapy. While I had paid those dues willingly a few times since then, I felt it was about time to renew for another year's membership. The light bulb above my head when I had an idea was a bright passionate red more often than not lately. I wondered if that was a symptom of a ticking biological clock or just lust.

But that train of thought stopped at the station when a car pulled into the lot and one of the reserved spots. Bruce Rossen got out and let himself in. I grabbed the clothes for Victor's last appearance on this stage and scrambled after him. I got to the door before he locked it again.

"Good morning, Mr. Rossen. Told you I'd be here early."

"That you did, Miss Chadwick, that you did. Good thing I believed you and prepared the contract last night... Shall we go to my office to discuss what's covered and other terms of the deal?"

"Sounds good to me. Let's go."

He led the way to his office very unlike his dad's. That was decorated in pastel pinks and blues. Bruce's wore vibrant colors in cherry and deep sky blues. More of a man cave or men's club atmosphere if you know what I mean. I felt the urge to invite him into my cave of pleasure, but fought it off. This was business only. Paying my annual dues would have to wait.

We went over the terms and costs for services to be rendered. I was satisfied but had a question. "Who writes the obituary notice?"

"Mr. Warsawski provided what he wanted. Pretty good prose if I recall it. Here's what he wrote." Bruce handed me a typed sheet of paper with a short paragraph that summed up his life.

I finished reading it. "Yes. That was good. Only one error. He wrote no known surviving family. I proved to the police and his lawyer that I'm his granddaughter. I wouldn't be taking care of the burial if I didn't. That needs to be changed."

"Good thing it's double spaced. Be easy to fix that." Bruce said. He scanned it into his computer, brought up the document, and edited it in a minute. He handed the corrected copy to me.

I read it and agreed to the change. The original that held the error took a short trip through the shredder to prevent confusion. Bruce printed more copies, and handed me one. He kept one. He also printed copies for the paper and radio station. He or one of the employees would hand deliver those before noon tomorrow if they estimated they would finish before the visitation times it listed.

"I'll wait until we finish preparing the body for burial to include the visitation, the wake if you prefer." Bruce clarified what I already figured out.

That triggered my memory. I handed over the bag of clothes and accessories I brought along and the part of his notes from the conversation with the doctor about his existing vagina that only needed to be opened. I pointed out the note that said he wasn't decided yet, and the carpenter's clothes to dress him.

I also mentioned "He sewed his own clothes. I think it's only right to let her have an outfit she made with her for this occasion. Will that be all right?"

"Yes, and will save delays later. Save you a trip to deliver it, too. There should be space in the foot of the casket for them." Bruce opined.

We signed the contract with the revised and final itemized bill attached. I got a billing invoice and a copy for my records. I'd need the record if the administrator needed proof to reimburse an expense.

"When do you expect the wake will start?" I asked.

"We usually start the visitations around six in the evening. End them at about eight." Bruce said. Then he asked, "Do you have pall bearers lined up yet?"

"No, but I'll ask my friends and members of the VFW and

American Legion I've seen with him at the saloon."

"Let me save you some time. Here are the post commanders' contact information. One phone call to each should get you all you need." Bruce wrote out addresses and phone numbers for the current post commanders and handed the slip of paper to me.

"Thank you. That'll be a big help."

We shook hands and I went out to the truck. Shad apologized for losing his cool, and I apologized for being grumpy. "We'll go home soon. I need to talk to Gunny first. I think a smaller pistol will be better for carry when I'm dressed up. I want his advice."

"Now you're starting to think defense with a capital D. Let's go." Shad really perked up at the thought.

I shared my planning with Shad, "Don't forget the undertaker's bill. Might as well stop at the bank and move some money from savings to checking while we're out. Bank is closer, so that's first."

After we got there, it took only about a half hour to get that transfer completed including a ten minute wait for the bank's doors to open for business and about five more to finish with the customer ahead of me. I'll wait until tomorrow to mail the check to the Rossens' Mortuary, or whatever they call it. Or maybe I'll hand carry it and hand it over the first night of the wake. No chance of lost or delayed mail that way. Specially if I get a signature on my copy of the contract and bill.

Next stop was Northwest sporting goods. The parking lot had more vehicles in it than that first time, but I recognized Gunny's truck. I went in, and started looking at the handguns. I found it interesting, and remembered some of the things I knew before my brain got clogged up with recipes, makeup, and fashions. I knew just what I wanted after a few moments, but no need to buy one. I already had one in inventory at home. The fog over the secret hiding place for Bear's collection lifted and I knew where it was. And what was in it.

I could use a few magazines for it, though, and some .45 Auto ammunition with 230 gr hollow point bullets. An inside the waistband holster would come in handy, too. None of the holsters displayed quite suited me, though. Another curtain opened and let me remember the project I started when I was he-Bear. I'd planned to make my own. Even had the materials in the work space in the basement. Just needed to assemble the parts to finish it.

That left only two things more to do here. First was to thank Gunny for telling me the trick to hitting close range targets. That had saved my life. I grabbed a sheet of paper from a notepad at the counter and wrote a thank you with the story of its use. If he didn't finish with customers in a few minutes, I'd just leave that and thank him sometime when business was slower.

Second was to pick up a copy of the deer hunting regulations. I liked to stay up to date on the rules, but this would be the third year I would hunt without intent to take one. Being out in nature was all I needed to call it a good day.

I'd read once that, according to at least one Native American tribe's beliefs, deer sensed when they were hunted. They also sensed when hunger was the reason. If the hunt was for food, and the hunter worthy, a deer would present itself as that needed food. Don't know if it's true or not, but I felt less guilty when I did take one home for the freezer after that.

The regulations made it an honorable hunt. It depended on the deer's decision whether or not I would have venison for the winter. I owed its spirit reverent thanks for its sacrifice if I took it.

Gosh! That trip to a siding took longer than I thought. Gunny came back from the range as the rhythm of shots came from customers shooting at the slow fire targets. "Hi, Gunny. Just wanted to thank you. It must have been fate. The day after you showed me how to shoot if I had to, I had to."

"I heard about that. Detective O'Doyle came by to check your story, told me what happened. Glad to see you're OK." he replied.

We chatted a while as I made my purchase. He paid me a compliment as I readied to leave. "I'll be there if you ever need help with another armed thug. Maybe not in person, but I will be with you in spirit." I offered the same in reply, then turned and left.

A short while later, Shad had his mid morning walk. I was in the uniform of the day again - jeans, a shirt, and comfortable moccasins. Lunch was simple and quick, burger and fries, shared in part with Shad as reward for his patience and to show no hard feelings about our disagreement.

After lunch, I looked for and found the collection of firearms behind a false wall in the closet. I did a few loads of laundry to ready Vic's clothes for the parish clothing bank. During the wash cycles, I inventoried the firearms. Gunny was right. Old military firearms from the 1880s, some of which were recent reproductions, to more current ones of the 1970s were the bulk of the armory's contents. There was a modern Winchester Model 88, a box magazine lever action rifle chambered in .308 Win. That and the M1A in that cartridge by the metric designation, 7.62X51 mm or 7.62 mm NATO, seemed well used and well maintained.

A shelf over the rifles and shotgun held manuals for each of the firearms I counted, holsters, cleaning gear, and boxes for three hand guns. The empty one was for the single action Vaquero I carried or kept in the night stand. One was for a twin Vaquero. The third was the one I sought - the Colt Officer's ACP. It was a shortened barrel and grip version of the G.I. 1911-A1 in .45 Auto. Much better size for concealed carry to my way of thinking. And his notes in the box said it was still close to the Government Model, within 30 feet/second velocity over a chronograph and calculated power. Not a magnum, but powerful enough to win any argument with an attacker.

A forgotten treasure was a range book for the M1A. The settings for the sights as 'battle sights' was already tested and recorded. I would test it myself to see if any changes were needed with this body. The computer printout for exterior ballistics showed a calculated result for 300 yards - Elevation 10 clicks up, Windage centered. With a center mass hold, that should be a good start and put the shots on paper to 300 yards That would make finding my personal battle sights easier.

The dryer's buzzer interrupted my voyage of discovery. I sorted and folded clothes, Put them in the bags for delivery to St. Michaels and St. James' Infirmary clothing banks. The 'dry clean only' clothes were already in two other bags. To me, this decision confirmed my acceptance of my new life, and gave a little payback for this chance in the bargain.

If you've ever folded clothes from the dryer, you know you have time to consider other things as long as they are short and concise sound bites. That last thought about payback triggered an internal debate whether Church dogma, thought up some fifteen to twenty Centuries ago, got it right.

It taught that we got one chance on a pass - fail basis. Some other religions and philosophies thought we came back until we got it right. What if purgatory was right here on earth in another life? Lately, the news supported the argument that living again would be punishment enough for minor sins and even some very serious ones.

I decided to go with the one chance option, but I'd welcome a chance for a do over if offered. That was similar to Blaise Pascal's answer about belief in God and reward or punishment in an afterlife for the soul. If I was right, I would be prepared for the decision and would gain all. If wrong, I wouldn't even notice whether it was oblivion or a do over. Of course, Pascal said it way better. Check the quote if you don't believe me. It's called Pascal's Wager.

The clock showed clothes drop off was for tomorrow or even later. The charities' offices were closed for the day. Also explained that empty stomach feeling. We had already delayed supper an hour. I walked Shad. The squirrel must have already gathered the choice, edible acorns because it was quiet. Then again, this close to sunset, it may have called it a day instead.

I hoped Mr. Loudmouth hadn't lost an argument over right of way with a car. His scolding was annoying, but he wasn't as bad a guy as I thought at first. I'd miss him if he was gone.

Supper dishes washed and drying in the rack, I poured myself a drink. I settled in and searched for a light movie on TV. Didn't find one on the schedule. It was crowded with boring period dramas that had a half hour story that took their two hour time slots to tell.

The others were shoot-em-ups. All action, shoot outs, and explosions burdened by a sketchy plot and minimal character development. Those weren't what I wanted to watch tonight.

I searched the DVD collection. Found Casablanca. Since I liked the acting, story, and the ending, plugged it into the player. A few hours later, I walked Shad for the last time tonight. On return inside, loaded the ACP and the spare magazine. Those went into my purse. The Vaquero went with me and rested on the vanity during my shower. After I dried off, it went into the night stand drawer. I prayed for the strength of body, mind and spirit to face my challenges, whatever they would be, and went to bed.

The Wake Days

Seven hours and a quarter more later, I woke. Pretty boring start but they were necessary tasks for a mere mortal. A brief thanks to the Creator that my eyes opened first, bathroom next, then kitchen to make coffee, say good morning to Shad as he joined me, then a more formal thanks to the Great Maker for giving us another day with good health, and toss in some mention of the world roughly divided into the Good and the Bad camps. The good got my prayer for a pleasant day and successful endeavors. For the bad, I wished the plagues of disease and confusion in their attempts to implement their plans. Made and ate breakfast in the hour plus until first light of dawn. Washed the dishes and left them in the drying rack.

The radio station came on the air with the National Anthem, followed by the morning DJ's station identification and the intro to the first song of the morning. Another golden old one, Buck Owens and his band got hearts beating and toes tapping with I've Got a Tiger by the Tail. God bless their pea pickin' hearts and the Bakersfield sound. It fought the blues at a moment when I needed the help.

I dressed for the morning's walk while the new machine, bought at a garage sale when the old one gave up the ghost, made twelve ounces of fresh brewed coffee. Because dressing was almost as automatic as the coffee maker, I started to back plan the day. Allowing for the first day of the wake at six to eight PM, an hour to apply makeup and get dressed meant supper should be finished by five thirty to allow driving time to the funeral parlor. Use another hour to shampoo and shower, then dry myself and my hair and fashion it into an up-do limited me to a frozen dinner, or one made in the crock pot, or the old emergency solutions of a PB&J or cold cut sandwich on toast.

The last was my choice for the day. I had ham and Swiss cheese slices in the refrigerator, rye bread in the plastic bag it came in and it was still mold free, and a toaster if my taste buds wanted it on toast. If I started to make supper at four-thirty, I could finish eating by five without wolfing it down. Add a little extra time for overruns, I had time if I started my shower at or before two-thirty.

That left the morning for myself and Shad. I readied for a walk with the canine member of my household. The next thought brought a grin. Whoever decided cats were the witches' choice hadn't checked with me first. Who would EVER pick an animal as aloof as a cat to be a familiar? Give me a dog. By nature dogs prefer to live in a pack, even one led by a human, on any day of the week.

That and I heard the cats next door talk after I got the gift to understand them.

They plotted the demise of dogs and dog owners so they could subjugate the other humans. It was not pleasant to overhear. Familiar, my butt. They despised us and only pretended to need us or to give a dang about us to make their conquest easier. I tried hard to keep from telling them they were done for because they'd be back to hunting for their food and living outdoors if I ever told their plans.

On second thought, there was always the chance it was disinformation or mere wishful thinking from two pampered and spoiled house cats that never killed a mouse or even thought about it. Better to keep the intelligence gathered as secret as deciphering the Ultra code machines was and kept under wraps for years after WW2 ended. I didn't need to be in a rubber room when the threat to the forest was imminent.

I pet Shad as I considered the chores I could tackle after the walk. First on the agenda was to pay bills. Those from firms in town would get a hand carried payment and I'd change the billing addressee during the visit as well as give them their check for the month. Those with out of town addresses would get a letter to do so with the payment. That would pretty much shoot the morning if I had any problems. Never considered that I'd get it all done in less time than I allowed.

A few minutes after dawn broke, it was light enough to walk on seen ground. Much more comfortable than stepping into the dark trusting that it was ground instead of a portal to a different dimension or a trap. "Let's go out, Shad."

Dang, those Sci Fi movies and horror films had planted some strange fears. Now I was a witch, something else I never considered. Maybe that's why those old fears were coming back.

The squirrel voiced its displeasure at our intrusion into what it considered its space. Shad reacted by sniffing out small caches of acorns, digging them up. and spreading the nuts over the lawn in the process. Then he snorted, "Now you've got nuts to find, you pea brain."

I swear I saw that squirrel do a double take before its lament started. Oh, how he wailed. It was truly overly mournful for only thirty acorns, after all. It probably would kill him if it were the main cache.

When the squirrel complained for almost five minutes, I heard Shad tell him to shut up. He shared the space with us as owners. He was just a tenant whose presence was suffered by this human. The squirrel spluttered, like many who have lost an argument, but did shut up eventually.

We were outside for full sun rise. For me, it was the first time in a long time I paid attention. The sky was partly cloudy, but the sun rose in a clear spot. There was a bit of reassurance in that. The world was still in one piece, the sun still rose despite the doom and gloom the media kept predicting. I renewed my intent to wake to celebrate every morning from then on.

Back inside, I made another cup of coffee and gathered the bills into a single pile. I chuckled to myself. From nothing on my schedule to a pretty full day. This being an adult had mighty big responsibilities attached. A prayer came to mind. "To Anybody listening, please give me the strength to do this well. Bear, and for all I know, Ursula Parker were good people called Home early. They deserve my best efforts and don't let me screw up." I exhaled my sudden anxiety and went forth with confidence that came upon me from somewhere.

I wrote the checks and made sure they went into the correct envelopes. Next, I sorted the firms with home town offices from those with out of town billing offices. It took less time than I planned to visit the offices of those with addresses in town even with the change of owner to be billed. After I mailed the out of town payments, and made a quick trip to the grocery, I was back home.

I answered Detective O'Doyle's call when the phone rang. He related that the coroner signed off on the cause of death and released Bear's body yesterday. I said that I talked to Rossen's and reached an agreement. He agreed they were reputable as far as he knew, and did a good job for officers killed in the line of duty. He had seen a couple in his eight years on the force, and been amazed by how good three looked despite horrible wounds in the photos of the bodies at the crime scene. That relaxed me some.

While at the phone, I noticed a message waiting. I played it. Eugene Washington, lawyer, called to report. He had filed the paperwork to start probate. The judge's clerk had us on the court calendar on the first of December at ten AM. He also notified the Public Administrator.

In relation to the farms near Witch Woods, there was also a glimmer of a chance that the state zoning board would hear a disputed county zoning board decision. A better chance the state's EPA would file an action to demand an environmental impact study before any trees were cut, or sales of farms for that golf course rumored to be in the works. The failure to do so already would delay their plans until it was done and reviewed.

He chuckled as he reported the Forrests didn't have a lot of friends in the state capitol, specially not after they tried to get the popular State Attorney General recalled three weeks into the new term last year. It wasn't even close despite the money spent trying to build opposition. They were also found guilty of trying to buy enough house members to pass a recall bill. Got a few of those legislators who failed to report the attempted bribery in trouble, too. The special elections to refill the seats emptied by guilty convictions at trial brought in a batch of new legislators and state government was no longer the retirement home for career politicians.

I returned Gene's call once late enough to expect him back at work after morning coffee to explain the call from him arrived while I was out. He reported more details. A younger Forrest son got charged, tried, and is now serving time at the state pen for the bribery fiasco. He laughed that a Forrest now served time. That brought a laugh to my lips also.

"Is it too much to hope this destroys that family's power in this area?" I questioned. The answer was a ray of sun in a cloudy sky.

Gene said it could ruin them if found guilty of unintentionally damaging or destroying an ecosystem under a state law passed last year. They would lose their licenses to be developers, not to mention the fines that would go with a conviction. Additionally, they faced long terms in the big house if it was an intentional failure to have the study. Gene chuckled, "They might be big fish in this small pond, but the state lake has much bigger fish that don't like them on both professional and personal grounds." I chuckled as I thanked him for the news and said good bye.

Then I called the Rossen Funeral Home. Bruce answered. I asked him whether the work on granddad would be finished in time to start the wake at six this evening. He said yes, and added, "Since he's shuffled off this mortal coil, we'll put the breast forms he wore on Halloween into the foot of the casket with the clothes you brought yesterday, and dress him as a carpenter as you want."

I asked what the revised bill would be. Bruce answered cheerfully, "We don't need an anesthesiologist, a large surgical team, or malpractice insurance when working on the deceased. The bill should be a little less than what we already agreed. It's $6,750, and $6,415 if paid in the week."

"Do it. Just let me know when he's finished so I can hold the wake and confirm the schedule for the funeral Mass."

"I understand. We'll do the best we can, and that's usually very good or better. Even our worst is still quite satisfactory. None of the customers has ever complained." Bruce paused.

It sunk in. He told a joke. One in very poor taste, but it still caused me to chuckle from the surprise that an undertaker show his sense of humor during a wake. Too, it did calm me. I realized anticipation of the day I'd spend had wound my springs too tightly. I needed to talk to a friend over a few drinks. Maybe after the wake tonight, or during if it went haywire.

"Thanks for the joke. It did help offset the day I've had, and it's only morning. I'll bring the check with me to the first night of the wake." I responded.

I left Shad in the house for the trip to pay bills. There were no surprises when I got back, so I felt I could leave him home for the wake. We had a quick walk and an even quicker meal. After the walk, I called Father Joe to tell him the wake would start today.

The radio broadcast the announcement for the wake at noon and every half hour after for the afternoon. I launched into the plan I had a little early to be sure I was ready to go on time. I explained the situation to Shad and he accepted why he'd stay behind when I left for the wake.

At the mortuary, I looked at Victor at rest. I felt he was at peace. I paid as promised. Then I sat in the chapel until the mourners and merely curious started to arrive. Protocol was for next of kin to meet and greet them. I was on my feet pretty steadily. The crowd grew slowly until about seven thirty when it started to thin.

A few moments of note. I met Gus that night. Besides the normal chit chat between strangers at a friend or family member's wake, I also mentioned that there were others in town who wanted to protect the ecosystem under threat. I had found an entry in granddad's journal that said as much. I fibbed a little when I said I didn't know what it meant, but I was for whatever saved Witch Woods. His eyes flashed with confidence at that remark. He knew now that he'd not fight alone.

Sue and Gene came and stayed until the end of the visitation. They were my crutch when I felt overwhelmed from time to time. It wasn't so much that Victor was dead as it was his friends and customers kind words about him. I thought I had talked to over fifty mourners, with that number more just mingled with the others. A quick glance at the visitors' log showed that my estimate was low.

As the last of the crowd dispersed into the night, I invited those two to drop by for a night cap. They declined. They used work tomorrow as an excuse. I drove home, walked Shad one more time and retired for the night.

The second day of the wake was almost a duplicate of the day before if you leave out the once a month bill paying and other boring stuff. There were more people to meet, and many stayed for the rosary led by Father Joe at the end of the evening regardless of their religion. They may not have shared the form of the prayer, but there was no reason they didn't offer thoughts in keeping with the situation.

A Good Man

After dawn and Shad's walk on Saturday, the gray sky of dawn stayed around. Fit my mood well. The funeral of anyone should be a solemn event, and gray skies contributed to that mood. After all, we the living lost the chance to make new memories with someone we held dear, knew, or should have known. I know. I never got to know my dad. Mom left before I was a teen, and my grandparents left before I finished college. I've also known others that left a hole in my life.

After the funeral and burial, that's a different story. We still have our lives to live, and a bright clear sky helps restore our optimism and hope. Without those, life isn't worth the toils and trials we face every day. Can't think of any? How about current or ex in-laws? Politicians? Internet acquaintances that drop you from their friends lists because of differing politics? The list is long, but is different for each person. You need to fill your list in for yourself.

For whatever reason, the day seemed to be moving at an unusually slow pace. For example, the oatmeal finally cooked in the usual ten minutes but it felt like an hour. Let's just write it off as a symptom of my anxiousness for it all to go smoothly. I abandoned philosophy for real life as I fixed a bowl of oatmeal with a long squirt of maple flavored syrup, a double toasted English muffin, to make it crunchy, with butter and orange marmalade, and some coffee.

Shad got his share of the muffin because he felt abused if he didn't share the people food. I figured he was worth it. He had given me early warning of the intruders. Not convinced I'd enjoy his kibble as much as he enjoyed his share of my muffin, but he had earned his portion.

Took my morning shower and dried with a towel and blow dryer. Brushed my hair straight and pulled it into a pony tail. Brushed my teeth and applied my makeup. Searched for and found my funeral outfit, a black sheath dress with matching coat, and even the big brimmed black hat appropriate for funerals. A memory of the funeral for which I bought it came to mind. A classmate and friend had died of a self-inflicted drug overdose of prescription painkillers. That was at the start of senior year and he would have graduated with my class. I missed him. Just another memory which wasn't a fond one.

Death came uninvited. It might have been me if I had followed that path. Instead, I stuck with beer and whiskey in moderation, and never together. I had heard the old saw, "Beer on whiskey, mighty risky. Whiskey on beer, have no fear." Tried it once and found that wasn't quite true in my case. I was better off to stick to what I started with. That one time I had too much of both was lesson enough for me. I learned my limits that time. And after I turned 21, it was legal to have in possession, unlike the drugs which too many used for recreational purposes instead of medical necessity. That's another instance of asking Can I? instead of Should I? at least in my philosophy.

But this was early morning. Neither beer nor whiskey was needed. I had all I needed just because I woke and everything seemed to work, from fingertips to toes, and so did all the other systems between those extremities. The day started well enough, and whether I made it to tonight was still an unanswered question. No sense worrying about that. It was up to the actions of myself and others whether I slept in my bed tonight or on a coroner's table. I just had to be alert for threats and avoid them or defeat them.

Which reminded me to move my stuff to the black purse. Be stupid to ignore Pete's advice. The fight hadn't started yet, but I had adopted the big D attitude that it could today. More likely, Junior Forrest still thought he had bought the county zoning board, so wouldn't start anything yet. It would start in earnest after we filed the appeal with the state zoning board. I used this grace period to establish the habit of preparedness before anything started.

I shivered mildly when I recalled the look in the intruder's eyes when he asked for the old man. I didn't want to be defenseless if, probably when, they came after me again. My magic wasn't yet powerful enough to fend off serious attacks. I could flick a light switch, throw a skillet, but that wouldn't be much help if more than one or two attacked.

It was worth the chance that I'd find a 'surprise' when I returned home to leave Shad behind. While he had traveled with me for short trips, this trip would be three, four, or more hours from start to finish. It wouldn't be kind to leave him in the vehicle so long alone. He had done well the last few times left alone, but I still wasn't positive it would be so every time.

He seemed to understand I wasn't leaving forever when I took him inside after the preventative walk between breakfast and my departure. I left him with the order to do nothing stupid that would get him hurt, but to guard the house while I was gone.

First stop was the church. I beat the hearse there by a few minutes, but they were still earlier than the pall bearers. Once they assembled, it looked like a well-executed touchdown running play when the whole thing came together for the service at nine.

I took my seat in the front pew after thanking the honor

guard of VFW and Legion members, plus the two civilians, Gus and Gunny. The other mourners filed in and filled the front fifteen rows. The rites for the dead took a few minutes before the low Mass started. It didn't take long and the pall bearers carried their burden back to the hearse. The caravan started for the cemetery and was there shortly. Again, the pall bearers delivered their friend and comrade to the grave site in almost practiced unity.

Father Joe gave a good eulogy that gave my former body credit as A Good Man and ended with John Donne's reminder, "Ask not for whom the bell tolls, it tolls for thee." The crowd dispersed to be at the saloon for lunch. I turned to watch the lowering of the casket into the ground. That moved me to vow that I would be a good person, at least the best I could be, when they buried me in my time.

I drove to the Spotted Horse and ensured they were ready for the small crowd headed here. Small crowd, my foot. By the time all were here, the building was at capacity of 150 plus the cooks, waitresses and bar staff.

Folding tables and chairs had been placed on the dance floor. Extra chairs had been squeezed in around the round tables in the usual dining area. A short line of folks waited at the bar to have their orders filled while the designated drivers found tables and drank coffee, tea, or soft drinks.

The folks mixed and mingled to chat with old friends, some made new acquaintances. A few chatted with me and I did my best to not break down. The entire membership of the coven, those I knew and those I had yet to meet, occupied a corner of the tables in the bar area. Even Detective O'Doyle dropped by to offer his condolences. He offered to drop by later this afternoon because he had some news about Victor's death.

Serving dishes arrived at the tables full and left empty. Except that it celebrated the final and permanent relocation of a human to a new neighborhood, this turned out to be a good party for the survivors. I remembered a few of these in my past life as Victor before I became Ursula. By eleven-thirty, people started to leave. They were all gone and cleanup by the staff began by quarter after twelve. Bob teased I'd get a discount. No unpaid leftovers for which to account or sell at a loss to clear then from the refrigerators.

Then he asked if I could be back by three. He needed a fill in barmaid. The one scheduled to work had called to report a slip and fall, and that she now wore a neck brace. I said "It'll be tight but I think I can make it."

"Look good today. Had a reservation made for the private room, and I'll need you to cover that room." Bob answered. "And these are big spenders who tip well, specially Junior Forrest."

"I'll be there with bells on. See you soon." I answered with a smile.

Yes! If this is that secret meeting with the zoning board, it was a way to listen to their plan like the proverbial fly on the wall, but better. I could testify at their trials.

I needed someone to house sit for this longer absence. Sue was handy. I told her the story and my intentions. She agreed. While she rode with Gene for the services, burial, and lunch, she rode to my home with me. We got to my house with some small talk during the ride, mostly about my chance to find the plan behind the plot.

It was a frantic rush from then after to the end of the day. First thing was a walk with Shad during which I explained the need to be gone a while longer. He agreed. I introduced him to Sue once we got inside again. Then it was the checklist for work.

Makeup, check. Tell Sue I was going to be better than a fly on the wall, check. Brush hair into an attractive style, check. Bra, not today, check. Low, tight scoop neck tank top, check. Panties, no, a lace thong, check. Denim mini-skirt, check. Tall shaft cowgirl boots, check. Ready to go, check. Say, wish me luck to Sue, check. Slip the Officer's ACP and a spare magazine into my purse as an afterthought, check. Scold myself for that possibly fatal failure, check. Ask Sue to watch Shad while I'm working, check. Find my jacket with the truck keys in a pocket, and drive to the Spotted Horse, check. Report in at two thirty- four, check. Catch my breath and calm down, check. Whew!

Find Bob, check. Get the estimated number of attendees, check. Found an order pad and wrote my name on the line for server on a dozen tickets, check. Tied on the carpenter's apron we used to carry change, the order pad, and a pen. Check and Ready. Whew again.

A Meeting Of Crooks

When I was ready to start my shift, Bob whispered, "Knock 'em dead, girl. Friendly smile with that outfit will ensure big tips. Damn, almost make me wish I wasn't married." He grinned.

Ah, that question was answered. He moved to the bottom of the queue just behind Gene. I'd never be 'the other woman', no matter how close the friendship. Notwithstanding that, I couldn't help smiling as the first private room guests arrived. They brought a tripod for a white board, and another for the maps I presumed were in a cylindrical carrier. It sure looked like the map cases used by the Driscoll Architecture draftsmen to transport their drawings.

I helped set up the display because they were helplessly fumble fingered with such simple equipment. Either they were extremely nervous or totally unfamiliar with manual labor. A much unkinder possibility was that they had already had too many drinks, or other drugs that destroyed their ability to perform simple tasks. The upside of that was that I'd be able to listen in, possibly in plain sight, if their faculties were already dulled by whatever they used.

As I spent time working with them, the smell of alcohol showed that was the cause. The truly inebriated big (a euphemism for fat in his case) man asked, "What ya drinkin', doll?"

I answered, "Name is Ursula, but I answer to anything

except being called late to dinner." Poor guy almost lost his teeth, he did lose a dental bridge, he laughed so hard. Yep, he was on something, probably too much liquor. I finished him off. "I don't drink at work, but when I drink, I like a Bourbon and Branch". I thought he was gong to laugh himself to death. Definitely and seriously inebriated. Neither of those old lines was worth more than a wry grin or a polite chuckle.

I helped him to a chair and had him sit with his head between his knees. I'd been taught that was appropriate for lightheadedness. The chubby young man who seemed to be in charge called over the other muscle and told him, "Guns, take him out to the car and let him sleep it off. If I ever catch either of you guys drinking too much again, you're both fired. Understand?" He turned back to the stranger he spoke to before the interruption.

Guns answered, "Yes, Mr. Forrest. I'll do that." He helped the other guy up. "Come on, Lou. You damn near got us fired again." He escorted Lou to a stretch limo and put him in the front passenger side seat.

I turned back to my work. The stranger wasn't in sight. Hmmm.

While that went on, Junior Forrest asked, "Sweety, can you help with the presentation after lunch? I seem to be a man short."

I looked around, saw no one else in the room. "Me, sir? The boss said I should do whatever you asked that didn't get us both arrested. I'd be happy to help with a presentation." Holy cow This was going to be even better than just listening in. "What do you want me to do?"

"About fifteen minutes of chart flipping on cue after you serve the after dinner drinks. Be worth a few bucks if you do it, more if you do it well." He winked.

"That sounds fine to me, sir. Count me in." Acting class

might pay off this time. I immediately switched to "sexy, almost but not really an air head mode", great for many roles in TV sitcoms or comic relief in dramas. Some girls use it in real life, then surprise their companions when they let their intelligence show.

"Fine. See me after dinner. My guests are coming in now. See to their needs, and bring me a glass of Pinot Noir to start after I welcome them. Put the drinks and meals on my tab if you don't mind."

"Yes, sir." I made a note of his requests and walked out to clear them with Bob. Used to this kind of thing, he adapted easily. He just opened a special key on the register used for private room parties. No lost or mislaid orders, or fooling with adding the tabs manually after.

One thing about living in a larger small town, I recognized the members of the zoning board because they were well known in town while they didn't recognize a nobody like me. Guns came in with the last of them, a stranger with a shifty look to him. There's the stranger again. Both took position near Junior, and the stranger chatted with the host of this shindig. While I don't speak Spanish, they spoke in what sure sounded like Spanish to me, and I recognized a few words that I did know. I looked at him to remember him again if asked to point him out in a crowd. He had the air of a boss of bosses about him.

The guests seated themselves and my work began. I took orders for pre-dinner drinks and scurried to the bar. Pinot Noir by the glass seemed popular. Of course it would. The main course was prime rib. Even someone on a beer budget like mine had read about red wines, especially Pinot Noir, with beef, possibly read the article about its ability to stand the stronger flavors of beef and game. One person ordered a Liebfraumilch and chicken fried chicken because it was a house specialty and her favorite. I watched as they ate and chatted, taking empty glasses away and bringing full glasses back.

One incident deserves special note. While delivering his drink, the president of the board slipped his hand under my skirt. I bent down to stage whisper, "Sir, I am NOT on the menu, so don't do that again. Thank you. Besides, if I were on the menu, didn't your mama teach you to not play with your food? Talk to me later about my fees if you're serious." Son of a beach actually blushed.

After the meal, dishes and old glasses cleared, after dinner drinks served, the presentation started. I took my position between the boards. Junior signaled and I flipped back the blank cover page which covered the other drawings.

The first page was a county map with a red stick on star showing the area of interest. The second page showed the township and range, about ten miles north of town, with a dark line tracing the boundary of the specific parcels of interest. That line followed the boundary of the State Forest on the east, Route 17 on the west, 25 Mile Road on the south and 28 Mile Road on the north. That looked to be about seven and a half square miles of land, of which about a third was rough ground now wood lots or pasture. Another third was rolling pasture with parts under cultivation for winter feed. The last third was gently rolling land that was currently cultivated for cash crops, the grains and pulse crops sold for human and animal food.

The brushy fence rows had always produced large numbers of small game, song birds, and even game birds and birds of prey. The wooded areas raised quite a population of large and small mammals that locals harvested for dinner. That helped keep the populations healthy because it reduced the number of over wintering critters so they didn't eat all the plants. Hunting was only fair and sound management without the large carnivores. Too, the humans fed the critters all year. Taking a few for food completed the circle of life.

I got my mind back on the present when Junior signaled me to turn the third page and announced that this area was the target. It showed the farms by ownership and estimated prices at agricultural land prices. An overlay drawing showed a country club and large outbuildings marked golf cart and machinery storage. Others were marked shop and warehouse. Scattered around the perimeter were small groups of houses on cul de sacs off a main road serving the interior. Other clusters of housing were on cul de sacs off the main roads along the edges.

The president of the board asked, "Are you sure this is legal?"

To the casual observer across the room, Junior just stopped to think. At a closer distance, I caught a glimpse of a hungry dog ready to fight for its meal. "Of course it's legal if you rezone the land as recreational and housing." Junior stated. There was annoyance in his voice before he calmed again. He assured them they could all make money buying the farms for agricultural land prices and reselling it as recreational land for three, four, or maybe even five times the original price paid. The meeting ended with no further questions.

I thought this might be an opportunity to determine whether the Forrests actually did eliminate their opponents. Or those they deemed too weak kneed to go the course of their schemes, as the president just showed himself. I'd watch the news carefully.

Happy hour started while I helped Guns carry out their displays. Bob dealt with Junior directly for the bill. On his way out, Junior spoke to me, "Buy yourself something nice. And see me if you want a better job." He slipped something into my top. I didn't see the denominations, but I recognized the color of US currency surely enough.

"I'll think about that. Thank you, sir." I said. But I was careful not to touch the bills more than necessary. After he left the parking lot, I got a pair of disposable gloves and a brand new sealable bag from the kitchen. When I removed the bills from my top, I noted the day and time of the transaction, who gave me the money, the amount and the serial number on the bills. and sealed them into the bag. Yes, you read that correctly. One serial number on all five Grants, $250 worth of funny money. Counterfeit, just like the scoundrel who copped a feel when he gave me the "tip."

Son of a beach. He had tipped nothing after promising a reward. That was a reason added to the land grab that put us on opposite sides for this battle. Now it was personal for the insult as well as to protect the ecosystem under threat.

I stapled the self-sealing bag shut and had Gene sign as witness to the beginning of this chain of evidence. Since he was a lawyer, I suspected that he could probably get a quicker and more serious response from the Secret Service anticounterfeiting folks than I could as a barmaid. Too, he could vouch for me that I wasn't the one trying to pass the fake bills, but received them from a pillar of the community. A pillar that leaned more than the Leaning Tower. A pillar that I hoped leaned too far over the line and would fall into ruin this time.

Duty to my boss led me to warn Bob about the funny money in case Junior paid him in cash also. I'd pretend to be an offended lady for a bit, but his tirade was truly offensive. I had no need to pretend. The language that Bob used was not fit for polite society and genteel ears, and not even some locker rooms. Maybe not even among drunken sailors on shore leave. He most colorfully questioned Junior's ancestry and honor to give you a clue. "F***ing" was used a lot. It might be funny if it wasn't the first time he blew up about getting stiffed by somebody he trusted.

The twelve Grants he received had the same serial number

as each other and the five I received. Bob stored them in his safe in a manila envelope. I moved away a little farther. As peeved as he was, better to give him space and time to calm down again.

Gene gained another client that night when Bob signed on. He also picked up a few points in the contest for my heart if he and Sue ever called it quits. He earned them. He remained calm outwardly despite confessing that inwardly he shook like the leaves of an aspen tree in a strong wind. After all, this WAS a federal case now.

"Does this mean we harpooned our Moby Dick?" I asked.

"Maybe. If we did, hang on for the ride of your life." Gene answered. "Or death if those rumors are true and this ends the way Melville's story does." he added.

The boss seemed calmer after his tirade in the kitchen. When he emerged, his face wasn't red any more. "Bob, Am I finished here tonight? If I am, I'd like to go home now." I queried as Bob approached us.

He said it was okay on condition that I came to work tomorrow. I agreed and clocked out after four hours work. I needed to talk to someone about the plans Junior outlined to the county zoning board. "Follow me to my place. Maybe we can plan to meet the threat so it doesn't take us by surprise. Besides, Sue is watching the house. I'm sure she'd like a ride home, Gene."

I went to the employees locker room to gather my coat and purse to leave. Francine stopped me on the way out. She reported that she, too, found the ride offered by that hospital orderly worth the effort of going with that one guy exclusively. I had a good chuckle about that with her. After I put on my coat and grabbed my purse, I drove home. Gene followed.

I reached the house first and went in. Found Sue watching television with Shad resting comfortably in his usual spot. Gene was behind by the time lost to one stoplight he didn't make.

When he arrived, he and Sue shared a monumental lip lock and hug. It was enough to show me I'd be the other woman if I continued to move on him. So much for my lust. Gene's ranking on my list of suitors tanked. Rats!

That left us little to discuss other than the scheme I witnessed while it was still "on paper" and not yet put into motion. We had a drink while we chatted. I related the story of the meeting that earned me the tip in funny money. That was good for a group discussion about what we'd do to derail Junior Forrest's plan.

The simplest action would be to report the counterfeit money to the anti-counterfeiting folks in the Secret Service. That would be up to Gene and his contacts who could put him in touch with the right people to get action from the Department of Treasury.

After we solved that dilemma, Sue reported that Detective O'Doyle dropped by. He was disappointed that he missed me but would visit tomorrow. She and Gene left together shortly after that. I walked Shad for the last time today. Another drink later, I went to sleep. As soon as my head hit the pillow, I might add.

Another Fool

I must have wondered "What's next?" during my sleep. The answer came at three AM. A cold nose poked me in the neck again. As I woke, that was followed by Shad's very soft growl. "What?" I whispered.

Shad looked toward the back door and whispered "Shush. Another fool thinks we're still asleep." He took a defensive position two steps back from the end of the counter along the kitchen's outside wall. I pulled the pistol from my purse and made ready to defend the house against unwelcome and illegal entry. The sound of someone playing with the backdoor lock came above the soft beeping my cell phone made as I dialed 9-1-1.

I got busy then and the dispatch operator only listened as the punk came in. I said loudly, "Hold it right there, jerk."

He challenged back, "Who's going to make me? You and what army, little girl?" He continued toward me at a measured pace rather than at a charge. Must have learned it was more intimidating to approach at a menacing slow speed in hoodlum school.

I used that to my advantage. I looked at the twelve-inch cast iron skillet on the stove. Might have been my imagination, but I saw it wiggle. "Stop right there, asshole." No time for a third warning. I focused on that skillet again and commanded it to fly hard into the back of his head. The skillet did as ordered and on contact, thudded to a stop. He pitched forward. I had intended to shoot low, but the fry pan made that unnecessary.

Shad looked as astounded as I felt. "Good job, Baba Two. You're getting a handle on your powers."

I wanted to kick the intruder in the face but didn't need to. The sudden stop against the bare floor broke his nose. He was effectively removed from combat. He'd be in the prisoner ward at the hospital, or maybe on the coroner's table, after the police arrived.

I wasn't sure which. After all, it was the first time I used that skillet for something more than frying food. I didn't know how hard to throw it at a head. Either way, it looked to me that I cooked his goose well done.

I reported to the dispatcher, "He came in right after I dialed and it went to hell fast after that. The housebreaker got hit with a skillet because he kept coming at me. He could use an ambulance from the look of him."

"Who are you, and where?" 9-1-1 asked.

"What? Oh. I'm Ursula Chadwick. I'm at my granddad's place." I gave her the address. "I'll turn the porch light on so they can find it more easily." Just before I switched on the light, I saw a van parked across the street.

I noted that the engine was running, and somebody in the driver's seat was smoking. I got the license plate number and wrote it down. Good thing, because the smoker quit daydreaming as the police sirens announced their arrival. He drove off fast. So fast he must have left some tire tracks when he turned short and drove over the lawn at the corner. I turned on the light when the patrol cars neared enough I could hear the sirens through the walls.

I'd mention that van when questioned unless they were complete assholes. If they were, I'd call Detective O'Doyle. Tell him directly.

Police and ambulance arrived soon after. The cops entered

with guns drawn, assessed the situation, then signaled the EMTs that the shooting was over. After they handcuffed the intruder, they holstered their pistols. That was when they started asking questions. They tried hard to get me to admit it was a lovers' quarrel until they found the fresh pry marks on the back door frame. That made them accept it was a forcible entry.

Well, with that conclusion, they moved up in my estimation. They weren't complete assholes. They were just guys with a hard job looking for an answer to make it easier.

I could understand that. No one likes to work harder than necessary. Their job just got harder, but they accepted that as just the way things are. I told them about the van and gave them the license plate number and told them it jumped the curb at the corner. They called it in to send out a BOLO (be on look-out) for the vehicle and driver, wanted for questioning.

The detectives arrived and took over the questioning. I repeated my story of what happened, included the suspicious van and its license plate number. A call to the dispatcher, plus travel time later, the Crime Scene Unit arrived. The sun broke first light. I excused myself to use the bathroom and change clothes. Also took Shad out for the first walk of the day. The supervisor of the CSU said it would be a few hours before they were done, and advised eating out.

I loaded Shad into the back seat, and drove to the truck stop with the twenty-four-hour restaurant. The food wasn't the best I'd ever had, but neither was it the worst, and it was served quickly and while still warm. Shad enjoyed his piece of toast and some sausage when I gave it to him as we left.

On the way back home, I stopped at a convenience store for soda pop and pretzels. I might need a snack if they took a long time to clear my house I parked in a dark corner at the store, so saw what looked like the van pull in. The driver dismounted and went in. I checked the license plate number.

Dialed 9-1-1 again and told them where I was and that I saw what I thought was the vehicle that was at my house when I was attacked. The driver was inside the store and they might be able to catch him there.

What seemed to be only a minute later, an officer knocked on my window. After opening the window, I told him what I observed as the van driver exited the store. He made a tactical error when he opened a can of beer while in the driver's seat. That was a violation of the no-open-carry-while-driving ordinance. The police closed in, cut off his exit, and had him under arrest They didn't need me to identify him for that crime. It was witnessed by two officers. I drove home.

On the way, I considered the small miracle of being in the right place at the right time with the right tools to do the right job. That got me in the mood to attend Sunday services. When home again, I found the house was empty of strangers. I dressed for church and applied subdued makeup. If I kept moving, I'd make it in time for the start of the nine o'clock Mass. I wore the go to shoes, my favorite loafers. At least they went with the khaki skirt and floral print blouse I wore under the khaki trench coat.

Shad came along since it was a pleasantly cool day. He wouldn't stay in an ice box or an oven, so he'd be safe from frostbite or from hyperthermia. We arrived on time. I entered the church without getting hit by lightning or a falling gargoyle, so figured I was safe here.

I took a seat in the middle of a pew in the back third of the church long enough before Mass started to find this weekend's responses for when the congregation answered the priest The hymnal had the words to songs it would sing at appropriate times. Two altar boys, a deacon, and Father Joe entered as the organist played the music for the entrance song. I stood, knelt, and sat with the others despite my years of irregular attendance on Sundays.

The gospel and sermon seemed to fit my situation. Gave me something else to think about besides that money grubbing developer and his plans for the woods. I did my best to include him in my prayers without asking for his success. At the end of the service, one of the nameless mourners at Bear's funeral invited me to coffee and a sweet roll served by the ladies of the parish. I accepted. Met a lot of nice folks, many of whom knew by now that I was Bear's granddaughter. Even more than the hot coffee and fresh cinnamon rolls the warmth I felt was, as the commercial says, priceless.

Spent a lot of time chatting, but was home well before noon. By then, skirt and blouse hung in the closet, replaced by jeans and a red buffalo check flannel shirt. I traded loafers for my camp mocs.

Shad was walked, fed and watered. I drank a cola. I was halfway through a pint of cola. Then Shad got that look. Someone was coming. After the last time, I didn't have a gun in hand. This time, I got one as the knock on the front door sounded.

I peeked out the window. That caused me to shove the pistol into my waist band. "Relax, Shad. It's O'Doyle. He said he'd drop by with some news about grand dad's murder."

Shad relaxed enough by the time I opened the door that I was reasonably certain Detective Sean O'Doyle wouldn't be his after-dinner snack. I opened the door and said, "Hi. Been expecting you. Come on in."

We passed the pleasantries of a friendly meeting as he did. We went into the living room. He said, "I see you're ready for trouble. Might want to get an inside the waist band holster, and make sure your shirt tail IS outside your pistol, not inside it."

I felt like a rank beginner, which wasn't unexpected. I was that in spades. After pulling the shirt out and ensuring it covered the pistol, I said "Thanks for the advice. Have a chair."

He sat in the recliner as if he carried the weight of the world. Not something you'd expect from a young man unless you knew he was a homicide detective. Or a small town detective used to simple cases With a complex one this time.

I sat on the sofa "You told Sue you have news about Victor's death?"

"Yes. I do have something." he replied, then explained.

"The bad guys were shooting 7.62 X 39 mm full jacket ammo from some imported AK47 type rifles. The customers who shot back used handguns of .38 caliber or bigger, mostly hollow points. Your grand dad was killed by a 7mm jacketed soft point hunting bullet, probably from outside the saloon. That's what the forensic team concluded from the deformed bullet, anyway. If that's what happened, your grandfather was murdered."

Holy shit! Excuse the French, but I was shocked enough to a let little of Corporal Bear slip out with the surprise. I never did anything to anyone in either body that would make them want to kill me. And all of the bar fights from my (Victor's) youth were from thirty or more years ago. I couldn't believe anyone would hold a grudge that long.

Well, maybe there was one. That hippie who objected to my service during 'Nam, and threw the first punch. He swore to get me someday. It couldn't be him, though. I read his obituary. It was in the local paper because his family still lived around here. He had moved to Haight-Ashbury in San Francisco and died from natural causes before Reagan's presidency. I read that in light of the prevalence of newspapers to use it as code for he O.D.'d on something or other in vogue at the time in that community, or something picked up from a used needle.

"Do you know of any enemies Victor might have had?" Detective O'Doyle's question brought me back into the present.

"Any bad blood because of business that you know of?"

"No, I don't off the top of my head. I wasn't close with granddad. As I said, he and grandma broke up when he went back to Viet Nam for a second tour. She gave back the ring. I met Victor for the first time when I started work at the Spotted Horse. I still didn't know he was my granddad on the night he died saving me. I showed you the paperwork that convinced me of that relationship."

Then I remembered the short entry on the calendar I saw when I turned the page into November. "But you might check with Gus Will. Victor's calendar showed a meeting with him for lunch the day he died. That was written in ball point. He wrote down after that they 'discussed land grab plot'. That was in pencil. Some photos I saw give me the feeling he would be quite interested in something like that."

"Why do you say that?" Sean queried.

I opened the end table drawer and pulled out a stack of envelopes full of photos. Took the top two and gave them to him. "Look for yourself. These photos show last year and the year before. He clearly fished and hunted there. Anything that would damage his favorite places or make them unavailable would grab his interest." I stated. "I'd like those back when you're done with them."

Sean looked at the photos, then reached into his jacket to pull out an evidence bag and his notebook. A minute later, he completed a receipt for property voluntarily given as evidence and handed it to me. "That will prove you voluntarily supplied them to further the investigation. Make it easier to reclaim them when the case is closed." he stated. "Maybe sooner if the lab crew can make prints from the negatives."

"Thank you. I appreciate that. They're a window into part of my family's story that I can't know without them."

"Oh. Better add that I filled in for a barmaid that couldn't make work because she wore a neck brace after an accident. That was yesterday afternoon, the day we buried Bear. I worked the meeting of Junior Forrest, some of his guys, a stranger who spoke in Spanish as well as English, and the zoning board in a private room at the saloon. One of his guys got drunk and I helped with the presentation. It sure seemed like a scam to gain control of land out near Witch Woods to me."

He visibly perked up as he made a note of that. We chatted a bit more before he left. While he was doing his job, I noticed his hazel eyes and strong jaw. If he were single, Sean definitely was, or at least could be, a rival for my hand. He definitely wore tested armor. Also noticed the mark of that ring he wore the first time we met had colored to almost match the rest of that finger and the dent was starting to disappear. Maybe he was single again. If so, it was recently. I filed the questions about his status for later if needed.

When Sean left, I walked Shad for a half hour or so. After that, I talked to Sue on the telephone. She had some news and wanted to visit. I invited her over when it was convenient for her as long as enough before five that I had time to listen. I had to report for work at the saloon by six.

While I waited for Sue or time to go to work, I checked the radio and was rewarded with a show of some of my favorite singers.

The front doorbell sounded. It announced it was show time. I turned off the radio and opened the door.

Definitely show time, just not the show I expected. Gene and Sue stood on the front porch awfully close together for acquaintances. Well, that would save me the decision to choose between being a lawyer's wife or the currently favored shadowy knight's spouse, specially if that was why he was so slow reacting to me I invited them in.

After the customary exchange of greetings, Sue and Gene

said, "We've got some news we want to share with you." It was a little spooky. They said it almost together and in harmony. That meant one thing.

I grinned. "You two are an item. Right? When's the wedding?"

Sue chuckled as she asked, "Is it that obvious?"

"Probably not to the general public or casual acquaintances, but plain to those who know either of you more than just as somebody to greet on the street." I stated the observed fact.

Almost from reflex, I also said, "Congratulations, both of you. Have a long and happy life together." After all the polite chatter finished, I offered them something to drink, even broke down and opened a fresh bag of chips and the dip I intended for the party for two when Stan got off the night shift at the end of next week. We chatted and emptied the bag of chips and container of dip.

When Sue excused herself to use the bathroom after her cola, Gene reported, "I called an acquaintance who called a friend who just called back. A Treasury Department investigator will arrive next week to check the story behind the funny money. There has been a flood of funny $50 bills with that serial number from this area." We agreed that was good news.

"Looks like I hired the right lawyer, Gene." He couldn't see my grin as I dropped the empty bag and carton of dip into the trash from his seat on the sofa but my voice gave me away.

He chuckled as he spoke again. "Wipe that grin off your face, Ursula. This is war. No time to smile until it's won."

"Right! Just like you're somber as a statue in the park. But the cause is just, so why not be glad to be on the right side or because something good happened or may happen?" I rebutted his statement.

"Just teasing. See you later at the saloon. I guess you're working tonight?" He said.

"Why, Mister Washington, I don't know if I'm flattered or

annoyed that you know my schedule." I hoped my chuckle softened my comment.

He whispered, "Not me. Sue keeps track to know where to find you if she wound up the story instead of the reporter. She trusts you big time. Besides, you told her you were working tonight."

When Sue rejoined us, we said our goodbyes as friends. The banter had not advanced Gene out of the bracket of those who stood no chance they might claim my heart, but it did improve his standing as a friend that happens to be a lawyer. My last words were, "Bring Sue, just to keep you honest."

We met again at the Spotted Horse. By then, I was in the "uniform" for a barmaid on a November Steampunk Sunday night - a replica late 1880's to early 1900s saloon girl outfit. Mine was red, which signified I was available, for a price. Relax. I hadn't had an acceptable offer yet. Too many cheapskates.

I mentioned that November Sunday nights were Steampunk Night at the saloon. We had a lot of folks who enjoyed dressing for the turn of the previous century with a seasoning of fantasy and science fiction. It was a lot of fun for many from out to fifty miles from town. Even had an occasional visit from folks who lived in the capitol 130 or so miles away.

We sold a lot of vodka dyed light green to pass as absinthe, the 1900's version of a love potion. Real absinthe wasn't available since it became illegal in the United States around the mid second decade of the 1900's. I think it was implicated as a cause for a sudden spike in illegitimate births or something. Added to that, a psychoactive ingredient was present in trace amounts. Too, absinthe was associated with the bohemian subculture of artists which caused a lot of bastard children on its own. That was enough for Victorian and Edwardian society to demand the end of its production worldwide. I think I read somewhere it's again legal, but don t bet on it for either its legality or its effect on your date.

Once an hour, we barmaids did the Cancan and some other dances as a group. The rest of the time, we laughed at the customers' bad jokes, engaged them in conversation as we brought fresh drinks, picked up the empty glasses and emptied the ashtrays. Not much different than a regular night except for the clothes and dances.

About a half hour after my shift started, Gene and Sue took a corner table and were joined by a very prim and proper middle-aged woman dressed in a contemporary maxi skirt suit except for the lace jabot at her neck, and her footwear. Those were full on steam punk, even the high top lace up boots with a zipper closure on the inside of the shaft.

After one of the dances, I had a few minutes to talk with Gene, Sue and Molly Pitcher. Really. She was named after the Revolutionary War heroines who carried water for the troops and manned the cannons when their husbands were wounded. She had a strong hint of Boston in her accent, and was the agent from the Treasury Department. I didn't need ask anything more. I even fought the urge to "help" to avoid interfering with her snooping, uh, investigating.

When they left a couple hours later and I had spent every break with them, I had Gene and Sues story. After I introduced them, they went to the same diner across the street from the court house for coffee. They shared a table because it was that or sit with strangers. They talked and coffee turned into lunch. That turned into a date and they hit it off very well. When Gene went out to start and warm up the car, Sue apologized for stealing my guy.

"He wasn't my guy, just somebody I dated a couple times. Don't worry about it. Have a great life together." I said.

My shift was over shortly after they left. I changed back to street clothes and went home. It was time for me to sleep.

Almost. First, Shad needed his last walk for the night.

I pulled the pistol when Shad acted strangely. He frequently glanced at the far back corner of the yard. I finally spotted the intruder and classified it as a feral dog or maybe a stray looking for home, smaller than Shad but big enough to give him a good fight. I challenged it, "Hey, dog, go home."

My speaking broke its concentration on whatever it was doing and forced it to realize that it would be one against two, not good odds. It took the logical path and lived to fight some other day by leaving at a ground covering trot.

Without a proximate threat, Shad relieved himself with due diligence in the corners of his territory (my yard) to claim this tract as ours, and proclaim that uninvited visitors were not welcome. I know he was satisfied from what looked like a bold swagger as he came back from the last corner.

We went in and got to bed shortly after. I had a daydream early, before sleep claimed me, that Sean tried to woo me. A shadowy figure kept getting in the way of Sean's efforts. That second knight wore battle tested armor also. If I thought about it when awake, it would be a certain distraction.

The daydream turned to dream as I surrendered to sleep.

A Slow Monday

Despite a dream that bordered on nightmare, one about evil forces challenging the forest's existence, I slept in to just after first light. I woke feeling rested as the sun rose above the Eastern horizon. I thanked the Great Maker for another day that Shad and I would share in reasonably good health and try to utilize well. Then I rolled into the day at a good cruising speed.

As I made a cup of coffee, I noticed an unusual brightness outside. I looked out the window. A thin skiff of snow sparkled over the lawn. Gave Shad some dog biscuits to keep him busy. Bathroom visit finished, I pulled on a walk-the-dog outfit, and called Shad.

"Shad, get your butt over here. Time for out." Shad stretched and came to me. I opened the door. Shad registered surprise at the white landscape revealed. "Let's go, silly." and we went out into the day.

He bounded down the steps and gobbled a few mouthfuls of the white cold stuff. Then he rolled in it until nature called more strongly than his urge to play. He marked the corners again, just to make sure others respected that this was our turf. The sunrise wasn't spectacular, more like an old friend I saw just yesterday but was glad to see again anyway.

The squirrel was getting used to the routine, it seemed. It was already in the tree by the time we went down the few steps off the porch to ground level. Shad did his dog things, which included sniffing around to make sure no ghosts or goblins, or really dangerous two-leg varmints, hid in the bushes.

I grinned when I realized I shifted into a defensive mode over the last few weeks. Still wasn't in the capital D mode, but much more aware of my surroundings than I had been before that creep got himself shot in my house or the one that lost his fight with a skillet. The term 'situational awareness' came to mind about the time Shad climbed the stairs and waited for me to let him in for breakfast.

We went in after. As I closed the door behind us, I noticed the squirrel come down the tree to gather more acorns. As hard as it worked, legend says, it must be a long, cold winter coming.

I made a hot breakfast after we went inside. It warmed me and Shad didn't seem to mind it either. The day was off to a good start. The morning show on the radio even played a few marches just to "get hearts pumping", as the DJ remarked. Took care of all the minor chores of being an adult in a house alone, save for the dog. You know what I mean if you've done it.

Stuff like washing the dishes from breakfast before the egg yolk hardened into a nearly integral part of the plate, straightening the bed, and fluffing the pillow. After the pots, pans, and breakfast dishes were washed and dried, I made a second cup of coffee and relaxed.

The morning news on the local radio station related the usual mayhem around town, the state, and the world. It must be frightening for those who worry about what might happen without planning what to do on the off chance it did and involved them. I added a PS to my talk with the Creator. I asked for strength of mind, body, and spirit to handle anything that came my way, and the wisdom to make the right choices.

Then I listened to the music that played for a few minutes. The fast tempo of old 1960s Rock and Roll put me in a good mood. Almost as good as some of the rousing Sousa marches did, I decided during the DJ's babble between songs. He was able to talk for hours and say nothing, just like some politicians. I once listened to one at a candidate debate that never answered the question but talked for a solid two minutes.

I stirred from my seat when I had the idea to check the Internet. Maybe I had some new messages. Or I could look for clothing patterns and a source for fabric that matched my desire to make another shirt after the first one turned out well. That would be more productive than just listening to music. Past experience showed that when I combined both, I felt better than when doing either alone.

Opening my desktop, I searched for sites that sold fabric. A discount fabric supplier site caught my eye. It was the one I used when I had sewn a sexy LBD (little black dress) for a stage presentation at school. The costume design and sewing course I took on the advice of my college advisor "to provide income while between parts" would make this a snap, or at least possible. I knew I could sew my own clothes if push came to shove. To make them at least as well as off the rack items was my goal, and I intended to reach that level soon as possible.

Checked my email and the local weather forecast. The weather folks expected it to warm enough that the overnight snow would melt by afternoon. I hoped they were right for a switch. I resumed my search for clothing fabrics and sewing patterns.

Came across a site that offered video tutorials of sewing from beginner to accomplished designer levels. From what they touted about their courses, it would be worth a serious look later. Saved that one as a favorite for future consideration.

Also found a few other sources for fabrics suitable for sexy underwear to warm winter coats. Just had to figure out how to use their different onsite search features. There isn't one that covered everything in an expected format. That was not a new problem for me and computer sites. I speak, write, and think in plain English. They think, speak, and write in specialist jargon. I've named it Geek. The word(s) they used sometimes defied common sense, or, more often, wasn't necessarily what I would I would call something. Time would take care of that, hopefully. Or I could start with stuff I knew, like corduroy, poplin, denim, knits, gabardines, even the synthetic fleeces. All were available in my language on a drop down list. Might even play with some of that polyester charmeuse, a poor woman's silk, when on sale. Its pluses were its machine washable, and sold for prices that weren't budget busting.

That was matched by a couple of sites that sold patterns for the necessaries of dressing stylishly warm or cool depending on the season. Always got a chuckle from that claim about suitable for winter. I once bought a coat the catalog copy called 'suitable for winter'. It now hung in the closet for early spring and late fall wear. Too warm for sixty degrees, not warm enough for under thirty if the wind blew. I'd guess the designers lived in areas with mild winters. They surely didn't live here on the northern high plains. I added a few of those sites to the favorites list too.

In any case, it passed the morning quickly. At ten, Shad had another chance to give the squirrel, Mr. Loud Foulmouth, his new name after an extremely vehement outburst, a piece of his mind and maybe a good scare. Dang squirrel didn't play the game. He started up the tree as the door opened and was quiet on a branch by the time Shad was on the ground in the yard.

Shad just did his stuff again and came back to me. Inside again, I made a quick lunch for two. A hamburger with a fried potato patty for me. Part of the burger went on Shad's kibble and left enough for me to feel satisfied when I finished. Cleaned up after the meal and turned on the TV and DVD player to watch an episode of Foyle's War. That was another treasure in the DVD collection inherited.

At three, Shad got another walk before we got in the truck. Stopped at a gas station to top off the fuel level before we headed toward Barbara's cabin in the woods. The snow from last night had melted. I gave the weather service a point for a good forecast. Only part of real benefit to me was it was easier to see the road or the potholes when the pavement ended. I drove slowly, enjoying the fall colors and even the bare trees that already dropped their leaves.

By four, we arrived at the coven's meeting place. I'd be way too early if I didn't enjoy Barbara's company. Too, Shad's mother, Sasha, had some time during daylight to catch up on events with Shad. I went up the back stairs and knocked. Barbara answered the door and welcomed me in. We chatted over a cup of coffee until the other members started to arrive.

As the newest member, I introduced myself to each member as they arrived. The first to arrive were the sisters Janette Washington, and Maudy Fields. A real surprise was that Sue Driscoll came as a member. It would be something to talk about later. Then Bunny Warren arrived shortly before Rose Flowers and Alice Zortmann. The last to come was Summer Holiday. More were expected, but waiting for them could take the rest of the day, maybe part of tomorrow. At least according to Janette.

The meeting started at five with a call to order by the president, Barbara Yeager. She reminded us the meeting would be run according to Robert's Rules. Summer was the secretary and read the minutes of the last meeting, then gave the Treasurer's Report. "Nothing in the treasury, no bills to pay."

When she resumed the meeting, Barbara gave us all a task. Find and bring her the Book of Shadows. Then we were to open it and read the words there in a five minute period. The roll was called alphabetically, and each of us was sent to find it in turn. All the others came back empty handed. With a first name starting with U, I went last. I saw a large book sitting on the coffee table in plain sight and called it to me. It came and opened to a short paragraph.

I read, "I accept the title Baba Yaga Too until the present holder of the title retires or comes Home. My purpose and intent is protect these woods with all my strength and powers, and not use the powers for personal gain. So help me God." I handed the book to Barbara. Took some time for all the other members to hug me and congratulate the new Baba. Barbara gave me the warmest and longest welcome of them all as she welcomed me to the coven and my new duties. No one stopped long enough to mention what those duties were. I figured I'd have to discover what they were on my own.

Next was old business which brought up "rumors of an attempt to isolate the woods". I was asked to speak about that. I related the meeting between developer Junior Forrest and the county zoning board I witnessed at the Spotted Horse. I also mentioned Gene's offer to pay for some posters. We spent some time discussing the wording.

After half an hour, when I realized that discussion without a motion under formal discussion was not in Robert's Rules, I moved that we develop a list of statements we wanted on the posters compared to how much would fit. Rose seconded. All except Summer voted aye. Summer was the sole nay vote, which she admitted was only because "There are few motions worth passing with a unanimous vote."

We moved on and held that discussion for about an hour more. Finally, Maudy moved to adjourn the session until next month at this time. Summer seconded, and this time joined the others in voting Aye. She grinned widely when she said, "Except this one."

After the meeting was adjourned, we finished the rest of the coffee, nibbled on some cookies, and chatted between bites and sips. I heard recipes and about the results of a church bazaar. The Bear part of my brain went to sleep from boredom. The Ursula part of my brain soaked it all in. By eight, the coffee was gone. Cookies left only crumbs on the plate. Time to leave.

We said our good - byes to each other and to Baba. Since I had a 4X4 pickup, I volunteered to be last to rescue any who got stuck going home. The potholes loomed as a real world problem for those driving standard passenger cars due to insufficient ground clearance.

I stayed behind until all were gone. Gave me a chance to ask Baba how I had been picked. She explained simply, "You saw the book, the others didn't. It chose you to be the next Baba." She also admonished, "Be a force for good and you'll live up to expectations."

A weak "Oh." escaped my lips. What else was I going to say? Except good bye and thanks for the invitation to the meeting. I put on my coat and went out. I called Shad once and he came running. No one was stuck, though a few tire tracks showed some potentially close calls that portended need for a follow vehicle when the snow and ice season came.

Once on pavement, those problems faded almost instantly. About two hundred feet or so allowed time for the mud to spin off the tires. A bear stood his ground in the middle of the road. I stopped, rolled down the window just a bit, and called out, "Mr. Bear. I'd like to get home. Please move off the road."

He said, "Then it's true. I understood you. You're the new Baba Yaga Too. Congratulations, Baba." and slowly walked away.

I went around him slowly and waved as we passed. By nine, I was home again. We made a perimeter check before going in. I had a drink, washed my face and hands, and went to bed. Shad was already asleep. I joined him shortly after.

142

Tuesday's Threat

Light from what I figured was the rising moon shined across my eyes. That triggered me awake. No dreams or nightmares remembered from last night. That's not unusual for me or many others according to that article I read a few years back by a guy who claimed to be a sleep expert. Those are the nights the brain does some housekeeping and clears out meaningless clutter if I correctly recall the thesis advanced. Translated to plain English, it was, "No one doesn't dream, but many don't remember the ones they had." It's something like the dog that chases, or is chased by, something in its sleep but is perfectly calm when it wakes.

It was bright enough to start the coffee maker without turning on the kitchen lights. I was alert enough to notice the garage door was open and the lights were on. At least now I knew it wasn't reflected moonlight but the light from the garage. I had time because Nature called too strongly to avoid a trip to the bathroom, but I went armed just in case. Two guys had broken in all ready. This might be another. Might catch me with my pants down, so to speak, but the pistol in my hand would be ready to change his mind, permanently if necessary.

When I dressed, I pulled on my jeans and stuck a spare magazine in a hip pocket. The pistol went into the waistband as I pulled on the chore coat. My cell phone went into the left pocket of the coat. The pistol moved from waist band to right pocket before I buttoned up. Shad was already at the door when I opened it. He was in the garage fast and cornered the bad guy under the truck. I heard the intruder yelling for help, or maybe just in fear of the dog.

I pushed the button to speed dial 9-1-1, and called Shad out to stand with me. The guy tried to run but stumbled when he tripped on something. He disappeared in a flash. Well, not quite. A small explosion only lifted him about three or four feet above the ground but flipped him onto his back. That caused his head to hit the concrete with a splat that reminded me of the sound a dropped pumpkin makes. I didn't know if he was just unconscious or dead, but he didn't move.

The dispatcher announced, "This is 9-1-1. What's your emergency?"

I reported, "I caught a guy in my garage. When he tried to run away, he tripped and blew up. That could only happen if he carried explosives."

"Stay put. I'll have officers there shortly." the dispatcher instructed.

"I'll be right here." I answered. I gave him the address. He must have been a little excited. He didn't mute his head set. I could hear him direct the nearest car to my location. I was about to form an unflattering opinion about the rookie when my knees started to shake. I moved to the steps and sat. My opinion about the dispatcher became more favorable. Shad acted as if all was normal as he went about his business.

If that blackguard was still alive, he wasn't doing at all well. If he was an assassin for hire, when the dog peed on him must have damaged his ego enough to make his wounds fatal. While I agreed with Shad's opinion, I did scold him mildly for expressing it openly. His grin showed he could care less, and wasn't going to waste the energy to try to defend his actions.

The police arrived as my knees quit their dance. They put up the crime scene tape until the experts arrived. There was a short delay until the bomb squad got there. They checked the body for additional quantities of explosives, confirmed he had fallen on a pocket full of blasting caps, and the dog sniffed the truck, car, and garage for any explosives left behind. Shad reported that the other dog didn't find anything.

The ambulance, coroner's crew, and crime scene unit came and started their work when the bomb squad said it was clear. I had gone numb as the shakes left and told the whole truth when questioned. The officers grinned when I told them about Shad's disrespect. The younger of them remarked, "Dogs ain't shy about showing their opinion, that's for sure." The older one gave him an elbow to the ribs, a silent order to get serious, but his own grin didn't fade.

A detective arrived in an unmarked car, but I couldn't see who it was. I was greatly relieved to see O'Doyle walk toward us. I felt a little less relieved when his opening sentence was, "Two in less than a week, are you at war with these guys?"

"If I am, they are the only ones that know about it. I haven't received a declaration of war at any rate." I replied. I continued, "I wrote the first one off as a guy who expected to find Victor. The second expected to find an empty house and I surprised him after he broke in. This one seems like I was targeted for some reason, though.

He continued to ask questions. I replied to all of them to the best of my memory. He excused himself as the various other personnel started to pack up to leave. He spoke with the supervisor of each of the crews but was too far away to hear the comments. But he smiled as he returned, so I breathed easier.

"Looks like you're off the hook. There is an extremely low probability you could cause that damage to his chest even with a shotgun." His grin widened. "Besides, they found some blasting caps and a few pieces from the wrapper for some commercial grade dynamite a few feet from the center of the blast". He paused. "That was one very unlucky fella."

"I wonder what he was doing in my garage, and why?" I said.

"It would be a safe bet he was up to no good." Sean replied. "There was some stuff under your truck and car. Bomb squad took it to the range for disposal. Sure looked like dynamite to me, but it could be candles or fireworks. You got someplace you can hide out for a while in case these guys are just the opening shots to a full blown war?"

"I might. I'd have to ask her first though."

"Then ask, because we'd like to put a couple officers in your house for a bit. Just to be on the safe side." Sean said.

"What about my job if I go into hiding?"

"You might be better off without it for a while. If they used explosives at your home, they're not above using them at your work. Already had one shooting at your job. Be a shame if they used a bomb and others were hurt or killed."

"Are you saying that those robbers that shot up the saloon were trying to kill me? Not just scare the customers?"

Sean spoke, "Remember I said it looked like a shot from outside killed Victor? It wasn't. No holes in the walls or windows. We double checked the walls. It must have been from inside. If it was, the robbery was likely a fake to draw attention away from the actual shooter who was inside. You said Bear pulled you down, which may have put him in the way. If they were gunning for him, there's another intended victim. Can you think of anyone that wants to kill him?"

That was new information, and a new question. "Not off the top of my head. I had a few guys who dumped me because I wanted a wedding before sex. I'll admit I wished they were dead for a few days, I suspect they felt that way about me, but to my knowledge no one left angry, just disappointed." I replied.

"Are you sure?" he asked.

"As sure as I am that I'm sitting here." I replied. As after thought, I added, "At least for right now. Maybe someone was angry, but how angry can a guy get over nothing more than a good night kiss after a movie, burger, fries, and a cola?"

"You might be surprised." Sean commented. "Most guys would get over it, but there are psychopaths, sociopaths, and flat out loonies in the mix. No telling about them."

"Geez! You sure know how to ease a girl's mind, don't you?" I teased. "Just put all the women in protective custody and all the men in jail for future attempted murder why don't you?"

"Not that simple. Almost as many crazy women as crazy men running around. Can't tell until they finish their plotting and planning whether they're potential killer or potential victim. Unless you wait until one is on trial and the other is in the casket, you can't be sure."

"I just thought of something. Not likely to be part of Victor's death, but could be related to the attempts on my life. That is if they're connected." I repeated my report about the 'special meeting' of the zoning board, and the hungry dog look on Junior Forrest's face when the legality of his plan was questioned. Asked how I knew about the plan, I reminded him that I was the girl who flipped the charts during the spiel. I also mentioned that he tipped an awful lot, in funny money, and we had contacted the feds about that.

Sean corrected me. "It could be related to Victor's death. Gus Will had contacted them to mention that he had spoken to Vic...Bear the day he was killed. Their topic was the land grab near the state forest for golf course and housing development. He himself had his windshield shot out on the way home that night. Same bullets were used in both cases."

"You mean that the rumors are true?" I asked.

"Which rumors?" Sean asked in reply.

"The ones that say the Forrests aren't too picky when picking friends or partners, or actually hire some killings to push their schemes forward." I said.

"Nothing has ever been proven, but some of the old timers on the force relate stories some of the retired cops told them about Prohibition era shenanigans. The Forrests are rumored to have been able to live high on the hog during the Depression because they had outside income from smuggling booze. Just like in the movies, those were bloody times. Rivals were gunned down in the streets, or died from 'hunting accidents' when no season was open." Sean related. "No one I know hunts in a suit with a vest and tie, or doesn't have a rifle anywhere near their body, or gets shot with a burst from a Tommy gun in a real 'accidental' shooting."

"I don't know if I just didn't wear enough clothes when I came out to walk the dog or if it's what you just told me, but I just shivered." I said. "Want to go inside or are we done?" I queried.

"We're done... for now. Go somewhere you can hide out. Don't tell anyone where you're going. I'll tell Bob that you've been attacked again and are not safe in town. He'll understand. His granddad was one of the saloon owners when they were called speakeasies until the mob closed him down." Sean suggested.

"Thank you, Detective. I appreciate that advice. See you when the shooting is over, I hope."

We parted company and I went inside. Shad was a bit out of sorts, as was I, because breakfast was late. The quick fix was a bowl of cold cereal and milk with buttered toast and a cup of coffee for me and a couple cups of killble in his bowl for Shad.

First call was to Baba, Barbara Yeager, to find out if she could let me hide out there for a few days. After another recitation of today's failed attack, she agreed as long as I brought some groceries. I was instructed to park in the barn to be out of sight when I got there. She also suggested I bring some firearms for protection, and ammunition to defend against a siege.

Also let Sue know I was headed to a safe haven. I answered her questions carefully to avoid giving away any details. She wished me luck. I returned the courtesy. I ended the conversation with a caution to watch her back. She might be targeted as my friend if they were after me instead of coincidental attacks.

I called Gene to find out if we could expect a decision about the estate in probate court while I'd be traveling until things cooled down. When he asked what I meant, I told him I had been targeted. He said he expected such things when we reported the funny money. He asked how he could reach me. I said I'd be somewhere in state, so should be able to reach me by phone. Gave him the same warning I gave Sue.

A fourth phone call reported my unavailability for work for a week or longer since I'd be out of town for my health. I found myself relating the morning's excitement to Bob. His last comment was, "You seem to attract trouble lately. Stay home until that wears off." It was followed by a chuckle, so I knew I wasn't fired ...yet.

I packed a pair of jeans, a skirt, flannel shirts, a warm sweater, etc., Also packed the Winchester Model 88, and the Officer's ACP with inside the pants holster. First stop was the state store for sour mash. They usually had a good price on the half gallon size. Stopped next at the grocery for milk, cereal, bread, eggs, sausage, a couple pounds of hamburger, canned vegetables and fruit, potatoes, and some kibble for Shad that Baba wanted.

Detoured past the sporting goods shop. I bought a few boxes of ammo for the rifle. Also bought a couple pairs of mid weight wool socks to wear in the chore boots.

The drive north to Baba's cabin was uneventful. She greeted me as though I were a returning prodigal daughter. We carried the perishables in and stored them.

The firearms and clothes were last, since they wouldn't spoil. When the truck was unloaded, I backed it into the barn, closed the doors, and went inside. Except during trips outside to walk with Shad, Baba regaled me with stories from her family history. Some made me laugh, others brought tears, all emphasized the relation between man and nature. A few hours after sunset we turned in for the night.

Don't know about others, but I slept well to the sound of wind in the trees and the night critters doing their thing. Once recognized, even the wolves' discussions with the moon was soothing. At least it wasn't banshees. I giggled at that thought and went to sleep.

Hiding Out

I was in a spare room on the east side of the cabin, so nothing changed in my usual schedule. The first hints of day woke me. I gave myself a few minutes to just marvel at that progression from night into day and later day into night. It's been happening for a long time. With luck, it will happen for a long time into the future. The only threats to that repeating pattern are beyond our control unless it happens because somebody doesn't ask should we when we need to ask it before we unravel the sweater.

Some may argue against the possibility the universe was designed by a higher being, a deity if you will. In my judgement, they just want to be at the top of the food chain and that's the only way their claim has a chance at being real. They'll never convince me it is just a lucky accident that the stars and planets move with such regularity that astronomers can calculate their future positions with regularity. If I were to bet on it, I'd go with intelligent design rather than chaos. That's a pale reflection of Pascal's Wager I mentioned before, to be sure, but it seems more correct than supporting the Big Bang with no explanation where matter came from if this was originally empty space as their theory was presented to me. You can't build something from nothing unless you have some mighty big power to use.

But, meditation over, I hopped out of bed. Startled Shad as I blew past him on the way to the bathroom. Came back at a slower pace and a pound or two lighter, stopped to scratch him behind the ears. Dressed for the outside. Went out as first light grew into day. Shad explored the new smells and aromas of this place. I sat on the porch watching him as dawn turned to the light of day.

A pretty sunrise was my treat for the day. I was so focused on that, only the squeaking board alerted me to Baba's approach.

I greeted her and she replied, "Brought you a cup of coffee. Mind if I join you?"

"Thank you. Please do. I enjoy your company." I said while I accepted the hot brew. "It's starting as a very pretty day, better than good enough to share with a friend."

We sat in silence as we sipped our coffee for quite a while before either of us spoke again, at least long enough for the sun to rise above the horizon. Barb broke the silence first, calling the dog with a simple announcement, "It's time for breakfast." I barely had time to think of the words and never got them out before Shad ran over and licked my face on the way inside.

Then Barb rose with an ease that belied her apparent age and went in. I joined her after giving Shad some affection in return. Breakfast eaten, I washed the dishes since Barb cooked, then joined her in the front room area. We chatted for a while when she announced it was time to tend the garden before her guests arrived When I asked for details, she smiled and said, "The bears are getting ready to hibernate for the winter. We always have a party for them. Another in the Spring when they come out. And don't fret, Little Bear, you're invited." She laughed gently.

I felt accepted by a family for the first time since Grandpa Pete left me alone. "How may I help?" I asked.

Baba grinned as she answered, "Just treat the guests with respect and they will return the consideration. Be of stout heart when you meet some of the them. They won't harm you."

"OK." An easy and expected answer to give, but I didn't

know what waited in the future. Had I known before I met the guests, I probably would have gone home to take my chances with Junior Forrest and his hired muscle. But if I had, I would have missed meeting the allies that helped save the woods. I'm glad I stayed.

"When you're ready, make yourself casual party pretty Many of the guests will become friends and allies if you give them the chance. Tell them what you know about the coming attack on their way of life and their homes." Baba said as she launched from the chair and went out.

I petted Shad and said, "You've heard the lady. Get presentable. Guests are coming." I followed my own advice and prepared for a party. After I washed up, I brushed my hair and tied it into a pony tail, I decided to wear the skirt with the sweater over one of the shirts I packed and the mid heel loafers. The chore coat would defeat the breeze if needed. I heard Barb come back inside and go into her room.

I decided a cup of coffee would be just the thing, so made a cup. Looking out the window, it seemed like a nice brisk fall day for a garden party near season's end. Neither too hot nor too cold, but seasonably comfortable as I went out onto the porch and sat in one of the chairs, I caught glimpse of a thin, low cloud of dust coming this way from the end of the pavement.

I was about to stand to go in to tell Barb about the possible arrival of a car when she came out. I called her attention to the dust cloud. "Is that one of the guests?"

"It may be. If it is, I know who it is. He always gets here early." Barb chuckled. "I think he likes the company." She paused to watch the approach. "I better make some more coffee." and moved quickly inside to do so.

As the SUV turned in to park, I got a glimpse of the driver. I relaxed as I recognized Stan Sharp, the Deputy. He looked rather dapper in his 'outdoors man' outfit - heavy flannel shirt, jeans, and boots. "Hi, Stan." I greeted.

He looked a bit surprised as he looked up. "Hi. So this is where you're hiding out. Well, this saves another unanswered phone call. How are you doing?"

"Pretty well. Could stand a bit more money, but I've got my health and some friends. All my body parts seem to be working. I've got food and shelter. Nothing to complain about really." I inhaled, "If I did, it would just be whining. You?"

"Pretty much the same." he replied with a chuckle. "Been a while since the gang got together last Spring. Be good to see them today."

"You seem very excited about this shindig. You don't get out enough, I'm guessing." I teased.

He grinned, and said, "Had too much going on before, studying at school after practices for the big game, studying for final exams, then working after the Sheriff hired me. But things are running smoothly now, enough that I plan to take in more of the social scene. Want to help?"

"Maybe. If this is a request between friends, I'll try. If it's a Court Order, I will fight it on advice from counsel." His stunned look was too much. I held a straight face for about five seconds before I laughed. "Of course I'll give it my best shot." I took his hand in mine and gave a gentle squeeze.

There's that commercial that says some result is priceless. This was one of those priceless moments in my life. I felt bonded to him as he squeezed back, firmly but not too hard.

Then he got even in a joking way. "Good. I really want to collect that cherry someday." He paused. Finally, the punch line, "Or at least one from that jar of maraschino cherries you keep around for your Manhattans." He grinned.

I giggled. "You've heard my best joke, spoil sport." I flashed an exaggerated pout while I whispered in my thoughts, "Maybe you can get the whole jar if you play your cards right."

Immediately, I hoped he didn't hear that.

He heard me. He bent down and gave me one of the best kisses ever, and it was just a light brushing of the lips. That kiss moved all other possibilities firmly into the also ran category as he opened his lead to five lengths and was going away in the last half mile before the finish line.

But this was a cross country race. There were obstacles to overcome yet in the course. There were fences and ditches still to jump. A fault could slow him to let the others catch and maybe even pass him. Such disasters would show his heart if he stayed in the race.

I recognized that wasn't in my control as long as we humans had free will. While I didn't wish calamity on the innocent, I saw no conflict to hope and pray that enemies were denied the Creator's assistance or suffered confusion when they tried to follow their plans, or that the 'Bird of Paradise would fly up their nose, and an elephant caressed them with its toes.' Apologies to the writer, and Little Jimmy Dickens, the singer of that old time hit song the first time I heard it. It just seemed to fit the way I felt right then.

While Stan and I were engaged in conversation moving toward setting a day and time for our first date, about a half dozen other families arrived. I was introduced to all of them. They were the farm families that would be affected by Junior's plan. That's counting only the human families. There were also representatives of other families that would be affected. From the mega fauna, like bears and deer, down to the wood mice and chipmunks, with a few winged friends and insects, they joined the party.

Stan and I helped Baba bring out lunch. There were foods suitable for the variety of dietary needs spread out on tables and the ground all around. All ate and mingled. Inter-species relations were tolerant, and even allowed for some joking.

Sue, with Gene in tow, was among the non-farm guests. She joked that they reversed roles this morning. She was ready to go, but he fiddled with his outfit for half an hour longer. It wasn't a party that he needed a suit with vest and tie, so fussed over what he wore. Even the bears laughed at that.

I was eventually given the chance to relate the plans I overheard while working at the secret meeting of the developer with the zoning board. There were questions. I answered as well as I could.

In his turn, Gene pointed out a nearly forgotten law, twenty years or so since signed into law in our state. It gave legal protection for the farms in the same family for three generations or more as a heritage farm. All six of the farms present thought they would qualify.

Gene also discussed how, even if they were forced to sell by future circumstances, they could restrict future use to agriculture for a century if the farm was registered before the sale. That was a fine point of the law. The farms had to be on the list of farms maintained by the state to qualify under that provision. If they applied soon, they would at least buy time to fight to keep ownership regardless what the local zoning board decided. He handed out application forms to all the human heads of household with the offer to meet to discuss the process and help complete the forms to ensure no technicalities stalled consideration. He urged them to start tonight.

His final point was a fine tuning of two ideas. Many have the opinion that farming/ranching is a way of life. He presented the argument that it should be treated as a business that supported a lifestyle if they ran it well. That also tied in with a mistaken belief that it was possible to live off depreciation and pay no taxes as a result. While OK to survive a bad year or two by using depreciation to pay family living expenses, to do so routinely prevented accumulation of money to replace machinery when it wore out. Paying fair taxes helped support the community on top of other benefits that would keep the farm in the family.

Both ideas raised some eyebrows. He convinced the farmers that both his ideas were plain common sense, just and logical. That was specially true with the current cost of machinery to run a modern farm and the payments on financed purchases. He pointed out that tax accountants didn't always take that into account in their efforts to lower the tax bills.

The meeting broke down into small groups for discussions or gossip. The elder of the farmers led that group, and shortly reported concurrence with the ideas. He also promised to have his paperwork done in a day or two.

While Gene took care of business with the humans, Baba talked to the four footed critters, then called me to join that group. We talked over possible roles to help delay construction if the developer jumped the gun. Mice and chipmunks volunteered to chew insulation off wires to short out ignition systems and instrument panels. Flying critters agreed to coordinate air strikes to foul the windshields with bombardments of whitewash (The stuff they have left over after the food is digested. If you live where birds fly over, you've probably seen the remains on a few windshields yourself.).

The bears promised to be active combatants if the fight started before they started their winter's nap or after they woke. Even industrial loader tires might not withstand their wrath, definitely not with some of the bigger and stronger he-bears. At the least, the vehicle windows would not be whole if even a rambunctious yearling or two year old put its mind to it. The cougars agreed the autos and light trucks wore tires that wouldn't take long if they intended that. The wolves agreed to serve as scouts to check on strangers and however else they could. One yearling wolf also pointed out that they could tear apart the upholstery, spread the padding around and mark their territory inside the vehicles if the bears opened the windows.

"Well, that will take the profit out of their plan." I chuckled. "Sounds like a plan to me." After Barb translated what I said into words they understood, the critters grinned widely. The wolf pack leader cried to the moon with a vow to do its part to help, and to convince the other packs to join the fight. His call was answered affirmatively by the other two packs in these woods.

It soon darkened with the approach of twilight. and the party broke up as all the guests save Stan went home. Barb offered a night cap to end the evening. The night chill made it a very good idea indeed. We retired to the indoors. Stan had a small drink because he had to drive home. It wouldn't do for a deputy to be ticketed for a DUI. Barb and I had larger drinks because we were already at home. We sat a while longer and chatted.

After Stan left, Barb said, "I felt that my grand nephew is smitten with you. I sense you are fond of him too. Perhaps you should consider making it permanent?"

"Ahead of you on that idea. Only one problem. My heart says yes. My head still says go slow." I answered. I explained, "I had a friend in college who was so sure, she set the wedding day for the first Saturday after spring semester ended. That was well before he gave her a ring and asked for her hand. He went along with the plans, but quietly resented being roped into the marriage. They fought frequently and divorced before the next New Year's Eve. Every now and again, I think 'what if they took their time?'"

I continued, "I don't want to make that mistake. Haven't the nerve to push him, though if he asks, I'm his."

Barb smiled and chuckled. "Sounds like a plan, to borrow what you said earlier. Still, you might consider a way to lead him to the right decision. Cook him supper a few times, and breakfast when it gets to that stage. It's a cliché, I know, but 'The way to a man's heart IS through his stomach.' Don't try to be a gourmet chef. Men like the comfort food meals the best if given the choice."

I almost launched the peanuts I chewed because it just struck me funny enough to cause a laugh. "Give me warning next time you expect to make me laugh. Please."

"Yes, Bear. I'll try to remember that." Barb, barely able to control her laugh, gave her promise at effort. "I expect you'll brave your home to start the plan. You're welcome back any time you need, but you'll never get that young man to ask if you're here and he's there. Specially if we get snowed in and cut off from visitors once Winter gets here."

"I see your point. I'll stay a couple more days to let the bas ....bad guys think I've run from the fight. I've passed on what I know, so not as important now to avoid all risks as to face them head on. Show those guys they're not as frightening as they think they are. A few more of them buried might even start them to trembling instead. I paused. "More importantly, if I'm going to war, a little training is in order so I know how to use the weapons I have."

After thirty minutes more conversation, I fed Shad. Then I took a little down time to relax before bed. I loitered over a whiskey while I listened to the news. Holy mackerel. The emergency room had been busy yesterday and this morning. Nothing too serious, but quite a few injuries from slips and falls. No telling how many felt they didn't need medical attention.

People forget during summer that they can't charge around on snow or ice as hard as on dry surfaces, specially when wearing smooth sole shoes. Been there, done that. as the saying goes. One time, it took nearly three months to feel normal again, though the limp from the bruised hip was gone in a few weeks. My pride took longer to heal, much longer.

Still, it was in the mid thirties. A southwest wind blew just hard enough to notice, but wouldn't have people chasing their hats. That should keep ice from forming tonight if it kept up until the melt water evaporated.

But there were a few jokes shared about the short memories many had for last winter's snow and ice. It all stems from those slapstick comedies from the early history of movies. The close-up of the banana peel was a sure sign of impending prat falls. Oh, I know. You should never laugh at another's problems, but I think it's a reflex to express relief it didn't happen to you. And most will try to help with at least a word or two after the laughter ebbs.

Finally, Shad got his last walk of the day. It was time to turn out the lights and go to sleep.

Stayed and Learned

Next morning, after Shad's walk and good mornings to the other critters awake then, I had a decision. As we ate breakfast, I told Barb, "Gave your idea some thought last night. It's got to be his decision to make it permanent. I can try to show him he'd be better off with me, but I can't give him the grounds to decide I had railroaded him and to file for divorce."

She nodded and I changed subject after another bite of food. "I will visit at least once a week if the road is open. Can I bring something when I do?"

She answered, "Some staples are always handy in the cupboard when you can't get to the store. Things like flour, yeast, and a smoked ham that doesn't need refrigeration would be very welcome if the power goes out. Oh, and some whiskey to keep the blood from freezing up." She grinned.

"Done. The grocery has a special on large bags of flour and those three packs of yeast for the Thanksgiving and Christmas baking season. If I can find a smoked ham, you'll have one next week. If not, there's a small butcher shop that sells unsliced cured bacon by the slab. Used to buy it for camping trips." I offered. "Any favorite brands of whiskey for the shopping list?"

She answered, "I've always been partial to bourbon, but I see no reason to buy the expensive brands just for prestige. Besides, as old as I am, if I can swallow it, it will do quite nicely. Some are a good buy for the money, and come in shatter-proof plastic bottles in the half gallon size." She chuckled. "But you would figure that out for yourself soon enough. Why pay for a half gallon and only get a quart because it has a big name label? Right?"

The conversation continued along those lines for a while. I even wrote a list on paper of what she wanted. Then she offered something that would be priceless in the coming weeks. It was a rite, or ceremony if you prefer, that summoned the Creator's protection for the home and its inhabitants. I considered that more than ample compensation to keep the old gal happy through the winter until spring came again.

Like the old joke about the fervent young preacher who drowned in a flood. He expected direct Divine intervention, so failed to use three chances to evacuate from the flood plain. It was told as a joke, but I saw its deeper meaning. It required an awareness of escape routes when faced with challenges to existence. It did not support blind expectations of dramatic direct divine intervention if we could take action to use a more subtle, 'normal' way out of danger.

The conversations for the next few days were just as pithy. We talked about exercises to increase my powers enough to be effective when I needed them for self defense. Those were important if the criterion was looking for answers to 'How do I survive this?'

Other talks answered the more immediate though somewhat silly concern of How do I lead Stan to ask the question? Barbara offered some ideas. The easiest were simple fixes for meals. Ways to add a little flavor to a can of something were primary. Easy fixes really, like cubing a slice of ham, getting the bacon crispy enough so it crumbled, or browning some hamburger and mixing them into some baked beans. First time I tried those, I had seconds. It was real comfort food that got to the table quickly. Another was to add a can of diced tomatoes with chili peppers to a can of beans or chili too bland because made to a recipe for the most sensitive palates.

The evenings were spent in pleasant chat, with a fire in the fireplace and a drink or two in hand. The last evening of this stay, I wrote down the protection rite and promised Barb I would use it. Hey Don't laugh. If it doesn't work, I'm no worse off. If it does, I'll accept the help from wherever offered as long as it doesn't cost me my soul. I'm rather jealous of that.

Waking that last morning, I saw ominous clouds gathering at the western horizon. While pretty at sunrise, they could bring a mess by evening. A small one if they brought low total precipitation. Different story if they brought a significant snow. Wouldn't know which until it was over. Spurred by the uncertainty, took my turn making breakfast to show what I had learned.

It took a while. Starting from scratch, it was more like brunch before it was ready. I made biscuits, sausage with gravy, and scrambled eggs. The biscuits and gravy had a much better taste than the canned sausage gravy on those biscuits in a tube that weren't baked yet. Don't get me wrong. The prefab meal was good for most days, but this from scratch was enough better to make the time and effort worth it for special occasions. Like, maybe, Stan's first breakfast after an overnight stay. -giggle-

Don't worry. I escaped from that distraction before the biscuits or the gravy burned. Barb gave me a B for effort, and a B-minus for execution. When I mentioned this was my first effort to make it from scratch, she changed my grade to a solid B for combined effort and execution. She urged me to try it often enough to reach an A grade. She even told me how to adjust a recipe for number of servings. There was no sense making a dozen biscuits when only two people sat at table, for an example. Who says you never use fractions once out of school? -grin-

When we had eaten, I packed, and was ready to leave. Since I planned to leave closer to noon, we had time to spare. We chatted about cooking and being a witch for a while.

As I said see you later, Baba responded, "You have the powers whether or not you accept the title witch. Use them well. she counseled. For now, you need to go home. You'll probably have more visitors. Not all of them mean you well.

I bid farewell until the next time and drove home. Saw nothing that indicated anyone had been here for a while and went in. I pulled out the protection rite and performed it. I didn't know if it would work, and would sleep lightly to do my part towards keeping myself safe. I made a trip to the grocery, the liquor store, and the butcher for the smoked ham that Barb requested. Doubled the butcher's order to fill my own cupboard while I was at it. After all, I too liked ham or bacon and eggs, specially when it was cold outside.

Afternoon passed and evening was an hour old when the phone rang. Sue called to find out if I were still alive. We chatted a bit. She promised to visit tomorrow. I agreed to that, but saw snow falling in the light of the street lights. I gave her an alternative if she wanted it. If we had more than a couple inches of snow, the city needed some time to plow the streets. I would expect her after the streets were open again. We left it at that.

The call from Gene was business. He reported that the farmers had filed the papers for heritage farm status. That's first step toward forestalling development of their land into a luxury golf course merely to enrich the Forrests and their partners. Part of the application was an agreement that they would not sell the farm before the state reached a decision, and if their farm was declared a heritage farm, they could limit use of the property to agricultural purposes.

Stan called around eight. We talked a little about his work

schedule with the winter weather warning in effect. Some folks were always surprised by the first real storm of winter. Fender benders, more serious crashes, and calls for tow vehicles went up with the depth of snow. He'd be busy until the storm ended.

We also talked more intimately about us. We and us never sounded as sweet to me before. I felt the probability that he would pop the question sooner rather than later was a lot higher. In any case, higher than the probability that we'd get a next day melt of the snow expected to fall tonight. This snow was still early to be around longer than a week unless brought by an arctic cold front. Anybody's guess when it would melt if that was the case.

After Shad's last walk for the day, I pulled off my clothes to change for bed. I looked at a satiny sleep shirt. I sewed it from some of the charmeuse fabric I found in Victor's stash. It let me feel extremely sexy for the mundane task of sleeping through the night, but I chose a pair of flannel pajamas. They'd be better suited to help keep me warm alone in a bed meant for a couple. I made up for that when I dreamed of Stan with me.

Turd's Day Night

I woke very early, about three-thirty, with just one thought. I need to break out the winter comforter if I'm going to sleep alone. Going by the wake up chill I felt this morning, it was past time to get heavier covers or sew up a blanket weight fleece sleep shirt. It would be quicker and easier to find my comforter. Still, I might just try a pattern for a tunic top with pajama pants in a fleece for lounging around the house when winter got here.

While the charmeuse night gown made me feel sexy, I needed a partner to share body heat during the Winter. That season's official start was only about a month from today. Winter weather could start anytime, maybe a couple weeks sooner or later. Still, it was late Fall, and cooled into the low or mid 20s overnight on a regular basis.

Nature called me, and I went to the bathroom. That task finished, I pulled my hair into a ponytail and dressed for the first walk of the day. It was still more than an hour in the future before dawn's first light would light the surroundings. That was plenty time for a cup of coffee. All I had to do was heat a cup of water and add instant. Shad joined me to see what was going on, and demanded some petting for his trouble. I sweetened his reward with a couple of dog biscuits.

I was half way done with my coffee when I realized I was nearly naked. I got the pistol and put it in my waistband, a spare magazine went into my left hip pocket, and a thin folding blade hunting knife in my right. There, now I was dressed fully to meet any physical challenges likely to come my way that wouldn't need a magic tool to meet. I sipped my coffee as I mentally patted my back. The chill I felt on waking left with heavier clothes and the warming beverage in my cup. And the sun now lit the horizon, but it is still about a quarter to half hour before first light.

That must be why I noticed the car cruising by without its lights on. Two could play that game. I turned off the kitchen lights. The street light provided enough light to see from the shadows of the living room. I wondered if this was another assault in the making.

When the car parked across the street, I was getting ready for the attack. Then I breathed easier. The young widow who lived there got out and went into her home. Good thing she didn't have kids. That baby sitter's bill would have taken what she made that night. Maybe she worked nights. At least that's how short her skirt was. I hated to think she walked the streets in weather like this. I hoped for her sake she had an indoor job. Perhaps even a generous sugar daddy.

My mind churned in the gutter I played in once upon a time. Seemed a near neighbor was involved in the oldest profession. That or she worked at one of the late closing clubs and had to shut down last thing in the morning.

I might get friendly with her just to find out which and get some tips if I wound up in that line of work again. That was always a possibility. If Stan stayed a deputy and some crack pot decided he hated cops badly enough to kill one, it could be any day or night. I shook off that thought.

That somber thought didn't last long before I chuckled to myself. That was obviously a left over desire from the Victor part of my brain. That might be why he dressed as a professional date for Halloween. I wouldn't hold it against either of them since I was a paid up member of that sorority, The Sisterhood of Soiled Doves. It was my back up plan to return to the trade if push came to shove. An old song came to mind, Ruth Brown sang "If I can't sell it, gonna keep sittin' on it." It's about a used chair, but even in Bear's youth, he figured it was a pro's lament camouflaged in double-entendre.

First light broke over the horizon at last. I pulled on the insulated jacket and my chore coat. We headed out. Shad sniffed around for any signs of invaders onto our turf while I meditated on the gift of good health I received daily so far. Looked like it was going to be a pretty day, so we spent a little extra time before we went inside again after sunrise.

I felt good enough to put in a good word by name for Pete and others who crossed the rainbow bridge recently or were about to at the end of their lives in the mortal world. I prayed they would receive mercy when they met with The Boss for judgement and added my name to the list recited in that request along with the anonymous others I never met.

After breakfast, I listened to the radio, more for weather forecasts than for the music between. The storm was still headed this way, but hit the mountains miles to the northwest of town. That had delayed its arrival by a day. It had to find its way around that wall to the pass onto our side of the hills, or climb over the hills.

Then I searched for that comforter I had. Found it right where I left it. The gremlins and house elves hadn't hidden it as quickly as they so often do. After I changed the bedding, I knew I'd sleep warm tonight. I put the blanket into the laundry to be washed and dried.

When businesses opened, Shad and I headed to the fabric shop. I found a heavy cotton blend flannel perfect for what I wanted, and it was on sale at 25% off regular price. It wasn't inherently sexy, but it was definitely practical for the nights I slept alone. I spotted some lace trim that would take the pajamas from frumpy to almost attractive. Also found a pattern for a sleep tunic with pants on sale at 20% off MSR. Somebody else had the same idea I had and made a commercial pattern. It matched fabric, pattern, and my needs. It even included three optional placements for lace trim. And it was rated as easy to sew.

I felt so good about that, I bought a large rectangle of firm foam, used for replacement sofa cushions, a heavy poplin in a camouflage pattern, and a long zipper to make the cover removable to sew a bed for Shad. He'd appreciate that when winter came.

I also bought some heavier needles and thread to put it together to last. It would give me something to do when the storm got here. The winter storm warning guessed it would arrive by six tonight. That put the pressure on me to make sure Barbara got the groceries and I was home again before then.

I dropped off my purchases at home. Let Shad loose to answer nature's call for a while before we headed North. While he did that, I gathered the bags of groceries for Barb and called to tell her we were coming with some provisions. She reported last night's snow was light, just a dusting. The sandy loam soil usually held the day's heat and drained well, so there probably wouldn't be any troublesome spots on her road until tonight's storm. The road beyond the pavement should be passable if navigated carefully. That would keep the trip from being an exercise in futility because I couldn't reach her cabin.

Shad and I were on the road early and made good time. Barb greeted us as I parked near the kitchen door. Three bags of groceries, two half gallons of whiskey, and a smoked ham went quickly with two of us carrying them. After storing the food in the refrigerator and pantry, we sat, drank a cup of coffee, and chatted.

Half done with her coffee, Barb asked a question I never expected, "I know I said the coven wasn't magical, just secret, but you have some powers beyond usual people. Have you ever considered being a practicing witch?"

It was an echo of the previous chat when she told me I was a witch. I answered, "No. I haven't. I didn't know there's a difference."

She explained, "I'm getting old and will move to the other world soon. I'd like to teach what I know to my successor before then." Barb indicated an old book, her Book Of Shadows, on the coffee table. "Please bring that book here."

I did so. Barb smiled and commented, "That's my 'Book of Shadows'. You saw it at last meeting, brought it to me then as now. When you opened it and read from it, you showed you're the one."

We ended our chat soon after. Shad loaded into his seat in the truck and we headed home. It took a while because I stopped to tow a low ground clearance sedan with license plates that showed it was state university owned. The occupants appeared to be grad students. An old joke came to me, "Too many folks educated beyond their intelligence trying to run this place." These were surely some to which that applied.

I got out the tow strap, attached it to both vehicles. One long pull while in first gear, four low (transfer case in four wheel drive, low range) freed them from the mud hole they managed to find. I advised them to report the incident to the mechanics at the garage, since the drag across the road might have damaged something. Also advised them to be more aware of road conditions.

They took another hit in my opinion when they greeted that advice with indifference, and neither thanked me nor waved good bye. Common courtesy was dead and common sense was dying if these were samples of the new generation.

On the paved roads, where I didn't have to devote full attention to dodging mud holes, I determined my questions were going to take some fortification to consider. I stopped at the liquor store on the way home. I bought a good supply, two five liter boxes of wine, one red, one white, a half gallon of 80 proof sour mash whiskey, and a case of beer. Seeing no sense being cheap about it after what I bought so far, I got some chips, dip, and pretzel rods, too.

I needed enough for more than me alone. After all, there were visitors coming, some of them friendly and welcome. Barb said so. Besides, a glass of wine, or beer, depending on the guest's tastes, would take chili or baked beans from the status of plain, ordinary food to a feast fit for at least a duke or duchess.

The back half of her warning was others wanted less friendly meetings. Even without magical foresight, visits by the turds of the world were likely, going by three recent experiences. Seemed to be the hand I was dealt since I decided to stand for nature over money. That also meant I was in conflict with a fool who figured he'd be rich before anybody noticed the damage he had done. His idea of 'highest and best use' was based on money he made instead of quality of life for the general population.

That was the opposite extreme from preservationists who wanted to keep things the same. It seemed to me from what they tried to do that was as when we all lived in caves. No use of any resources. That made them feel environmentally friendly. A different philosophy, but still a lowering of the quality of life for most of us. Clearly, they hadn't thought this through, or are blinded by today's fad if they thought it wouldn't interrupt their lives. The energy to have their lives as is, to cool their wine, or make their espresso depends on fossil fuels, at least for now.

Too bad "conservationist" had been misapplied to the preservationists in the names they chose for the organizations they supported and the stories written by the media. Gifford Pinchot must be spinning in his grave. The man, a true conservationist, helped President Ted Roosevelt lay out the National Forests. As first head of the national forestry service, he believed conservation was based on the idea that you could use resources wisely for the benefit of the population. That is my stance, as unpopular as it is among the preservationists. Let them live in caves. I'll take a well built house with central heat any day.

I shook my head, called Shad back inside, and poured myself a drink as I heated a can of beans and browned some hamburger for dinner. It was bubbling merrily when I heard a squeak from the porch stairs. I was ready when turd one came through the back door. He wore the beans and a new bump on his head after contact with the pan. Yes, dear reader, I swung it as hard as I could. I think I cracked his damnably thick skull. He deserved it.

As he went down, turd two came through the front door. I drew my pistol and ordered him to stop right there. He didn't. Then I willed him to freeze and waved my free hand. He became a statue.

I knew them. Lou lay unconscious. I kicked his gun across the kitchen floor, then approached Guns to take his away. I teased him, "You've got the name Guns, but a girl just ended your career. How's that feel, tough guy? More like a turd that got flushed?"

I backed to the phone and dialed 9-1-1. The dispatcher recognized my name from the caller ID and said hello. I returned the greeting, then outlined the situation, requested an ambulance as well as police. In short order, the police arrived and handcuffed the aggressors. The ambulance carted them to the hospital. The detectives arrived and questioned me.

That's when I let loose my best ad lib lines ever, "I guess this was bound to happen on Turds' Day Night." At their blank stares, I explained I knew both of them as employees of Junior Forrest, and how we met. That raised eyebrows. I was asked about that meeting. I told them that Detective O'Doyle already heard the full story and gave them an outline. They left after a while. I guessed they went in search of O'Doyle, maybe Junior Forrest, if they wanted some answers. Or they'd drop it as unimportant. I expected that. The pair struck me as not measuring up to the ability to see the big picture Sean by himself showed.

As for myself, I decided I needed more practice. The most powerful magic was of no use if used too late. When needed, it had to become natural to use it without thinking. And sometimes, the evil doers just needed to be shot. I'd spend more time at the range, too. I tended to think a lot when cleaning up messes, like the spilled beans. Finally got that done.

I took Shad out for his last walk of the day. On return, I wondered what happened to Sue. I figured her plans changed or circumstances got in the way of her planned visit. I showered, and went to sleep. I slept warmly under the comforter. I heard the wind pick up and the tapping of snow flakes on the window. That took a strong wind to do that. The storm arrived a few hours later than expected, but no less fierce.

A Few Days Of Quiet

Habit woke me a few minutes before dawn peeked over the horizon. The snow came hard last night as I went to bed and still fell when I woke. The forecast last night said it was going to be cold, too. I used the heavy wool socks for the first time since I bought them. Before I heard the weather on the radio, I considered possible additions if the socks proved inadequate if Shad spent a long time for his relief walk.

Before I panicked, I listened to the radio weather. The socks should be enough. While single digits was cold, it was still above zero. The winds weren't bad either. Only ten to twenty miles per hour with gusts to twenty seven. I'd be fine if I protected my skin. While I hated what it did to my hair, I pulled on a watch cap to cover my forehead and ears. Also wrapped the lower parts of my face with a thick wool muffler until only my eyes showed. I laughed inwardly at the thought - just call me High Plains Ninja. The winter weight parka went over that with the hood up. Insulated leather gloves should be warm enough at these temperatures. I called, "Come on. Time for out."

Shad paused for a second when he saw the white, then seemed oblivious to the weather as he charged out to frolic in the snow. He almost disappeared in a drift fifteen steps out from the stairs. I moved slowly to check the depth of snow against the tops of the chore boots. While close ankle depth most places, only the drifts were deeper than the boots were tall and it was a fluffy snow that didn't flood in to cause wet feet.

Shad exploded from the other side of the drift and rolled and jumped and had what appeared to be a very good time for himself. Then he calmed down and checked the yard for yeti or bigfoot. When he didn't find any of those, he marked the corners of our turf as a place where friends were welcome, enemies would be dealt with harshly. In my turn, I made some snowballs and let Shad chase them down.

But it was harsh enough weather, we were back inside after only fifteen minutes. Unwrapping from the outer wear took almost as long as wrapping up to go out. The skies were what photographers called cloudy bright from sunrise on. That demanded flapjacks, sausage, and eggs for breakfast. Plenty of maple flavored sugar syrup gave almost instant fuel to the metabolism to re-warm my legs from the chill. Jeans are great, but they have limits, and the weather this morning was chilly enough to defeat them.

I spent the time after breakfast checking supplies in the sewing cache and found the owner's manual for the sewing machine, thread, needles, some patterns - a few that I thought I'd buy but wouldn't need to order now - and a few yards of fabrics that would let me launch an effort to sew my own clothes. Add the fabric I brought home yesterday, I'd pass the storm sewing an increase of my wardrobe.

After the second walk, Shad took a nap. I spent the time before lunch sewing a tan corduroy maxi pencil skirt in my size. Victor had marked the changes he needed for his size, but didn't deface the smaller sizes so it was easy enough to use the my size on the printed pattern. It was a good though loose fit, easily fixed with a bigger seam allowance and darts at the waist before I added the inch shorter waistband.

Took a break for lunch. After we returned from the third

walk, I turned on the lights in the sewing room and finished the skirt. Not as good as I hoped, but much better than I feared it would be. I judged it remarkably good for a first effort without an instructor watching over my shoulder. I wore it for the rest of the day. It was fun to wear something I made myself.

I decided that called for a celebratory drink. I mixed a stiff one - two shots, more or less, poured by eye and a guess, with a splash of cool tap water. A short while watching TV for the evening news and weather. The prediction was the storm would pass around midnight. I knew I'd get some exercise shoveling out when it stopped snowing.

I bundled up again and took Shad for his fourth walk. I finished the drink when we came back. Searched the library of DVDs and found one I liked. I watched that for the two hours it took. After the fifth walk for the day, I was ready for bed and sleep.

Last thought for the day was 'Today was a day with nothing but normal happenings. Judged by the past week, that was unusual for being so ordinary.'
*****

Pete sat on the bed when I woke. "Good morning. A week already?" I asked.

He answered, ***"Sure is. Better keep your mind on getting through this first. Don't worry about Stan. He's as hooked on you as you are on him. He had a rough night, though. A lot of fender benders, stuck vehicles, and one bad accident with serious injuries."***

I couldn't help the grin when I replied, "That's good to know. Makes getting through this more important. I'm glad Stan is OK."

"Just keep your mind on the business at hand. You'll do better. So will he. The guys who work for your opponent, they're a different story. They're smart and make their living

getting rid of road blocks for their boss." Pete counseled.

"Now that's a downer. Any more 'good' news or advice?"

"Not right now. Just know that you're doing well. Keep alert. I'll be in touch again when you need me, or next week." He said as he poofed to wherever he went.

Awake after that short exchange, I answered the call of nature, got dressed for the outdoors. Just in case of need, I put the pistol in one coat pocket and a spare magazine in the other. Shad waited at the door, and we went forth into the dawn. The fresh snow was almost boot top high, or sixteen inches deep, but squished down at my steps. It would likely melt in a week or two, but would likely leave some ice in the shadows or on the roads and sidewalks tonight if temperatures fell below freezing. For now though, breakfast could wait for some play time.

Shad was quite adept at catching snowballs lobbed in his direction. If he missed, he was also persistent in his search for it. After a half hour, we went back inside.

Breakfast was quick and easy. A bowl of oatmeal with milk, some toast with butter and preserves, coffee black. Radio news, weather, and sports had some interesting items but, this time, the music had been why I turned it on in the first place. I liked this station because the first hour was classic music. Grandma Joyce got me used to listening to it while growing up.

No, not classical as in Beethoven, Bach, and Mozart. This was classic country like Patsy Cline or Hank Williams, pop like the McGuire Sisters, Pat Boone, or Perry Como. Those were mixed with rock from the Shirelles, Supremes, Buddy Holly, Fats Domino, and Chuck Berry, all still popular after the British invasion that brought the Tornadoes with their hit 'Telstar', first British record to chart in the Billboard Top 100, the Beatles from before 'Yellow Submarine' and the heavy metal take over, with some big bands that still played on radio in the 50s and 60s even if the band no longer existed. Back when the band played accompaniment to the singer rather than drowning him or her out.

Much easier wake up listening than the marches played the second hour. Of course, I concluded with a chuckle, if a person slept in that late, they deserved it. While not guaranteed, marches might help get them moving quickly enough to be at work or school on time. At least they worked that way for me when I was in high school.

I pulled on my coat and boots to go out again. My task was to clear snow off the drive, sidewalks, and stairs. Snow of this depth took effort to clear, but I finished in two hours or so because it was the fluffy type rather than wet, wind packed variety. I wanted to use the time before any of the businesses opened to clean up and dress for people contact as I shopped, or visited my lawyer. When, maybe if, the streets got plowed out. Then again, this was weather for snowmobile suits. I didn't need to change.

As I put the finishing touches on my makeup, Victor dropped into my thoughts with the comment that I was losing his influence, though not his memories. They were boxed, labeled, and put in the basement of my mind. I was becoming the girl whose body I wore. That was one I'd have to decipher later. I had a full morning of errands ahead of me.

The day after the Thanksgiving Week Storm for this year offered different and limited plans for me. The streets needed to be plowed and snow removed before anybody got anywhere. The announcement of a snow day on the radio included advice to call ahead to find if your destination was open for business. My date for tonight was in question. My errands were delayed until afternoon IF they got the streets cleared by then. I sighed with resignation.

I made another cup of coffee and considered my situation.

Stan would have to do something imbecilic, like seriously peeving me to the point of starting a blood feud, or getting killed, to drop out of first place in the race for my love. I already liked him a lot, so he led.

There was another, Sean, still in the race, but many furlongs behind right now. That was complicated by his official duties to investigate the criminal invasions of my home. Even were he single, it would be unseemly to become romantically involved right now.

I spent the day inside except when Shad needed to go out. I sewed a lot. Got the flannel pajamas done and wore them during the evening. Shad had his new bed to sleep on. Spoke with Sue in the early hours. She apologized that she didn't make our chat, but she was snowed in at her apartment. I told her no problem, since it was obviously not fit weather for man or beast the last day and a half. We made up for that with a discussion numerous topics for about half an hour. We agreed to meet once the streets were cleared.

After I watched "Miracle on 34th Street" , Shad and I went out for the last time today. When back inside, we warmed up a bit and turned in for the night.

Next morning, after the routine tasks completed every morning, I started to plan the stops I'd make when I started my errands when a 4x4 ATV parked outside. The doorbell rang. I answered the door to Gene. He offered to take me to his office to film my deposition for the trial in case Junior's minions successfully silenced me. My planned first stop was Gene's office, so I accepted the ride.

On the way, he explained he planned to introduce me to two people. I already sort of knew Gus Will. The other, Bob Josepski, was my godfather and boss, so we weren't strangers.

They would witness my deposition. When we arrived, he sat us at a conference table. I answered questions into the recording camera as a video deposition in case unable to testify in person. Gene made copies with intent to send one to the State Attorney General, another to the US Attorney handling the case the feds would bring for passing counterfeit money unless there was a plea bargain that put him in witness protection.

I hoped with a clear conscience that Junior Forrest wouldn't get such a deal. I thought I was entitled to hold a grudge against anybody who tried to have me killed. After all, I was being reasonable. I wasn't asking for his head, just a long prison term. I didn't want the guys that actually printed the funny money to slide, but wouldn't mind if they got parole or cut a plea deal while Junior served hard time for his whole sentence. The money they made from criminal activities would get them in trouble again sooner or later anyway.

After almost an hour which included frequent checks of the owner's manual and adjustments to the camera in use for the first time, I finished my deposition. I traded seats with Gus, a witness to my testimony to serve as a witness to his. His was just a half hour before another round of musical chairs. I grinned. In a little over two hours, we had ended the Forrest dynasty if the prosecutions resulted in convictions.

Screwed them good and proper payback for the way they tried to screw the people. They were toast on the charcoal side of done. I hoped to be at the trial to listen to the guilty verdict. At least to be well enough to hear it on the local news.

Without my own transport, I asked Gus if he'd give me a ride home. He said he'd warm up his truck. As the last one to leave Gene's office, I invited him to a chili supper if he brought Sue. When he accepted, I gave him a hug. Why not? He was a minor hero for finding a way to topple the enemy.

As I walked to Gus' truck, I passed the hardware store.

The window display showed a medium size crock pot on sale. I'd been thinking about replacing the one I broke, so stopped in. Left the store with one of those and a brand new two cup coffee brewer to replace the old one. That one gave up the ghost some mornings ago. Garage sales provide good bargains on occasion. The items may have a long life left in them, and maybe not. Some things should be bought new. Coffee makers for one.

That triggered a thought about dinner tonight. How hard can it be to make chili? Not very if I used canned chili seasoned beans, diced tomatoes with jalapeno peppers, a little chili powder, some onion, and browned ground meat. I ran through the menu. Something crunchy to accompany the chewy beans and meat, and something to drink. The meal was already in my cupboards, even some beer to wash down the tortilla chips.

Gus dropped me off. Noted the slush was melting well, and it would be mostly gone by later tonight if it really did stay in the 40s overnight. Tomorrow would be a good time to deliver Barb's grocery order. Pulled into the drive and got all the packages moved inside, sorted, and washed the pot of the crock pot and let it dry. As if on cue, Sue arrived just in time for lunch.

We ate, and chatted the afternoon away as I opened cans and mixed them to start their warming. She agreed with me that the major companies used recipes for the least tolerant palates to label their product hot. I added the can of spicy tomatoes and it was much improved. About an hour before supper, I browned about a half pound of ground beef and stirred it into the tomato and bean mix already in the pot. I was pleased with the result. Not so spicy that it raised sweat on the brow, but with a small bite. Grandma Joyce would have rated it as mild, but the canneries would label it 'Super - Hot'. It would not be offered for sale because it would only sell to the initiated, a sure recipe for failure. It was that in comparison to what they called 'Hot. I rated it as palatable on the safe side of too spicy.

Sue called Gene and awaited his arrival. I used that time to wash and refresh my makeup. As I looked at myself in the mirror, the urge hit to open another button on my blouse. A second look in the mirror and I buttoned up again. I didn't want to display that much to my friend's date, definitely not in her presence. Walked Shad one more time before dinner. Noted the snow had either melted or settled enough to offer several inches clearance to my boot tops.

Gene arrived the 'polite' fifteen minutes late. Here in private with no witnesses, he confirmed my diagnosis that he was ready for private time with Sue by the way they embraced. But he was also ready for supper, and that was priority for his grumbling stomach. .

The chili was just right. Hotter than the factory canned variety, but wouldn't cause discomfort. Brought out the analyst in him, but his discourse on the two types of heat possible with chili can be distilled to two sentences. Thermal was the temperature. Chemical was the level of spiciness. Sounds boring and was. Still, it made sense when you think about it, and safe dinner table talk.

Stan dropped in on his way home from work. He enjoyed some chili too. I introduced him around the table. Sue made a joke about our local Law and Order episode with a cop and a lawyer at table together. That brought some chuckles. She and Gene left at seven, about an hour after supper.

Stan needed a pair of ears to listen to his exploits during the Storm. That was boring too, until you factor in the personal relationship growing between us. I actually enjoyed it just because he was talking to me like I mattered to him. I know. My goose is cooked, figuratively. That's OK with me. He is every bit a MAN, like the old time stars: Wayne, Mitchum, Price,

Arness, and even looked a bit like Marshall Dillon in the early episodes. I'd be his Miss Kitty any day he asked, and maybe his Missus someday.

A few beers later, we cuddled and chatted on the sofa while we watched TV. Nothing momentous happened, but another month might bring more. He left before we got out of hand, about nine PM. I walked Shad for the last time tonight, stored the leftovers, cleaned the kitchen, washed dishes and my face, and was asleep by ten. I dreamed the shadowy figure lifted the visor of his helmet and he wore Stan's face.

Skip A Week

Not a bad melt off after a Chinook Wind blew for ten days. The Native Americans were right when they named a warm west-southwest wind the Snow Eater. The melt was quick, but not so fast that the creeks and streams overflowed their banks. The weatherman said it was partly because, while the snow fall had been deep, the moisture content was low. Low spots without an outlet did fill with water too deep to ford without a very high ground clearance vehicle, but most had a route around them.

It took almost two full weeks for the last traces of the storm to soak into the ground. That delay postponed my visit to Barbara's house until today. The silver lining to that cloud was I was more or less confined to quarters until the snow melted. The wait for the melt let me practice my magic enough to have confidence in my powers. It was still a workout to focus on lifting the refrigerator, but it was getting easier. It would make moving it easier to clean behind it. Also let me get better as a seamstress. I sewed winter weight clothes without major flaws. Some approached factory made items.

Too, I learned to answer inquiries when questioned how I got the gun from Guns. Thought fast enough to stretch the truth a bit without an outright lie. I told the detectives I aimed at him and ordered him to freeze. Then I got him to hand over the revolver before the squad car arrived. Actually, I had managed to hold him in the freeze until I heard the footsteps of the uniforms on the stairs before I released him so they could handcuff him. There wasn't need to explain Lou lying in the middle of a pool of chili with a dent in his scalp matched by one in the pot I hit him with. See? No lie. Just used words with a common meaning that fit special circumstances with a slightly different connotation. Sometimes, it would be a lot easier just to shoot the beggars right off the bat.

The time to melt the snow delayed my trip to Barbara's until today. I packed a change of jeans, socks, underwear, and a couple of sweaters. The plan was to stay three days to get some training, so I packed more than for a day visit, but still not a lot unless you count the weight of ammunition and firearms. I took the Officer's ACP, the M1A, and plenty ammunition for each. I was still more confident with shooting than with magic. We drove to Barb's on dry roads until we ran out of pavement. That was interesting times I can guarantee. But we got there with only a few pounds of new mud under the wheel wells.

Barb and Sasha greeted us as soon as the engine stopped. We carried in the supplies I brought. I carried my bag in and put it in "my usual room". Then we talked about what happened since I was there last over a cup of coffee. She was quite amused when I related my victory over Junior Forrest's hired muscle, Guns and Lou. She particularly enjoyed how I told the police what happened without revealing my powers but told them what happened.

Barb said I was beginning a wondrous journey that had rewards if I stayed on the side of nature. We'd explore that tomorrow. Supper took little time with two cooks, and cleanup went as quickly with two dish washers. It reminded me of times I had been there with grandma Joyce. It felt natural, so very natural.

We put the dishes away and immediately dirtied two glasses

with the nightly medicinal dose of ethanol to ease the aches and pains of old age and to help the young sleep as antidote to the caffeine. Bourbon works quite well in that role. I don't advise it if you drink too much from habit or alcoholism, but for those who can call it quits after a glass or two, it works quite well.

It was time to sleep this night. Baba called the dogs. They came racing up the stairs, slowed to a fast walk across the porch. I had seen old newsreels played with contemporary movies from the 40s and 50s at the theater for old movie buffs in town near the college. When they came inside, they displayed a dignity and bearing rarely seen in people outside the English monarchs. At least that was the impression I got.

The days and nights passed quickly as I learned to speak and listen to the animals and birds of these woods. Baba gave pointers on when and where to use my powers, and exercises to get used to them.

The third morning, I woke to Peter's Hello, ***"Ursula. Got some news from the Boss. You're doing good. Keep it up."*** He paused then said, ***"You might want to add deputy Stan Sharp to your friends. Gunny Sharp seems to think that would be a good thing. You'd be able to help him, both personally and professionally, is the way he put it last night."*** He paused, ***"Of course, that's up to you."***

"That free will thing again?" I asked. He nodded. I grinned as I told him, "Well, we haven't even had many dates yet, so way too early to know whether I'd agree with any certainty. I admit I enjoy his company as a friend already. Up to him to make the serious move and ask." I answered.

"Might solve that problem if you asked Gunny for a lesson with long guns. You're still a novice there. Leave setting up the meeting to him. If he meant those requests he sends several times a day, he'll work it out." he said with a definite twinkle in his eyes.

"Are you trying for guardian angel or the Cupid Squad?" I laughed.

"One and the same thing as I read the manual." he laughed back. *"By the way, I noticed the local theater group will advertise for help putting on their next play. You might be interested in one of the jobs they list to put your education to use. If I get busy with another client and miss the news, tell me what happens."*

"I'll watch for it when they run the ad. I'll see which job they offer. Don't know if I'll audition for a part." I tried hard to keep the whine out of my answer. "I might try for the part of the saloon girl who saves Destry's life from the villain's bullet. Marlene Dietrich had that part in the movie."

"That would be a big break for you. Just remember, there are more jobs than as a performer even for a local production. They are important roles, too." he said with a wink. *"See you next week unless an emergency comes up. Then I'll be right here with you. Bye for now."*

"Before you go, I better tell you that you must have missed the memo. Stan and I are dating pretty seriously, though not often when he has the night shift."

"No kidding? That's great. Fits into the plan for you, too. Bye." Pete said as he started to fade.

"Next week then, Lord willing." I thought as he poofed off to wherever he spent his time. I stretched, rose, took care of my need to use the bathroom, and dressed for the day. Shad and I took our first walk today under the scrutiny of a barn owl lounging on a tree branch. "Hi. You'll have the yard to yourself when we're finished." The owl was silent.

After breakfast, Barb gave me a verbal score card and charged me to keep practicing. We said our goodbyes and Shad and I headed home.

I was lost in thoughts of magic, and being back in theater when the announcement of the Lone Pine Players came from the radio. I almost missed it. At least I caught the station's invitation to call for information if we missed the contact number for the group. Once home, I called the station and got the information I needed.

Plenty of time before most businesses closed. I brushed my hair and fashioned it in a ponytail. Didn't need makeup if I were going for a costumer or stage hand job, and definitely not needed to talk to Gunny over the phone. I used the time to give Shad some affection, and to give the firearms some care. Amazing how much can be done well before five PM when you wake before dawn, specially to the tempo of Sousa marches. I had to grin at that thought.

Finally, time to call Gunny rolled around. I phoned. I used the ploy that he said to call if I needed help. I explained I was already planning for defense when the snow melted, and my lack of knowledge and confidence cost me more that one shot during the past deer season. I wanted to learn enough to feel comfortable if either game offered a harvest shot next season, or a goon threatened mayhem next spring.

He asked for time to schedule a session at the rifle range. I agreed to that and mentioned I had need to be out of the house for a while later today. He could leave a message on the answering machine. He laughed and said it would be a day at least until had the schedule worked out. I joined him in laughter and apologized for unrealistic expectations.

I also called the contact for the theater group. Miniver O'Grady was nice on the phone, and asked for a run down on my experience. Supporting roles in my drama class at college didn't draw much interest. That I had made costumes and done some back drops for other plays did. Maybe I wasn't meant to be a celebrity, despite those elusive dreams of stardom, but a gaffer or seamstress offered more subtle rewards. Miniver seemed quite taken with those abilities and that I had even studied those as minor fields while earning my B. F. A. in acting. She asked what I was doing for a living now. I told her I worked as a bar maid at the Spotted Horse. She said, "Hmmm." and added they'd be back in touch when closer to the start of production in January. I said thanks and hung up. Wrote that down on the calendar.

I had a few minutes of fantasy about claiming stardom from obscurity, then came back down to earth. Whatever job they wanted done, I'd do my best. I guessed I was addicted to the aroma of grease paint, even second hand because worn by someone else. That's an addiction, though harmless unless it inflates the ego, as surely as addiction to any of the narcotics.

But it was time to get the supplies Barbara wanted. I gathered my things. Shad got a short walk to prevent accidents, and we were off. The liquor store was first because Shad wasn't as prone to sample a bottle of sour mash as he was a few pounds of hamburger. The grocery had some all-purpose paper in a suitable weight for letters by the ream and envelopes by the box so those were on the list there, as were whole grain white and rye flours, yeast, caraway seeds, salt and other seasonings. All told, these plus what she already stored, should get her through to Spring.

We headed North and made good time. The usual routine was in place, so we unloaded the groceries, then sat at the kitchen table and chatted over a cup of coffee. I reported the goings on in town, and even the possibility of working on the Spring production, whatever the Lone Pine Players chose. She smiled and said one sobering thing. "That's fine, Bear. Just don't lose sight of the real task at hand."

"I know. The protection of the forest is priority. Still should leave time for work on a play in addition to working for a living and working to save the ecosystem." I replied.

"What's going on with Stan?" she asked.

"Not sure. He seems reluctant to get past 'friendly acquaintances'. Been worse since he drew the night shift. I feel like I'm the one left with one cigarette in the ashtray, like that Patsy Cline song." I sighed 'Part of it is that I'm busy at the saloon. He's busy with his patrols. We don't get to spend much time together." I chuckled and opined, "One thing sure, he doesn't act like he's not interested, more like he's preoccupied."

"That's too bad. One good thing I see is that he's still friendly. Might be handy to have a friendly deputy later on, so don't give up yet. If it comes to it, stay friends even if not romantically involved." Barb grinned.

"I'll keep that in mind" I laughed. "Getting on to time to head home. See you next week if not snowed out."

We parted. I loaded Shad into his seat, got into mine then started the truck. A helicopter flew over. Looked like one of those Hueys in film clips and war movies including the flat olive drab paint job but without military markings. I cursed the failure to bring the camera today. Won't be a next time for that. A small camera will be as much part of my regular load as the pistol and a spare magazine. Better add some compact binoculars in the glove box too, I decided.

I headed toward Route 17 slowly. I'd rather not get into a shootout if I could help it. Bursting onto a rendezvous would likely bring one on if my suspicions were realized. I didn't have any proof, but I felt strongly these were smugglers of some sort of contraband.

There had been reports in the state of injuries and deaths after other accidental confrontations. Survivor statements described similar helicopters met by nondescript vans before the shooting started. Enough to give anyone pause unless they had a death wish. I certainly didn't.

As I neared the start of the pavement, a van turned onto the road. The helicopter took off, circled once before heading south. I slowed my truck to a slow walk and finally stopped when concealed by some spruce trees. A long five minutes later, I resumed my trip home.

Not far from Route 17, State police and sheriffs vehicles with their lights flashing blocked the road and officers surrounded the van. Two grubby guys that I took to be the occupants stood to one side with hands held over their heads. Another sat near the van already handcuffed. A fourth lie face down in a puddle of crimson. I stopped about a 100 yards distant until waved in and drove slowly nearer.

I stopped as signaled to do by the deputy in the road. I followed her instructions again when told to dismount the vehicle. Hey, I'm not stupid. Do what The Man, or The Woman in this case, tells you and you reduce the chance of getting shot by mistake. I stood for the frisking, enjoying the banter with the officer. She was polite, and apologized for the inconvenience of the stop. I explained that I had delivered baking supplies to a friend who lived closer to the lake. When she asked, I told her it was Barbara Yeager.

She looked up when I said that and asked, "Is she still living back there?"

"Yes. Met her during the Fall and we hit it off. I deliver groceries about once a week, weather permitting."

"You're the new girl in the coven then." she whispered. "My mom belongs too. Good thing you're standing up for the ecosystem these farms and the forest. I would too, if I had the time."

I whispered back, "Thank you. Makes me glad I joined to know others give a hoot." Then I spoke. "Been busy?"

She said they were. There was a new drug dealer in town, and he was ruthless. Made some enemies among his competition. That's why they just busted a shipment of whatever the lab determines, but it was likely drugs. One of the guys decided to shoot it out rather than just stop for the search. That's why even office personnel were here.

While we talked, a wrecker hooked up and towed the van to the evidence lot, an ambulance removed both wounded to the nearest hospital, and the state police took the two standing to the nearest barracks for questioning. I would just be speculating except Officer Morgan, the one who searched me, explained what was happening as it unfolded. I was given the go ahead to leave, said good bye to Officer Morgan and waved to the others as I drove out and toward home.

It was a short drive, but long enough to give me time to consider writing a book about this when the dust finally settled. Might be a good idea, I decided, specially if Stan didn't warm up to the relationship I once held as a real possibility. So far, it might even make a good romance movie.

I got home and walked Shad. Since almost supper, lunch was light. A slice of bologna held by a slice of bread with a beer. The five o'clock news and weather held nothing earth shaking. Gunny called and we agreed to meet at the old gravel pit south of town around noon on Saturday, two days from now. Minerva called and asked me to meet some of the group this afternoon. She had told them I worked at the saloon and they were interested in listening to me read for the part as a saloon girl in a presentation of Destry Rides Again.

I agreed. Why not. I grinned. After all, it was a good movie in its day, back when the studios still took westerns seriously. I took a short nap after Shad's walk and was at the Civic Center on time. They handed me a script and had me read a few lines, then asked if I minded being a tart.

I asked, "How do you want to play this? As a conversationalist drink seller dance hall girl or as a Soiled Dove?" I had to explain the difference. Knotheads wanted to do a play in an Old West Saloon and didn't realize there was a hierarchy for Fallen Angels.

The director had a wicked grin when he suggested 'Go for Soiled Dove, whatever that is."

This was going to be fun. "I need a guy to play off to do this right. We can use the stairs stage left for now, but it should be stairs up to her room in the actual production." A lean cowboy looking guy hid in the back. I'd give Stan a bit of razzing. "Hey, Tex. Come on over." He looked around like there was somebody else I could be talking to. "You. The guy looking around for rescue. Get up here, Stan."

Stan finally acknowledged he was the guy I meant and came forward hesitantly. "This is play acting. Don't take it so seriously. For this scene, you just helped drive a thousand head up from Texas to this Kansas railhead. You've been eating barely cooked beans and drinking coffee made with whatever water was available for three months without seeing anybody not working for the same outfit, definitely haven't seen or talked to a woman since roundup for the drive started. Got that?"

"Yeah." he said

"Try it again with a bit of respect, and say 'Yes'm'. OK? Even the ladies of the evening were given respect back then."

This time he said it right. "Yes'm."

"Mr. Director, Am I just shilling drinks with conversation, or am I relieving him from pent up desires and some of his pay?"

"Go for the relief this time." the director said.

Holy cow! I had Stan where I wanted him and permission for the seduction scene I was about to play. "Ready, Tex?" He nodded. "You've got the pay for the drive in your pocket. You're thirsty and horny. You want to have a good time. Come in and go to the bar. I'll be along shortly after you order your drink."

He grinned, "Yes'm."

The scene was a smash with the director. I knew because he actually clapped as we went to my pretend bedroom. He asked how I had those lines for that. I confessed I had the part once before but never performed it because my granddad died and I had to go home for the funeral. He asked about the version for a drink pusher who just talked.

I told him, "That's easy if you remember Miss Kitty from the TV Gunsmoke. The broadcast code back then limited her to just selling drinks. If we had the same code as in Real Life during the real cattle drives, she was probably the Dodge City equivalent of Tombstone's Dutch Annie the madam of a cat house, and did her best work on her back. I did some research for the part."

He said, "We'll probably need both versions. One for the matinees, the other for all adults. I think you've got the part."

"Thank you. I'll work on both versions. And you too, Tex. Much easier to do the part with a guy acting as sounding board."

Tex, Stan, answered, 'Yes'm." General laughter broke out.

I went home as others read for parts. Shad got his walk, I showered and went to bed. Just before I slept, I answered the question nagging at me. It was simply that Stan Sharp looked different in jeans, work boots, and a big hat than in his deputy's uniform with pressed trousers. I was impressed with him in uniform. I was in lust with him in tight jeans. I grinned myself to sleep. Excuse me, but this dream is my secret. I'll share it only with Stan. I will tell you I woke still wearing a grin, and a slight sheen of perspiration.

Thanksgiving Break

Morning passed in the normal routine. Boring stuff, so I won't tell you again. It was the last morning for a while that would be routine.

Around lunch, the phone rang. It was the day manager at the Spotted Horse. I had an unexpected week off from work. The guy that plowed the parking lot turned too quickly for conditions and skidded into the corner of the building. Repairs would take at least that long. That called for a minor celebration. Had a beer with lunch and took a short nap after I washed the dishes.

About one-thirty, I woke and launched into a project at the sewing table. Not too hard, but taught a few new ideas and let me merge the top from one pattern, the skirt from a different one and sleeves from a third. That took a bit longer than I wanted, but I was done in time to make supper. Tomorrow, I would trace the patterns and make sure they fit together. Day after that, I'd use some lining fabric to test the pattern, my cheapskate's version of a muslin. Lining fabric was half the price, less if on sale, of actual muslin. On the fourth day, I alter the pattern to make it fit if needed.

Supper wasn't super, just my favorite TV dinner in the 4-for-$5-when-on-sale-bracket. Just because I didn't feel like cooking didn't mean my taste buds were dead. My choice was simply made. It was a lot easier than making a chicken fried beef patty from scratch, and left enough calories in my allowed daily intake to include an after dinner drink or two.

This evening's plan called for the first episode of the series I found this afternoon. I called Sue when she should have been home from work. Left a message when she didn't answer. That plan shot, I'd watch the movie alone. It was one of the shows I missed when they were first run on TV. It was a western that caught my fancy from the description on the jacket. It was slow moving, heavy on the character development instead of action, but it made sense for the topic.

Not one of the typical love at first sight bull manure modern romances, but the building of mutual tolerance, each for the other. That grew by steps into friendship into attraction into a life long commitment. The couple faced challenges together, some with immediate action, others of long duration that required perseverance.

After two hours, the happy ending was welcome when it finally came. At least I found it so. Even went misty-eyed a few times and had to wipe a few tears at the end. That was a really good movie, unlike too many made now.

Before bedtime, Shad needed a walk again. No, he didn't tell me, he showed me through his proximity to me. He had a favorite corner in which to nap until he needed to answer the call of nature. Then he lay down closer to me when the urge hit him.

During the walk, I considered my feelings about Gene. While he was a nice guy, no sparks flew. Then, about the time he and Sue got together, his calls quit coming unless they were business related, and were lawyer to client. That was about the time I went back to my regular schedule at the saloon so hardly noticed it at first.

No need to tell anyone about Stan yet. This one might fizzle out like a candle in a rain, and I didn't want to build their hopes or mine just to jinx it. Shad finished his last walk with a happy smile on his face. We were asleep soon after.

Time passed quickly, I sewed a few more skirts and dresses, figured out how to load pictures from the camera to the computer and print them. And I shopped for groceries for daily needs, the Thanksgiving meal with guests and supplies for Barbara.

After Thanksgiving, I settled down after the flurry of cooking my own dinner shared with both Sharps, Gunny and Deputy Stan. Except that they graciously took home large shares of the left overs, I faced my own share of 'turkey for a week or more'. That was the only part of the feast that brought fear for my waistline and weight.

On first of December, I went to court. The hearing on the evidence of my lineage was held. The Administrator of the Estate reported Victor Warsawski's assets were marshaled and accounted for the debts owed by the estate. The will was entered into the court records. Two weeks after court, the judge signed the order. My rights as sole heir with a claim on the assets left after the bills were paid was now a matter of record.

I held a small party at the Spotted Horse that grew as long time customers joined in if only briefly to offer their well wishes. Even the crew of the company Victor founded joined in to eat some pizza and drink a few beers. This seemed to be a celebration of memories, based on the stories of kindnesses he provided to those he knew. With the information, I could see him now getting close to turning his quota of rocks into gravel. It was humorous to imagine him breaking rocks, swinging his sledge hammer in high heels.

I got home after I left the last inebriates to their own devices. Shad had his last walk for the day. I slept well through the night and woke to Pete's visit at dawn. "Good morning, Pete.

How are you?"

He answered, ***"Fine as frog's hair. You seem to be doing well enough too.***

"I am. Got my health. I'm not privy to the workings of the cases, but the arrests in both Junior's counterfeiting case and the drug smugglers caught as I witnessed give me hope." I replied.

"Now is too soon to claim victory. Don't forget the silent partner in all this. He's still loose, and I'd expect that he's very miffed by the loss of that shipment. Think about it. Why were they looking for that much land to start with?" he stated. Pete continued. ***"Seriously think about that. I'll be back soon to see how you do with the answer. Your final goal is in that answer. "***

"You mean the protection of the woods don't you?" I queried.

"Just awake and saw that. I'm impressed. Now I see why you were picked for the physical part of the task. See you soon. Bye." Pete said as he started to fade out. The fade stopped briefly for a few seconds for his last words, ***"Be a good idea to visit Baba this afternoon. Clear your calendar for the day. It may be a long night."***

"Really know how to make a girl's day, don't you?

Pete chuckled. ***"You're more than a girl. You're a warrior with powers. Remember that. Remember, too, you have allies. For them, it's not just a nice place to visit. It's their home."*** The fade out was quicker from then on.

I frowned while I worked out what Pete meant by what he said. It dawned on me as I rose and dressed for the day. Of course I had powers. Baba had taught me well. I was a warrior thanks to that part of Victor I now claimed as mine. The rest fell into place. I could communicate with, or at least speak at, the birds and critters who lived in the woods. Some of them could explain it to ones that didn't get it. They were natural allies in a fight to protect the woods because it was their home. And some of the bears were still up true to their word they wouldn't hibernate until later. The wolves were active all winter, and had promised to be available if it came.

After the morning routine, I had a few things to check out. The book store usually carried plat books of the county. I could use those to have the legal descriptions of properties that might be targeted for acquisition by those I considered the villains of this plot.

The court house held the Clerk and Recorder's office. That's where I could track recent changes of ownership or leases. With luck, my search would be quick enough to eat lunch before I headed up to Baba's. I was curious to see what was so important that Pete had urged me to be there this afternoon because of a special need to do so. I felt but couldn't explain a certain dread of what I'd find.

But my errands were completed by ten thirty. I walked over to the new Sheriff's building. The blond brick stood out from the red brick or gray poured concrete of surrounding buildings. A ceremony open to the public celebrated the recent promotions. Corporal Sharp was now Sergeant Sharp and Sergeant Sharp was quite pleased to see me.

I told him what I found during my search this morning. He seemed interested, specially by the clerk's comment that a recent lease was brought by a very unusual Sidney Greenstreet, as an old films buff, she recognized the name of an old time actor who was rather rotund. The man who claimed that name for the lease was quite the opposite. Shortly, he introduced me to the Sheriff himself. I repeated my story. This time, I mentioned her name. The sheriff rose to his full six foot some height and walked over to the court house with a handful of mug shots.

"Does he always just walk out on a social visit?" I asked Stan.

"Not always, but I've seen him do it often enough to sense he found a clue in what you told him. We've been fighting a new gang in town. A lease of the roughest ground on the Johansson farm could be important." Stan answered. We kissed good bye and I left feeling good after what he told me. I HAD done something to help.

I also noted that he had become more ready to act on impulse with me since he got the promotion fifteen minutes ago. The raise that came with it may have been enough for him to consider a steady girl if not a spouse. Rehearsals for Destry would begin after Christmas, so I'd see him more often then, and there was always the practice for the un-staged activities 'upstairs' before when the script arrived. -grin-

But today, right now, I needed to get home, finish lunch in time to get to Barbara's before whatever Pete had in mind when he suggested I make the trip happens. The suspense about what that event would be was growing to nearly insufferable. I just hoped I was up to handling 'it', whatever 'it' was.

I decided on another bologna sandwich. Tore a piece to top Shad's kibble, and treated myself with a full sandwich since only a handful of chips went with it. I loaded the truck with equipment, food, and drink, called Shad and he took his seat. A half hour later, I was only another half mile to go to be there. A car pulled out of her drive, followed by a guy on foot running hard.

A half dozen wolves loped along behind the parade. The driver didn't have much experience on gravel roads, judged by wild changes of direction made. It caught up to him when one of those turns led him straight into the biggest pothole on the road. He skidded off the road and stopped with the car kissing a large pine tree. The guy running jumped into the car and slammed the door behind him.

"Sir Wolf, why were you chasing these guys?" I asked the

pack leader.

"Baba Two, they were prowling around Baba's cabin. We feared for her safety. I gathered some of the young ones and by the time we got back, the two in the car and another were pounding on her door and yelling loudly." he answered.

"What happened to the third guy? You didn't eat him, did you?"

The wolf snickered, "Didn't eat him. He saw us coming, panicked, fell down the stairs. Knocked himself out when he landed head first. Two of the yearlings and a senior watch him." He was quite pleased with himself and his pack.

"Do me a favor? Watch these two also. I'll check on Baba, and call the police. Will the wolves be able to slip away when the deputies take over?"

"We'll do that, Baba Two. Been doing it for years. I'll post one of the older of the pack down the road to signal us when they get here." He agreed.

"Thanks." I drove quickly and jumped out of my truck. First thing was to add Shad to the guards for the unconscious brigand "Watch him." I instructed.

I let myself in. Barbara lay on the floor unconscious. I checked for breathing. Her pulse was weak but regular. No need to start her heart. Her breathing was shallow but steady. No mouth to mouth needed. No visible bleeding either. Her right leg above the knee was at an unnatural angle where there were no joints though. I dialed 9-1-1.

When the dispatcher answered, I told her about the guys in the car, another in the back yard, and Barbara unconscious on the floor with what looked to be a broken leg. She would send two patrol cars and an ambulance. Almost as an afterthought, she said she'd also have a wrecker coming for the car. I confirmed the location and she rang off.

I attended to my friend and mentor. Her pulse was stronger,

but I didn't attempt to rouse her. Better that she was unconscious if the leg was broken until the EMTs arrived. They'd have pain killers with them for her trip to the hospital. She'd need them if she woke before they got there.

The first car arrived about fifteen, maybe twenty minutes after I called in the emergency. The second car and ambulance came into the yard about five minutes later. I looked out when they arrived. Shad was the only guard, but he was strategically located near the bad guy's head. I doubt the ruffian would have moved if he regained his senses. That was a moot point anyway after the deputy handcuffed him.

As the EMTs split, one for the unconscious hooligan in the yard, assisted by the deputy, the other came to Baba's side. I reported what I observed. He confirmed the appearance of a broken leg, but wouldn't give her a shot until she woke and spoke. Too much chance that any analgesic he had in his kit might shut down her brain. Even I saw the logic in that decision.

Together, we readied Barbara for the lift onto the stretcher. I arranged the backboard as instructed. After the deputy and the other medic got the asshole handcuffed to the ambulance, the four of us got the backboard under my friend, lifted her onto the stretcher, and got her out to the ambulance. I confirmed they were headed to the hospital in Lone Pine since it had the nearest emergency room able to handle Barbara's injuries.

The ambulance left first, slowly to offer the smoothest ride possible. The deputy left next. When they were out of sight, Sir Wolf came out from the bushes and trotted over.

"Those guys came to, so we growled a bit. They sat still after that. They may wind up in the psych ward if they tell that story." he chuckled. "I'd guess we scared them good, judging by the smell of them. Strong enough odor we could smell in from outside the car."

I could guess what he meant. Fear is not a very attractive

cologne in any species. Worse when it causes the lumpy drawers syndrome (they poop in their pants).

"Baba is alive but hurt badly. They took her to the hospital. I'll check on her after I close up the cabin." I stated. I also thanked them for their help, and asked, "Do you think you can stay close to watch that no others come to cause damage?"

"We already do that. Part of our duties as the closest and largest pack. The shifts are already to go into action." Sir Wolf answered.

"Then I'll leave it in good hands uh, er, paws." I giggled. Sir Wolf did also. "I'll be back tomorrow. Do you think we can have a strategy planning session with all the leaders before noon?"

"We will pass the word, Baba Two. You're in charge until Baba is home again." he said.

"See you then. Thanks again for your efforts today." I said. He turned and trotted off.

Shad spoke up. "We better get home so you can make evening visiting hours."

"Stay on guard while I make sure the house is secure. Don't want any food left in the oven to start a fire or anything like that. I'll be right back." In the military, they call that a fragmentary order. That memory had come back from the storage of Bear's gift to me. It also gave me the idea to arrange the defense to use the strengths of the different species in my 'army'.

I went in and turned off the oven. Tasted the cookies that baked during the incident, and shared one with Shad. After I ensured ashes in the fire place were cold, the windows were locked, and all the normal measures when leaving a home for a vacation were completed, we drove home.

I made supper. After the dishes were washed, called the hospital to check on visiting hours and whether Barbara could have a visitor during that time. When told yes, I asked the nurse to let Barb know I'd be there. Freshened up and we were on our way to the medical center.

We arrived. Shortly after, I had my visitor's pass and the room number. Faith, the nurse that watched over me like a mother during my visit, spoke to me before I went in. "She's very tired, keeps talking about going home, so keep your visit short."

"Hi, Barbara. How are you?" I spoke my greeting.

"Hello, Ursula. I'm doing well enough, but I think I'll be going Home soon. I feel too old for this anymore." she said. "I was getting something from the cupboard when there was a banging at the door that startled me. I fell, and next thing I know, I wake up here."

"Don't worry about those guys any more. Two of them came roaring down the road. Driver lost control and crashed. Sir Wolf and others watched them until the sheriff's deputy arrived. After I found you and a third creep outside, the ambulance brought you here for a check up and any repairs needed."

Barbara thumped the cast on her leg and commented, "So that's why I've got this thing?"

"I guess so. I did notice it looked a tad strange when I got there. That's why I called for an ambulance."

"So you did make it. Good girl for keeping your wits about you."

We chatted a bit more before she started to doze off briefly every now and again. I told her I'd be back tomorrow. That's when she said, "No dear. Go to the cabin and muster your allies instead. I fear the visitors today were just looking the place over. Your first responsibility is to protect the woods, and I have a feeling it will be best done soon."

A smile crossed her lips. "And I think now that Stan has his sergeant's stipes, your romance will heat up a bit." She chuckled then got serious again. "You can handle the threat now. Do your best. It will be good enough." She paused and then said, "Now go and let me get some sleep. I'm old and need my rest."

"See you. Rest well and get better soon." I said and left.

There was a message on my answering machine when I got home. The hospital called. Baba had gone Home. Not to her cabin at the woods, but the one where she would face the Maker and get the address for her next domicile. After I returned the call and gave my consent for the autopsy, I prayed that He is merciful when she is judged.

I raised my glass to her for the first drink. Then I prayed for the strength to face whatever came and had the second drink for myself. I told Shad and he joined me in mourning her passage to the other side.

We took our last walk for the night, then turned in with heavy hearts.

A Gray Day Brightens

Morning came on schedule. The daily routine was compressed to allow us to get to Baba's cabin as the sun rose above the horizon. That was a minor logistical miracle in itself. I took some rifles and ammunition for them this time, as well as the usual handguns. Perhaps it was an over reaction, but better to have more than needed than not have enough.

As I took in the last load, an owl landed on the porch railing. It said, "I saw many trucks coming your way here. More than three stopped at the end of the hard road. Men got out and seem to be waiting for something."

"Tell as many others as you can that the enemy comes. Meeting as soon as they get here." I told it.

I spotted a mourning dove in the branches of a near by tree. I got its attention and said, "Tell the birds to keep an eye on those men. Report any activity.. Tell the squirrels and chipmunks to do what they can to slow their advance and generally make their lives miserable."

Sir Wolf arrived with most of his pack. Only the nursing mothers stayed back. He reported the other two packs would be here by seven ready to fight for their homes.

A grizzly bear arrived. He said he was here to fight for his cousins. He had lost his home to development and searched for a new abode. He wanted to save them the same disruption to their lives. About a half dozen black bears joined with him.

Then another grizzly bear, and yet another arrived. Details of their stories differed, but the driving force behind their decision was saving their homes. They were joined by several dozen geese and ducks and hundreds of grackles, robins, cardinals, blue jays, magpies, crows, and other birds I didn't recognize. Even the insects still active this late in the year came, or sent a representative.

I stood on the back porch to speak to the army. I passed the word that Baba Yaga had died in the hospital, and we fought in her memory as well as for ourselves. These men who attacked us now were responsible. We held a moment of silence for her, then I sent the critters to their posts to form a defense in depth.

The smallest critters, the insects up to the snakes, were tasked with slowing the attack by distracting the men and causing confusion. The mice would make noise in the fallen leaves to let the enemy know they weren't alone but were watched. The copperheads and timber rattlers were given the choice to ambush the men or just join the effort to distract the attackers. A few older rattlers opted for the ambush. They could strike in a flash and disappear into the leaves. They had the ability to make the enemy's lives miserable.

The ticks insisted on the right to ambush also, since they were small and often unnoticed before they bit and drew blood. They spoke eloquently and I authorized such attacks. They were joined by the ants who felt the same.

The deer came out of the brush to offer their services as lookouts. After all, they were very good at hiding in the open, masters at hiding in the undergrowth and timber. We accepted their offer and dispatched them on reconnaissance patrols.

The birds would do "bombing runs" with their ability to drop 'whitewash' during flight, or climb higher and send back reports of their aerial observations. Having suffered with just a spot of whitewash in my hair or on my windshield, a massed raid at the least would affect the attackers' morale for the worse.

The squirrels, rabbits, and others of that size up to the deer would use their natural abilities to disrupt and confuse the thugs who marched on us. The beaver could drop trees across the road to hamper the progress and set them up for the ambushes.

The larger carnivores and omnivores, wolves, cougars, and bears, would form the last line of defense to funnel the men into a killing zone that I would use to maximum effect if one or two made it. It was a gray, foggy day at dawn, so it should help them to herd the men into confusion about which way they headed if they tried to move through the trees instead of along the road.

When the sun rose above the horizon, aerial reconnaissance flights started to report movement by the foe. They were moving down the road without a care in the world, certain there was no opposition except the old woman who lived down the road to the lake.

They were wrong and would pay for their smugness. The woods and its residents were organized against them. While they might win, they would know they were opposed, and greatly outnumbered. I just hoped the only casualties were on the enemy side of the battle.

Without air support of their own, they wouldn't pay attention to the passing birds. Their first attack would be a surprise to the men. The medium (duck) and heavy (geese) bombers lifted off and started their bombing runs. Flight after flight of them. You may wonder if they had any effect. Let me remind you that a fifteen-pound goose produces a turd as big as a small dog, and dropped from two or three hundred feet has a significant sting when it hits a body. It won't stop them, but it will demoralize them a bit, perhaps even distract them from ground level threats until too late.

Aided by the trees the beaver would drop across the road, they'd be slowed, or, better yet, move into the tall grass off the road to avoid the bombers. That's when the copperheads and rattlers will strike, that will make the enemy vulnerable to the ticks who need a good meal before winter. And that won't save them from the smaller birds agile enough to strike below the tree branches with their own loads of whitewash. A few of the robins, crows, magpies, blue jays, and cardinals could deliver large load for birds of their size.

The ground recon element reported the rise in stumbles and falls among the road bound invaders. Two gave up because they found it impossible to walk after being snake bit. Others with only strains or sprains helped them back to the trucks.

The pack from the northwest had the men rounded up and sheltering in their vans shortly after they arrived. Safe bet they never expected such stiff resistance. That was compounded when many of them left their "fire sticks" leaning against the vehicles in the panic to escape the wolves. There were two that carried theirs into the truck, but those were nearly useless until cleaned.

Reports from that field detailed that one guy forgot he had a solid plug of mud in the muzzle from his fall. Blew up his rifle when he tried to shoot at the wolves. Scared himself enough to faint dead away. The other checked first, found his bolt was frozen to the receiver and wouldn't open. The others started saying their prayers to prepare for death. That's when the first deputy arrived on the scene in answer to my call for reinforcements. They willingly surrendered because the wolves lay down to watch while the deputy used the supply of long heavy-duty electrical wiring ties to restrain them until other deputies arrived.

Meanwhile, the eight left to continue their march started to notice wolves on both sides of the road moving in the same direction, shadowing them. They paid so much attention to the wolves, the three grizzlies had to stand up in the road to their full height to be noticed. The black bears used that distraction to encircle them from the rear. The wolves tightened the circle. I willed all the humans' weapons to be wildly unreliable, and inaccurate.

The skunks moved in to gas the foe. After the vapors dissipated, I walked calmly through to face the defeated men. Told them to drop their weapons or I'd let the animals have at them. An unbeliever tried to aim, but a bear ran over him, turned back, and stood on his rifle with his hand under it. He gave up and joined the others sitting along the road with hands on their heads.

Not surprisingly, they surrendered with abject failure plainly showing in their faces and in their body language. The only thing left to do was wait for the sheriff's officers to take them into custody.

It wasn't a long wait. The sound of gunfire evidenced more that the six guys in custody were there. A pair of officers had started walking down the road. They watched the capture and were jovial as they approached. They called in the deputies and others. It seemed the rest of the sheriff's department, some state troopers and some town police arrived minutes later.

Even the sheriff, William 'Wild Bill' Donovan, came himself. He saw the number of men caught and commented, "Baba is still here it seems." He looked at me and winked. "Same story for the papers?" he asked.

"I guess. My friends and I are just happy to have witnessed the courage of your officers." I replied. It was better for the general public to believe law enforcement handled it without help. To make sure the assistance from the residents remained secret, I cast a fog on the hooligans' minds that made it seem a nightmare from the night before. It would support the sheriff's claim of befuddled minds under the influence of mass hysteria to counter the criminals' stories as a bonus.

We, my army and I, would keep a low profile, fly under the radar.

He chuckled, then said, "I was worried when Barbara died. Should have known she had her successor picked before she let that happen. Did she say anything to you when you visited?"

"She said, she needed some rest because she was old and wanted to go to sleep. She also talked about going home. I didn't notice during the visit, but thinking back on it, she seemed ready, even willing, for that trip. I missed it when her voice hinted, she used the capital H home." I answered.

"Don't blame yourself. We never want to see family go to the other life. That deafens us to what they really say near the end. I know. My dad and mom both talked that way before they died," Wild Bill stated. "Missed that call both times."

"Thanks, Sheriff. That helps some."

He took off his glove and offered his hand. I returned the courtesy of a firm hand shake. He welcomed me to the family, the protectors of Witch Woods.

I invited him back to the cabin for some coffee. He declined because he wanted to supervise the arrests but asked for a rain check. He would be kept busy for a while so I granted that request.

I sent runners and birds to send my thanks to the army in the far reaches of the woods. Those close by received my thanks directly, and I allowed entry to the granary for the whole army as long as they were orderly. Good thing I found that spell to insure all got a full stomach from the supply there.

Hours later, the police had all the attackers in holding cells. Will Lumber had cleared the trees blocking the road. One truck took the light branches to the beaver homes near the lake.

The trunks and heavier branches were loaded on the truck or the trailer it pulled after it returned from the beaver town. The chainsaws went quiet. Peace at last, at least for now.

I returned to my home in town and made supper. Shad got some fried burger as top dressing for his meal and the chill left my bones, thanks to a drink, the warm meal, and a happy movie from the collection of DVDs. "The Quiet Man" always had that effect on me, and I really liked the way the Duke, John Wayne, let Maureen O'Hara play her part cleanly, with no attempt to steal the scene. Maybe that was why I wasn't interested in most of the movies made with little guys as stars, or in Real Life wimps.

Shad's last walk for the day and a warm shower followed by sleep ended my day.

Over the Holidays

During the first two weeks after the first battle of Witch's Woods, I slowly moved some of my things to Baba's cabin. If another snow came while I was there, I wouldn't have to wear the same outfit every day. Even spent a few nights just because I felt like it. I wondered if I could sell the house in town for enough to pay cash for this small farm with enough left over to buy that Appaloosa mare and the necessary tack and accessories - saddle, bridle, blanket, hoof picks, brushes, first aid supplies for the horse, and on and on..

Mid December, weather set in to leave us a white Christmas. The city went over budget for snow removal for the month. It got bad enough, I quit work at the Spotted Horse because I couldn't make it in the days I was at the cabin when it blew a blizzard. I spent a lot of time there now, reading the journals of previous witches. I also read the Book of Shadows to increase my armory of powers. In my spare time, I cooked both meals and potions. Take it from me, you want to make sure you don't add supper ingredients to the potion bubbling on the stove. Those were some wild dreams.

One was a second battle for the woods. Twice as many men and the wannabe drug lord himself in charge. I saw the commander of the attacking force. He was two faced. Polite and charming in one. Cruel and deceitful in the other with a strong ambition to be the biggest drug dealer in the state on his way to controlling the neighboring states soon after. With his first group of henchmen now in jail for hunting out of season with full automatic weapons, it would be after the snow melted before he could try again. At least, I saw it that way in that dream.

My Christmas included an engagement ring from Stan. We started practicing for the honeymoon to make sure we got it right then. -giggle- I think he liked that very much from the smile on his face.

Toward the New Year, the scripts for the play arrived. After reading it, specially my part, I had a flash of inspiration and designed a costume for my character. I started gathering the fabric, shoes, and accessories needed for a lady of the evening in the 1960s, also known locally as a Honky Tonk Angel. Since it was rather risqué, made a drawing to show the others before I started sewing it for the performance. I grinned at the thought of publishing a coloring book for hookers, and their customers.

A Chinook Wind blew again starting on Valentines Day. Lincoln's birthday brought the warning from the sheriff that they had a suspect for the drug trafficking in the county. They ran a picture in the newspaper with the article. He reminded me of that stranger that talked to Junior the day I gathered the details of the land grab. I told the sheriff on a trip to town. Hombre muy malo was Ernesto Gonzalez, very evil man indeed, and a known drug lord that wanted to be The Kingpin of this state's drug traffickers.

By March first, the snow had melted and ice left the lake in Pulaski State Forest. Hints of Spring started to show throughout the county. Don't let it fool you. Meteorological spring was still three weeks away. Even on warm days, a winter coat was handy from sunset to a few hours after sunrise. On the cool days, it was handy all day long. Cold days might even take a sweater under it to stay comfortable.

I had rehearsals, and didn't want to miss any. My Stan was there and it wouldn't get any closer to the wedding if I didn't go. We spent those nights together in my house in the city.

I spent a lot of time at Barbara's cabin during this period by choice. No more involuntary stays because of snow. My time there was spent well. I was now a fair to middling witch, and my army of residents was gathering for the next battle. Even the bears came out of hibernation and visited the barn for food regularly. I started to buy bulk grain and dog food because cheaper by the ton than for fifty 40 pound bags. That gave me a chance to discuss the best use of the bears' strengths with the bears themselves. I did the same with the wolves from all three packs that lived in the woods and the cougars, mountain lions if you prefer.

The engineers, the beavers, would help to funnel the enemy into a narrow front by felling trees. The deer would scout the intruders' moves again. The geese rather enjoyed the experience and volunteered to bomb the humans again. A week or so later, the ducks said the same thing.

The mice developed a taste for electric wire insulation, but also learned to spit it out after they got the flavor out, much as humans treat chewing gum. They could disable the ignitions on most vehicles quickly. That would make the survivors walk out or ride as prisoners in law enforcement transport.

Birds joined as they arrived from their winter stays farther south. The fast, high flyers were able to cover the woods to scout or to deliver messages. In a pinch, the larger ones could deliver prodigious bombardments of whitewash and some even taught the rest to add solid projectiles, like stones, similar to dropping shellfish to open them for a meal, to other birds of prey.

This would be dangerous, but we were determined. We

would fight for our homes, protect them from the drug lord's minions. With that thought, we prepared. The air and ground arms ran maneuvers and trained in combined arms operations during the day for the next month as I rehearsed for the play in the evenings. The Witch's Woods Home Guard was ready for whatever came our way.

April Fools

In other news, the trial for involved members of the Forrest Clan resulted in Junior's and Senior's sentences to ten-year prison terms. They weren't long enough, as far as I was concerned, but much better than if they walked out of the court room with verdicts of not guilty. There was a bit of extra punishment when the State charge of failure to have done environmental assessments to protect the ecosystem brought permanent loss of their developer licenses and nationwide notices of that prohibition. The judge included some advice during the sentencing hearing that was appropriate. "Use your time in prison wisely to learn a trade. Your wheeling and dealing days are over."

They also had to liquidate all their property to pay the fines. They were no longer rich. Not even middle class. They were broke, and broken. Empty shells where once they were envied for their lifestyle. Their big house on the hill was now a Bed and Breakfast, or at least would be after it passed inspections. That also broke their spirit. They used to swagger. Now, they shuffled along in the restraints on their way to the prison bound bus.

Closer to home, the play ended and the cast party was scheduled for the night of the last performance. The applause at the final curtain call had all the cast members strutting as they entered the restaurant. I glanced back as I went in.

Two men followed the crowd at a distance. One thing

bothered me about them. It was cool but it was not heavy overcoat and ski mask weather. I found Stan and related my observations. He smelled the same rats I did. We both drew our weapons as secretively as we could and found positions which offered some protection from the expected gunfire. The sheriff was at the bar getting praise for finding the source of the drugs. Withdrawal during rehabilitation was hard on the kids, but not as hard as death from an overdose.

I saw the shotgun barrel before I saw the man holding it. Stan had a better angle on the hall from the main door. He took aim and called out for the man to drop his gun. The second gun cast a shadow and opened fire. Both men entered while working the actions of their pump shotguns. Stan fired at the first guy. He dropped his gun as he crumpled to the floor. I aimed and fired at the second guy. He dropped his as he found his right humerus was broken. The broken arm made a pump shotgun the worst possible choice.

The shooting was over in about five seconds if you include the "Drop it and lie face down on the floor." command Stan issued. In second six, I was ordered to cover him as Stan moved in to remove the shotguns from easy reach and handcuff the one with the broken arm. The sheriff provided cuffs for the one that folded and replaced me as the over watch. Stan called in for ambulance and police and joined the sheriff as they waited for the response.

The only casualty on our side was the piano. Temporarily out of tune but repairable, though it would take a master craftsman to heal its scars. At least it wasn't a Steinway. Those are expensive tools for concert pianists. Most folks I know use electric keyboards. The better of those are indistinguishable from real pianos to the average ear. I can't tell the difference even at the bargain brands level. That's why I don't play any musical instrument more complicated than those with an on-off switch, a tuning dial, and a volume knob.

But enough time on that track. The guy who crumpled came to. Seemed he was frightened into a faint when he was shot. He didn't mind seeing his victims bleed, but shut down when it was his own.

Some of the cast at what was left of the party reacted to the unexpected violence. Most obvious, the festive mood evaporated at the first shots. As the EMT's cared for the wounded hired guns, the city police questioned the onlookers. The play's director issued an invitation to a postponed party.

The sheriff and old gray hair, the detective from an earlier incident, questioned me. I got a warning ticket for discharging a firearm inside city limits, and hearty handshakes from both these officers of the law. They were unanimous in their conclusion that it would have been much worse if I hadn't noticed the threat, warned Stan, and joined the fight to even the odds.

Gray hair moved off, but Wild Bill stayed to talk a bit. With a wink, he whispered the question, "Little bit off your turf, aren't you?"

"Why do you want to limit me to just the woods? I live here in the city, for now anyway." I whispered my answer with a wink.

"Do gooder, huh?" he teased.

"Might say so, Sheriff. Might just be doing my job wherever I need to."

"Well, I can accept that. But be careful." Suddenly serious, he reminded me the wannabe drug emperor of the state was still out there. "Gonzalez is used to getting his way. Watch out for him."

I set his mind at ease. "My friends and I have prepared for another battle for Witch Woods. We've had maneuvers and are ready."

"Same group you had last time?" Bill asked.

"Same group plus reinforcements. "We smiled at each

other and went our separate ways. I found Stan.

"Take a girl home when this is over?" I asked.

"Sure thing, soon to be Mrs. Sharp." Stan answered with a broad grin on his lips.

We took adjacent stools at the bar and talked while the police and crime scene unit finished up. It wasn't long before the witnesses finished their preliminary statements. A short while later, the CSU finished. We were released to our homes. Except Stan. He came home with me.

We had a drink each and went to sleep. Well, not right away. We had some gymnastics to take care of first. It was the consummation of our marriage during the betrothal, an old custom from times past when marriages had to wait for the next visit of the circuit riders with authority to perform marriages.

He rode me hard and put me away wet, but made sure I was warm during the cool down. He was the only one stiff the next morning. I helped him work it out. Rode him slow and easy until he was limber again.

We were interrupted by a scratching at the door. I rose and answered the summons.

"Sir Wolf, what is it that you're here so early?"

"Some men came last night, camped out just the other side of the boundary to these woods. Thought you should know." he answered.

I answered, "There was an attack on the sheriff in the city last night. I think it was related to the newspaper article he wrote about a bad man. Better sound the alert." I looked out and saw the first hint of the coming dawn. "Make it Condition Yellow. And start to watch the men. Take action if the situation requires it."

"Yes, Baba. You'll know if the situation changes." Sir Wolf turned and went down the stairs and out of the yard. Soon, his howl sounded and the animals started to form battle groups and manned defensive positions.

The Second Battle
Of Witch's Woods

I returned to the bedroom and started to dress. On a lark, I dressed as a movie witch. A few flyovers should unsettle the invaders, specially if I hit a few of them with the one pound rocks I could carry. Those would carry a kick from 200 feet, and my will could steer them like a guided missile to my target.

After a short discussion, Stan was assigned to guard the castle keep. He would watch the dirt road, the most likely approach to the cabin. If he saw the ruffians coming, he was to call the sheriff for reinforcements.

As a last measure, I asked the Great Maker to protect the cabin and those in it. Shad and Sasha would do their part to help because they could hear noises farther away than Stan could. Every extra second to prepare would be worth a lot during the battle once joined.

At first light, I let the dogs out to do their thing. The "land mines" of poop were laid in the grass along the road. When they came back, I gave them their instructions to help Stan guard the cabin.

The owl arrived as I prepared for take off. "Good morning, Mrs. Owl. Anything to report?"

"The 'wop-wop-wop' brought another man to the group at the edge of the woods. He seems to be in charge of them."

she reported.

(In case you haven't guessed, it was easier to teach the critters to call the flying machine by the sound it made than helicopter, a word not in their vocabulary.)

"Maybe I should pay them a visit, just to let them know they're up against more than they suspect if they attack. Tell the others about that. See you later." I gathered ten one pound stones and put them in the musette bag that hung over my shoulder and took off at tree top level toward the west. The reflection of light from the windshields of trucks and the helicopter gave away their location. That gave me time to plan my attack.

The chopper was my first target, specifically the rods that controlled the pitch of the blades. I intended to bend them enough in negative pitch that it wouldn't lift off the ground even if the pilot tried to get it airborne. The result of that hit left it a big fan rather than a flyable machine.

Next strike was to the tail rotor. That bent until it would hit the fuselage until it broke off. In turn, that would cause loss of control of the yaw because nothing canceled the main rotor's rotation. That would make the helicopter spin. Two well aimed rocks and it was an expensive pile of scrap metal until repaired.

Next targets were the windshields of the trucks. They were still drive-able, but it wouldn't be pleasant for the people inside, specially if a star burst kept them from seeing the road.

One more rock hit the coffee pot. Hot water splashed onto the two nearest goons. I doubted they suffered more than first degree burns on exposed skin. One of them got most of the heated water which soaked his clothes. The other made his own clothes wet. Again, no serious injuries, but the wet clothes and minor burns certainly would spoil their day.

I headed back east, with notes of their probable strength in numbers and weapons. The guy in nearly new khakis took a couple shots at me without aiming. The last rock hit him square in the nose. It was mildly satisfying to see the red drops soil his new, shiny shirt. I let loose with a loud laugh echoing the mad scientist in the old movies. "Mwahahahahahaha". (I still found the witch's cackle hard to do right. I had to practice that after this was settled.)

A mile in, I split the large predators into three elements. One pack on each side of the road. Their instructions were to herd the men onto the road without getting hurt. Sir Wolf, leader of the Southwest pack, took his group south of the road. Wolfgang, leader of the Northwest pack, kept his group on the north side. The bears retired to form the stopper in the funnel on the east end at a narrow spot of the road.

Those of you who are familiar with the term have recognized a Denied Center defense. You make your enemy reach the wrong conclusion that they have found the weak spot in your defenses. As they move down the center, your flanking elements close the trap. It offers them only two choices - die or surrender. Either way, we win, they lose.

Going by the thugs in the first battle, this batch exploited weapons and superior numbers to get their way against their victim(s) in the concrete jungle. These jackals, however, were playing as visitors here. We had home field advantage.

A magpie took position on my right and reported the men grumbled as they started their march without breakfast or morning coffee. If we kept them grumbling, they would become reluctant warriors sooner. All the better for the defense if they were dispirited. The wolves on either flank would certainly unnerve some of them.

I thanked the magpie and landed. "Attention, Ticks. Fresh meal coming if you're ready for them. So far, they're walking down the road." Always nice to be cheered even by the tiny critters.

I took off and found Wolfgang. "Hello. How are all of you doing?"

Wolfgang answered, "These guys are in terrible shape. Already stopped for a breather twice."

"Think you can get them on the road winded enough they'll take a break? I've tipped the ticks that they'll be on the road." I laid out my plan.

"Oh, you are a tricky one. We'll try." Wolfgang agreed.

After a "good hunting" to the pack, I headed back to the cabin with a stop at the bears. I told them my plan to move the ambush up because the men were already getting winded. We'd be here all day and part of the night if we waited for them. I asked if they had anything they could do that would get the enemy to stop long enough for the ticks to board them.

A young bear volunteered to engage in a play fight. "It always stops the tourists." he opined.

"Pick a dance partner and have at it, about a half mile up the road." I consented to the idea. "Just be careful. These guys probably aren't sportsmen. They may try to take one of you for a trophy even though season isn't open."

"Don't worry. We're used to that. We've got a spot that let's them see just enough to get interested, but plenty of brush to keep them from seeing us for more than a half second, we just growl and shake the bushes to give the impression that we're fighting. Our sister sneaks out and liberates the cookies if they leave an open package on the seat." he boasted. "We split them equally between us if we get any."

Another piped up, "I hope they have some chocolate sandwich cookies this time. I really like those better than the green berries we usually eat this time of year."

"I've got a guest at the cabin I need to check on. Be back in about half an hour, or send a messenger if you need me sooner." I took off for the cabin.

Minutes later, I landed and went in. "Stan, call the sheriff. Tell him no rush, but to get here as soon as possible. There are twenty-six of them. The pilot won't be leaving soon. His chopper has been disabled. One guy looks like he's in charge. The others are mixed, old pros and first job thugs from what I saw." Then I added, "I love you."

He stopped dialing, and smiled. "I should know better, but I love you too." He finished dialing and reported to the sheriff when he answered. They spoke a while before he hung up.

"What do you mean 'you should know better'?" I queried.

"Just that your first priority is protection of the woods. Never pictured myself married to a witch with your powers." he stammered.

I grinned. "Get used to it. It's not so bad if you go with the flow. I can cook more than just potions, you know." The tension disappeared from his voice when I added, "And I used no magic on you last night except the love that we share. You seemed to enjoy that. Besides, no one in their right mind pictures themselves married to a witch except those with evil intentions."

"Now, get ready. We've got bad guys to fight. They should be almost to the ambush site by now. Take a rifle in case they have some fight left in them." I advised.

I needed only change skirt for jeans and I was ready. We dog trotted along the road a mile, until we met the bears. I whispered a greeting.

Berenger replied and reported, "They are squabbling among themselves. A few ticks should break the weak ones, and those who have never been comfortable in the outdoors outside a city."

"That's good for us. Let's use that to our advantage." I replied. Then I sent a thought to the bad guys. "Are you going to be killed and eaten by the warriors of the woods, just to help a greedy madman?"

I let that work for a few minutes before I broadcast a second question to those men. "Why are you here when you could be safe and warm in the city? There are too many animals in these woods that can kill and eat you before you die waiting to do just that."

The body language of about six of the enemy changed from mildly annoyed to cautious. Instead of watching the trail, they started to be suspicious of every noise coming from the woods by which they were surrounded. The mice and chipmunks did their part to make last year's leaves rustle with hidden menace.

A flock of birds silently took perches in the tree branches over the road. When the men were under them, they loosed a rain of whitewash. Shouts of surprise rose to the heavens, then curses.

I signaled the heavier Birds of Prey to start their bombing runs. The hawks dive bombed the men with heavier rocks, and the eagles dropped the heaviest loads. The men tried to cover themselves, but to no avail. Many of the rocks made solid contact with the men's bodies and heads.

I sent another thought to the men. "Even the smaller animals are against you. Your actions are meaningless against these rightful residents of the woods. Listen to the meat eaters who now surround you."

The men started to search the woods around them. Their heads swiveled from right to left and back. Many showed fear, all but one showed concern. That was the guy in the shiny new shirt with the stains from his nosebleed on the front of it. In full light of day, I recognized him as Ernesto Gonzalez.

I hit him with a hint that his greed is responsible for this peril to all their lives. The wolves gave a few howls, the bears a few growls. It unnerved a few of his party since it was so close to them. Not half as worrisome as the silence punctuated with soft rustling in the leaves which followed from the reactions. The men seemed to gather into small groups, four or five seated or kneeling in clusters looking out.

Even Ernesto started to show signs of worry when all of the groups refused to let him join them. It was time to let them know this could end without more blood spilled if they piled their firearms away from their groups and sat with hands on their heads. The thought went out to them. I even used the ploy to suggest directly to Ernesto that if he did so, he would save his own life as well as all of his men's lives.

A moment later, I sent visions of the hell he would live in if anyone died trying to carry out his plan. Even he had a conscience to bother him into a rubber room if he lived but his relatives died. I helped him decide. I used my telekinesis to take the pistol from his hand and dropped it 10 feet away.

A dust cloud from the road signaled arrival of the reinforcements. I sent out another thought "It would be a shame to die for a lost cause, now that the sheriff was coming.

One of the younger guys got up and put his gun in the pile, and soon all the others did the same. When the sheriff's deputies arrived, I dismissed the army with a well done. The deputies soon had all of them hand cuffed and loaded into transport.

Sheriff Donovan came over and whispered, "How the he—ck did you get these guys to surrender this time?"

"Not while you've got that body cam on you. I'll tell you sometime when it's just you, me, and the cabin, and maybe Stan and a bottle of whiskey." I grinned as I added, "But I'd bet these guys say they saw a witch flying and kept getting ideas from the blue about being eaten by animals they never saw just to help a loco hombre."

(I told you I had practiced and was a fair to middling witch, didn't I? I was just a little bit pleased that we had rounded up the gang with no deaths. Cuts, bruises, and tick bites don't count.)

"Oh. Better check them for ticks and tick bites. There are a bunch of ticks where they were sitting. Some may carry Lyme Disease too. I've read what that does if not treated early. Some lawyer would try to make money off a case that you didn't check them. Just protect yourself and the county."

"Until I make it back to hear the truth, I'll just run with the story that an alert neighbor spotted a group of men armed with firearms when no season was open." He whispered again, "Good job, Baba. We can use the stories we hear during interrogation to prove Ernesto over there was involved in the land grab and counterfeit ring. With the enemies he's made, he likely won't make it to his release date this time."

"He's been in prison before?" I asked.

"His rap sheet takes more than a page just to list the charges that he was fined for or jailed." he answered.

"Good job by you and your deputies, Sheriff. Stay safe." I offered in parting.

He started to leave, but turned back. "You too, Miss Chadwick." Next, he spoke to Stan. "And you. Take some time off. I imagine you'll find something fun to do with a couple of days." He turned again and strode off to his car.

Rather impressive sight to watch that convoy leave. I turned to Stan. "Let's go home, dear."

He grinned from ear to ear as he spoke. "OK. Be interested in your side of the story I just witnessed."

"You heard what the sheriff said. They wrapped up the mob after an alert neighbor called in that armed men were moving in the forest." I replied with a wink.

"Yeah. Right." he challenged with a smile and a chuckle.

"You've heard the song, and like the singer, that's my story and I'm sticking to it." Then I tickled him until he laughed, pulled him to me and kissed him passionately. "Besides, the sheriff usually leaves out any mention of help he receives from we poor, untrained civilians. Gets him elected every time."

He responded by tickling me until I laughed. He led me behind some screening brush. Two hours and a half later, I removed leaves from my hair and put my clothes back on. If I'm not preggers, I don't know what it will take. He took me to the moon and stars beyond, and brought me back safely three times, once the first time he entered me. The trip extended to the edge of the galaxy the next two times.

I warned him that he better do that from now on or the marriage would end with him a frog, but I giggled with the thought. He laughed his dare to me, "You'll have to kiss me back to being a prince if you try that."

We walked back to the cabin hand in hand and talked. Our discussion centered around a wedding in the next month, just because of my feeling. We agreed on a small church wedding if we could get one scheduled. If we couldn't, we'd get a justice of the peace or a judge to join us legally, and do the church part when we could. Since this was a more or less rush job, we'd keep it small.

I let Shad know that he was going to have Stan as my other partner as Stan showered. After I finished mine, we dressed to visit Father Joe to arrange the wedding if we could. We drove to town for that and other errands.

At St. Michael's, Father Joe said he could marry us Saturday two weeks from now, or we could wait until October. The schedule was already full for every weekend between. I looked at Stan. He nodded. We said, "Saturday in two weeks." That was done.

It was going to be a busy two weeks. I stopped at the fabric shop for cloth and notions necessary to sew my wedding dress. None of the traditional white fabrics excited me, but a bright

Kelly green, the shiny green of new leaves, almost jumped at me. What could be better than the color of Spring? And it came in a nice poly stretch charmeuse that had a gentle sheen.

At the drug store, I picked up a handful of pregnancy tests. As I paid for them, the clerk tipped me that the women's clothing store had a special on those stretch jeggings that looked so good on Sue. I detoured to that store. It was a good price. I bought two pairs. Also spotted a cute sweatshirt that proclaimed "One made it past the goalie." I bought one, just in case.

The stop at the Spotted Horse went well. Bob, my godfather, was thrilled to host the reception. He even stretched the rules for the family discount on meals and rental of the private room for the rehearsal.

We were back home at the cabin, with many of the errands completed, before sunset.

A Blur of Activity

Don't know how I did it, but I made it through until the wedding. Must have been because I asked for the strength to keep it together and was granted that request. Pete had been a regular visitor to cheer me on, which helped a lot, specially after a pregnancy test showed positive.

Stan moved in overnight occasionally since we weathered the attack. I found those very pleasant, and found no reason to turn him into a frog. -grin- He also visited regularly for meals after his days off and he went back to work.

I brought out the DVD collection, some photos, and other inherited items. The girls at the saloon and the guys, employees of the construction company I sold last year, helped move heavier items.

Things moved quickly. After my new bed and some other keeper items made it to the cabin, I sold the house in town to Sue and Gene. That provided more than enough money to buy the cabin from the estate, and to pay off this year's property tax. Even with those outlays, I had some left.

While it wasn't a fortune, it was enough to buy a nice Appaloosa mare from a breeder, and the necessary tack, equipment, and supplies. I met Bill Donovan at the farm supply store when he was tacking up a "horse for sale" flyer. He explained that the horse was sound, but, at only 15 hands, 900 pounds, was too small for a man his size to ride in horse shows. That interested me. I guessed he meant that he looked bigger than the horse when mounted. That seemed reasonable based on his height and weight. He had played defensive end, after all. We dickered a while, reached a mutually agreeable price, and I agreed to buy Smoke, the gelding's name, if sound of wind and limb and we got along with each other.

I arranged to have Dr. Fred Stone, the vet, check him. He gave the horse a clean bill of health. When I visited Wild Bill's place a few days later, Smoke and I seemed to get along well. It wasn't the mare I wanted, but the price was right for a first horse. At five, he was calm enough to make a steady trail horse, young enough to be with me many years, and might, with training, make a horse to ride in the local saddle clubs monthly fun barrel races and for mounted shooting matches. Importantly, Smoke and Shad were friends almost instantly.

As things came together, it became easier to cope with the small bumps in the road of life. After minor repairs to the barn, a good cleaning of the stall and surrounding area in the barn, I made Smoke comfortable. I rode the trails around home for a bit almost daily and Shad came along for the walk. The statutory blood tests came back with an OK to marry and we got the license to commit matrimony.

I finished a wedding dress that could do well on the red carpet at an awards show. Didn't bother me when Sue pointed out it was a little racy for a wedding dress if made as I planned it. Easily fixed by sewing the outseam lower at the slit, down to almost knee high, and left the rest from there to the hem open for ease of walking. I didn't tell her I used a basting stitch because it was easier to open so it would be a thigh high slit for later wear. (Heeheeheehee, pronounced with a definite cackle undertone because I've been practicing that.)

Since it was short notice, I only had Sue as maid of honor, Francine, and Faith as the bride's maids. We had a discussion and decided to honor the colors of the spring flowers, like rose, lilac, and apple or cherry blossoms for their dresses. Francine said I would be a Venus man trap in solid green. We had a good laugh when she explained that a man that got between my legs would be there for life.

I waived the bridal shower and bachelorette party because there was too short a time to fit them in before the wedding. If held the night before the wedding, we'd still be hung over at the wedding. Noticing their frowns, I offered up what I could mix from the liquor cabinet on condition we started right then.

That sure enough put a hole in my supply. Those girls were thirsty, and were staying the night, so had no fear of need to drive home. We arranged their bivouac after the third drink, and roasted hot dogs and marshmallows over the fireplace flames. None of them noticed my drink was iced tea with a cherry in it, just in case.

We were asleep by ten PM. I was up with first light and had breakfast ready when they woke. We all made it to rehearsal in passable shape. That went smoothly and the rehearsal dinner also. Stan and I left them dancing. He took me home, to the stars again, and left by midnight so he wouldn't see me again until the wedding.

The wedding went well, all members of the cast remembered their lines. For as little time that was available for the notice, the ceremony was well attended. Stan was one of the heroes of the drug gang arrest according to the story the sheriff put in the paper, so was responsible for a good part of the crowd. I contributed the members of the coven, and some customers from the saloon. The usual attendees from town came just because they went to all the weddings and funerals. All in all, the church was nearly full.

The reception lasted well into the night, but Stan and I left for home at an appropriately early hour. That is the custom in this neck of the woods. It allows the newly weds to consummate the marriage before 'normal bedtimes' or they got too drunk to drive home.

With the ebbing of adrenaline now that we were at home and had returned from another trip to the edge of the galaxy, sleep claimed both of us. The last thought I had was: 'If Stan keeps this up, he won't ever have to worry about becoming a frog." -giggle- I looked forward to the rest of our lives together and fell asleep in my husband's arms.

www.ingramcontent.com/pod-product-compliance
Lightning Source LLC
Chambersburg PA
CBHW020107310726

48970CB00002B/514